This book was donated to the
Maury County Public Library
by Mr. Kenny Holcomb
(former Columbia resident)
& Random House books

TELL ME LIES

ALSO BY PATRICK COOPER

I Is Someone Else

O'Driscoll's Treasure

Wings to Fly

TELL ME LIES

PATRICK COOPER

DELACORTE PRESS

Published by Delacorte Press
an imprint of Random House Children's Books
a division of Random House, Inc.
New York

First published in 2006 in Great Britain by Andersen Press Limited.

www.randomhouse.com/teens

Educators and librarians, for a variety of teaching tools, visit us at
www.randomhouse.com/teachers

Library of Congress Cataloging-in-Publication Data
Cooper, Patrick.
Tell me lies / by Patrick Cooper. — 1st ed.
p. cm.
Summary: In England in 1969, nineteen-year-old Stephen leaves his conservative home, where he is haunted by a troubled past and dread of the future, and is drawn by an old friend to a commune, whose charismatic leader speaks of finding freedom to live in the moment.
ISBN 978-0-385-73270-3 (trade) — ISBN 978-0-385-90287-8 (lib. bdg.)
[1. Hippies—Fiction. 2. Communal living—Fiction. 3. Drug abuse—Fiction.
4. Coming of age—Fiction. 5. Vietnam War, 1961–1975—Fiction.
6. Great Britain—History—Elizabeth II, 1952– —Fiction.] I. Title.
PZ7.C78765Tel 2007
[Fic]—dc22
2007002407

The text of this book is set in 11.75-point Sabon.

Printed in the United States of America

10 9 8 7 6 5 4 3 2 1

First American Edition

TELL ME LIES

PART ONE

Cling to the truth and it turns into lies.
Understand lies and they turn into truth.
Truth and lies are two sides of the same coin.
Neither accept one nor reject the other.

ZEN MASTER TAIGU RYOKEN (1758–1831)

Chapter 1

"The Truth will set you free." That's what Detective Sergeant Harrison said. The Truth—nothing less will do. All right then, Sergeant Harrison, this is the truth, the way it all really happened.

It started when I met Astrid again. And I met Astrid because I'd gone to see Rob in London. And I'd gone to see Rob because my mother told me to. And before that . . .

Before that, I wanted something, but I didn't know what it was. Just the wanting would come at me in quiet moments, the sense of a hole inside me waiting to be filled. I wasn't unhappy, just a bit bored. I went to Sixth Form College and sat dreaming through the lessons, then last summer I did my A-levels.

I finished the last exam early. I should have waited for the others and gone with them to celebrate, but I didn't feel like it. I'd meet them later anyway. Instead I walked back home the long way, past the railway and along the river, enjoying being out in the sunshine after the stuffiness of the exam hall.

My mother was lying in wait when I got in.

"Well, Stephen, how did it go?"

"Okay."

I tried to slide off up to my room, but she blocked the way.

"What were the questions?"

"You know. Usual things."

"I hope you got plenty of quotations in."

"Don't worry, Mum. It was fine."

That seemed to satisfy her.

"I'll make a cup of tea."

She moved away from the stairs, and I headed up them.

"It's okay, I don't want tea. . . ."

"I'm putting it on now," she stated firmly.

I shrugged. There was no point arguing.

In my room I slumped back in the old green armchair, closing my eyes tight and breathing deeply. I was safe here, more or less. Even though my mother went through my drawers while I was out, it was my own room, with my own atmosphere, somewhere I didn't have to perform for anyone.

Part of me was still in the exam hall, scribbling down hasty sentences about Shakespeare. I thought I'd done okay. I'd written what I was supposed to write, without thinking too much. I thought now, though, about Prospero in his magic kingdom. It seemed to me that Prospero liked his island; he didn't want to go back to his old life. But everyone else couldn't wait to get out of Prospero's paradise.

I wondered how the others had done. I should have

stayed and asked them—Jude, in particular, struggled a bit with Shakespeare.

Anyway, that was over now. I could forget about *The Tempest*.

I opened my eyes. The sun was shining through the copper beech tree, filling the room with golden light.

"Stephen! Tea's ready!" my mother shouted shrilly up the stairs.

We had tea in the garden, with a robin singing and the scent of roses.

"We should have a celebratory dinner—" my mother started.

"I'm going out with my friends tonight," I said quickly.

I thought she'd object, but she looked relieved.

"What a pity! Never mind, we'll do it another time. As it happens there's a Conservative meeting tonight. Old Pearson Clarke is standing down at the next election, so we have to select a new parliamentary candidate. . . ."

She paused expectantly.

"Will it be you, Mum?"

"I should think they'll want somebody younger, wouldn't you? Have some cake!"

She sat back, fixing me with narrowed eyes. "So-o-o. What were you thinking of doing now?"

"Well, I thought I'd have a bath."

"You know perfectly well what I mean," she said

severely. "What are you going to do over the summer? You can't just sit at home, you know, twiddling your thumbs."

"Oh, I expect I'll get some work," I said randomly. "They're looking for bar staff in the pub."

My mother nodded approval.

"Good idea. So many young people nowadays just seem to hang about all the time. Taking drugs and wasting their lives. Such a pity . . ."

She tailed off. I munched the cake. Once I'd finished it, I could go back upstairs.

"Anyway," she continued, "we'll have a party for your birthday, of course. Perhaps Rob would like to come."

"I don't think so, Mum."

"I don't see why not. After all, he is your brother. He'd come if you asked him." She looked at me accusingly. "You should go and see him, now that you've finished your exams. Go up to London. We'll pay your train fare. Tell him to come to your birthday party."

"It won't be any use, Mum."

But I knew she wouldn't listen, and that she'd go on at me until I went to see Rob and asked him. She'd never let go.

We had a good evening in the pub that night. I was a bit of an outsider in the group, but they were easy to get on with. Mostly, though, I was just aware of Jude. She kept smiling at me, and I couldn't help smiling back and catching her eye. Her leg rubbed against mine under the table. I didn't know if it was an accident, but I liked it.

I walked her home. She took my arm and chattered away as we walked through the empty streets to her parents' house: tipsy chatter about her little sister, about a film she'd seen, about her holiday in Spain.

We reached her parents' house and stopped by the streetlamp. Jude held on to my arm, but she stopped talking, and her silence made me feel awkward. She turned to face me, suddenly serious.

"Stephen, why are you so—so not available? What's wrong with you?"

I was taken aback. Was there something wrong with me? I thought I was normal now, doing the right things, being ordinary. But she was right too. I always held back. I didn't want to get involved.

Her face was close, so sweet and open. I couldn't help myself. There wasn't anything to say. I put my arms round her and kissed her.

It was she who pulled away, in the end. She touched her finger to my lips and whispered, "Good night, lover boy!" then ran up the steps to her house.

I walked slowly home, wondering what it meant. Was I in love with her? I wasn't quite sure, but I thought I could be.

The next day I went to the pub to ask for a job, and they wanted me to start immediately. Later Jude came in with a couple of friends. My heart missed a beat when I saw her, and I was waiting for her to say something. But she only smiled, as if we shared a secret.

I knew I'd have to go to see Rob sooner or later, so on my day off I went down to London. I hadn't seen Rob for a while, and I hadn't been to his flat before. I got off the bus at Notting Hill Gate and walked past a row of fancy shops: swinging London, where long-haired guys wore purple flares, and girls with spaced-out eyes wafted around in velvet and lace and a haze of patchouli. It was nothing like my hometown—more like being in a foreign city, with the smell of incense, and rock music blaring from the boutiques.

Behind the main road was a maze of backstreets. Three black guys with colorful hats sat on some steps sharing a joint and watched me walk past through reflector sunglasses. Two girls in miniskirts passed, giggling, barely seeing me, absorbed in their own world.

Rob's flat was in a basement, down cracked steps sprouting weeds and toffee wrappers. I rang the bell a few times to no effect, and was turning to go when the door opened and there he was, unshaven and bleary-eyed, looking as if he'd just woken up, which he probably had. He blinked at me in surprise.

"Hey, Stevie! Come on in!"

He led me into his sitting room. It was dark and damp, but someone had tried to make it nice, with embroideries hung on the walls and a smell of incense, so it felt secret and safe too, like a cave.

"I'll get myself some coffee," said Rob. "How about you?"

"Thanks."

He went to the kitchen and I sat down on some cushions in one corner. There wasn't much other furniture: an old sofa, a table with a typewriter, and piles of books everywhere.

"Looks like you've been writing," I said as Rob returned.

"Yeah, well, a bit."

"I saw one of your poems in the *Poetry Review*."

"Yeah, they'll publish any rubbish in that. . . . You didn't show it to Mum, did you?"

"No. She showed it to me."

Rob grinned.

"No escape, is there?"

He gave me a mug of coffee and sat on the sofa with his.

"So here you are. I've been expecting a few people to walk through that door lately, but you weren't one of them."

He looked me up and down, critically.

"Christ, I don't believe it. How can you dress like that? Those trousers—they look like they've escaped from a museum."

I didn't say anything. It was never any good trying to defend myself against Rob. I didn't like my clothes that much either, but they were what people wore in St. Albans. I couldn't see what business it was of Rob's though, so I just drank my coffee.

"Thinking of moving to London, then?"

"No. I'm working in the pub for the summer. I'm going on a business studies course in September."

"Business studies? *You?* What the fuck's that about?"

"It's what I want to do," I said quickly. It wasn't really true, but I was irritated by his assumptions. "I don't believe in all this hippie stuff. . . ."

"Whose idea was it? Mum's?"

"Not really—" I started, but at that moment the door to the bedroom opened and a girl slid herself round it, blinking at us vaguely. She had a white face and long straight hair and was wearing only a man's shirt—one of Rob's presumably.

I stared at her. I couldn't help it.

"Who's this, Rob?" she asked.

"Oh, just Stevie, my little brother. I told you about him, didn't I? The one who washed up in India and I had to ship him back."

I winced. It might have been true, but he didn't have to say it like that.

The girl pushed her hair out of her eyes and squinted at me, then smiled.

"Hi, Stevie!"

She padded across to the kitchen. "Any coffee for me?"

"Yeah, there's a bit left," said Rob. "You'll have to wash yourself up a cup, though."

He turned back to me.

"That's Melanie. She . . . stays here sometimes. Anyway, what brings you here? Looking for some hot business tips?"

In spite of myself, I laughed. Rob stretched his arms back, relaxing.

"Hey, Stevie, look, you should come down and spend some time in London, see what it's like. You could stay here for the summer, get a job somewhere, meet girls. You'd see something different. You'd have a great time. London's where it's at."

"Where what's at?"

"It. Everything. Girls. Music. Poetry. Politics. Life."

"Politics? I thought that was Mum's thing. . . ."

Rob shook his head in disbelief. Then he reached for his tobacco tin and started rolling a joint.

"Where have you been, Stevie, these last two years? Haven't you heard there's a war on?"

He meant Vietnam. My mother talked about it sometimes (she was for it), but I'd never taken much interest.

"Yeah, well, I suppose so—" I started, but Rob interrupted immediately, jabbing his finger.

"*So coat my eyes in butter / Fill my ears with silver / Stick my legs in plaster / Tell me lies about Vietnam!*" he quoted. "You've a lot to learn, Stevie!"

Melanie came back in with her coffee, and Rob heated a lump of hash with a match, then crumbled it into the tobacco. I watched with some alarm. I hadn't smoked dope since I came back from India, and I didn't want to. My memories of that time were fractured and far away.

"Anyway, how's things at home?" asked Rob. "How's the Colonel? What's the Mouth of Darkness up to?"

The Mouth of Darkness was what Rob called Mum when he wanted to be rude and look clever. It made me uncomfortable again.

"Mum's been short-listed by the Conservatives."

Rob clapped his thigh.

"To be an MP you mean? Yeah, she'd just fit in with those shit-arse geriatrics. Christ, one shouldn't laugh though. . . ."

"They're having a family party for my birthday," I went on quickly. "She asked me to invite you. Maybe you too . . ." I looked at Melanie, hesitating. I'd have liked her to come, but I couldn't quite visualize her with my parents.

Melanie smiled vaguely, but Rob had put down the half-made joint on the tin lid and was staring at me.

"So that's it, huh? That's why she sent you. I knew there'd be something. She's always trying to pull me back into her web. I won't come, and she knows it. Stevie, why do you always have to be such a good boy? I liked you better when you were mad. Look, give up on those people, they're half dead already. Live a little, Stevie, you owe it to yourself."

He picked up the joint and licked the gum on the paper.

I stood up. I suddenly felt disgusted with him, his rudeness, his patronizing. But there was no point in saying anything.

"I'm going."

"Okay," said Rob without looking up.

I turned round briefly at the door. Melanie pushed back her hair and rolled her eyes at me.

"See ya," she said pleasantly.

"You can come back," said Rob without looking round. "You probably will."

The light seemed very bright outside. The black guys were still sitting on their steps and watched me pass. I don't know if it was because of how I looked, but they started laughing.

I had all day, so I lingered outside the boutiques. I looked at myself in a mirror, a drab figure among all the color. I made a sudden decision, went in and bought a pair of orange 'loons that hugged my thighs and spread out wide around my ankles, and a tie-dyed green-and-purple T-shirt. When I looked in the mirror again, I saw a completely different person. The black guys wouldn't laugh at me now.

I put my old clothes in a plastic bag, thinking I might hang around a bit, maybe buy a record or sit in a coffee shop. As usual Rob had unsettled me. He was a complete pain, but I couldn't help feeling he might be right, that I might be missing out on something.

Back in the street, I stood for a moment with the buzz of people and traffic and music surrounding me, enjoying my anonymity in this colorful crowd.

And then I heard a voice, calling to me through the hubbub.

"Stevie!"

I didn't believe it at first. It was a voice from the past that shouldn't be here.

"Stevie! Hey, Stevie!"

My heart started racing. I wanted to turn away, to melt into the crowd, but at the same time I didn't want to. My past was coming back to me, and I couldn't, or wouldn't, escape it.

"Stevie!"

She was sliding towards me through the crowd, as beautiful, as stylish, as perfect as ever.

"Stevie—it is you, isn't it? You remember me?"

Oh yes, I did remember her. How could I ever forget?

Chapter 2

If I hadn't met Astrid that day, my life would have gone down a completely different path. Or would it? Was it really only chance that brought us together in that place, that moment? Spencer once said that what we think is happening outside us is really created by our own consciousness. I didn't understand exactly, but I can see that there were urges inside me that I was barely aware of. Perhaps it was what people call destiny.

At any rate it wasn't what I'd expected, to be standing outside a shop with some hippie name like Granny Takes a Trip, dressed up in my new gear and watching Astrid weave her way towards me. I wasn't sure if it was what I wanted either. Astrid belonged in a half-forgotten past of glittering seas and vast mountains, precious but hidden, so I could often believe it hadn't happened at all. I had a sense that if she reappeared in my life, it could only mean trouble. Yet I had a choice. I could have turned my back and walked away, pretended not to know her. But I didn't. Destiny called, and I accepted.

"Stevie!"

She was in front of me, pushed close by the crowd, smiling.

"I knew I'd see you again one day. I knew it!"

I couldn't think of anything to say, but I smiled back. My heart was still pounding.

"Hey, you look real good!"

"I just bought some new clothes," I said awkwardly.

"You are taller," she said. "But I would have known you anywhere!"

She put her hand on my arm.

"Hey, we must talk. Let's go somewhere we can sit down."

She led me into a basement café where they played Grateful Dead records. Three long-haired guys with round pink sunglasses sat blankly in one corner— grannies taking trips I supposed—but otherwise it was empty.

We bought cups of peppermint tea and sat down opposite each other. And suddenly we were both awkward, lost for words. Astrid looked down at her hands, and I felt a shiver up my spine as I remembered how I had last seen her—the beauty of her body, the gentleness of her touch.

It was half thrilling, half embarrassing. But it was over, past, forgotten, another time, another world. We were different people now. I hoped she wouldn't mention it.

"Are you still with Jerry?" I asked, to break the silence. Jerry was her boyfriend when I'd known her before.

She looked up.

"Jerry? Oh no. No, I haven't seen him since . . . Well,

we never did get on too well really, did we? Remember when I walked out in Istanbul?" She laughed nervously. "No, Jerry's all past. All over. I have a new life now."

"Yeah. Me too," I said.

"What is your life? Tell me."

I wished I hadn't said anything because it was all meaningless, but I did my best to make something out of living with my parents and doing my A-levels. It was surprisingly easy to talk to her. She listened and smiled and nodded, and felt like an old friend, which I suppose she was.

"And the old life?" she asked. "Don't you remember it sometimes? Don't you think about Afghanistan? Don't you sometimes wish you could be there again?"

"Not very often. Nobody's interested here anyway. It's all like a dream."

"Dreams are real too." Astrid smiled mysteriously. "You know what I do? I have a little book of dreams. I keep it beside my bed, and when I wake in the morning, the first thing I do is write down what I have lived through in the night. Do you remember your dreams, Stevie?"

I shook my head.

"I don't think I want to."

She reached out and touched my arm with those long fingers.

"Oh, you should, Stevie. You must remember your dreams."

I moved my arm back. Her touch was waking something in me, something I'd rather stayed asleep. My own dreams were full of violence and fear, and I didn't want them, any more than I wanted my past. It was too dangerous—too much feeling. I needed to keep a lid on things, like everyone else.

"I'd better get on," I said. "I've got a train to catch."

It was a lie, and I blushed.

"Sorry!" said Astrid.

I had no idea why she'd said that, and it flustered me. I knew what I ought to do. I ought to finish my tea, say "It's been really nice to see you again, Astrid," give her a peck on the cheek and cut her out of my life forever. But I didn't. I just sat there with my mouth half open and my gaze shifting round the Moroccan hangings, the bored girl at the counter, the three stoned guys, the sign saying CAPITALISM IS A CARNIVOROUS FLOWER.

Astrid leant forwards, her eyes seeking mine.

"Listen!" she said intensely. "The past is gone, I know. I've changed, and I guess you have too. We were both very young then. We don't have to talk about that. But when I saw you in the street just now, I was so happy because I knew we have more to give each other, you and I. I want you to meet somebody, Stevie. He is very special to me. He has changed my life. He is waiting for me in the park right now. Will you come?"

She was gazing at me and she was so beautiful—why was she talking like this to me? I looked back into her gray eyes and saw nothing but friendliness, softness, warmth. And a promise: the granting of secret wishes, wishes I hardly even knew I had.

"Well, okay then, I guess I could take a later train. . . ."

I still have in my mind an image of Spencer the way he was the first time I ever saw him: a short, well-built man of about thirty, with loose clothes and dark hair beginning to thin, waving a stick in the air as a big black dog danced around him. He threw the stick, and the dog charged after it and ran panting back to drop it at his feet and gaze up expectantly into his eyes. That was all: a man playing with his dog in the park. But there was something about the way he moved, an elegance and a balance, that drew my eye even before Astrid pointed him out.

She ran over to him, excited.

"Hey, Spencer, I just met an old friend—Stevie—someone really special."

Spencer straightened up as I approached and he smiled. His smile lit up his face and made me feel that in that moment nothing could delight him more than the sight of me walking awkwardly towards him.

"Hi, Stephen!"

It was odd because Astrid had introduced me as Stevie, but he called me Stephen. He always called me Stephen, and she always called me Stevie. I never knew why.

"Hello," I said.

He took both my hands in his and looked in my eyes for a second. I felt uncomfortable and looked away.

"Meet my dog," he said, giving the dog a pat. "He's called Chinook, after a lost tribe of native Americans from the Pacific Northwest, where I come from. I'm

Canadian. It's also a wind and a U.S. Army helicopter. Chinook, meet Stephen. He's a friend."

Chinook snuffled up to me, and I patted his head. Then we walked together across the park. Astrid took Spencer's arm, and Chinook ran round us in loops, coming back to Spencer to be petted, then running off again. We chatted and it was relaxed and easy. Spencer told me he'd been traveling for years, but he was going to stay in England for a while.

"It's a good country to be in right now. Hey, you know what? Our place is just a couple of blocks down here. We're going home to make a meal. Why don't you join us?"

They had a first-floor flat with a big living room—no damp basement like Rob's. Sunlight streamed in through the window onto a thick blue carpet strewn with cushions. A man who Spencer introduced as Ray was sprawled there reading a magazine. He seemed an odd friend for them. His hair was matted, and he looked as if he hadn't washed for weeks—a wild man come in from the woods. He stared at me for a while, then grinned, showing bad teeth.

"Yeah, man."

"Make yourself at home," said Spencer. "We'll fix the food."

Chinook went obediently to his basket, and I sat down next to Ray while Astrid and Spencer disappeared into the kitchen. Ray scratched his hair and stared at me.

"Nice house," I said, trying to make conversation.

"It's not a house, it's a home!" said Ray. He chuckled to himself and withdrew into his magazine.

A bit later another couple arrived called Louise and Tim. Tim was friendly enough, but there was something odd about Louise. She looked lovely, with long, dark hair, but her gaze wandered aimlessly, and Tim was protective of her. Astrid came out of the kitchen and got us all chopping vegetables and mixing salad, then when everything was ready, we sat cross-legged in a circle on the carpet with a cloth spread between us, and Spencer brought in big pots of vegetable curry and rice. I hadn't eaten all day and it smelled good. I was ready to start, but the others closed their eyes.

Astrid noticed my confusion.

"We sit silent before we eat," she explained. "It makes the food taste better."

Once again, I could have found it embarrassing, but in fact it felt quite natural to close my eyes for a minute, smelling the curry. A bit like saying grace. And when we did start to eat, I enjoyed it. After Rob's smelly basement it was great to be in this big, airy room, with people who smiled and took trouble over food.

"Eating well is living well," said Spencer. "We're moving to the country soon. Then we'll have our own vegetables, fresh from the soil. We'll have our own eggs too, from our own chickens. Maybe a cow. What do you say to a cow, Ray?"

"Moo!" said Ray through a mouthful of food.

Then, after supper, Astrid poured out green tea in

china bowls, and everyone went silent again and looked at Spencer, who was sitting quietly, holding his bowl so that the aromatic steam drifted up towards his nose.

He looked round at each of us in turn. This time I didn't look away. His eyes seemed to pierce into me, seeing everything about me but without judging in any way. It was a strange feeling, as if for a few moments he turned my world upside down and gave it a shake.

He looked back down at his bowl and breathed deeply.

"There's not much to say, is there? We're here. Just here. The smell of green tea . . . the cars passing in the street . . . the comfortable feeling of good food. Just here . . ."

Spencer paused. I looked round the group. Everyone had shut their eyes apart from Astrid, who was gazing at him with a half smile around her lips.

"We're here to find freedom," he continued at last. "Not freedom to do things, to become things, but deep freedom. The freedom of the Self. Freedom that comes in *not* doing, in *not* knowing, in not holding on to our separate identities. The vastness we can only experience when we are nobody, when future and past fall away with all that bondage of thought, and there is only this moment, this moment, this moment. . . ."

He stopped again. The light from the window was shining around him so that he seemed to glow. This moment, this moment . . . It was like something I'd heard once before and forgotten. I shut my eyes and heard the traffic outside and music filtering up from the flat below, but I was also aware of a silence that was almost a presence, filling me and refreshing me. I sat comfortably on the cushion with little thoughts running through my brain, like what time the trains went home and whether I should tell my friends about my birthday, and felt for the first time that day no urge to go anywhere or be anyone.

Spencer took another breath, and everyone stirred.

I opened my eyes. He was looking straight at me.

"You're welcome with us, Stephen, any time," he said.

What was he on about? There was something weird about it all, but clean and refreshing too. Nobody else I knew sat in silence like that. We were always looking for distraction.

Once again I mumbled something about having to catch a train. This time Spencer nodded amiably.

"Yeah, sure! We'll be seeing you."

Chapter 3

I meant to go back there. I really did. I had felt something special and warm from Astrid, and Spencer intrigued me. We'd swapped phone numbers, and it would have been easy to give them a ring and go down to London for a day. Yet I couldn't do it. Their lives were too distant from what I was.

The summer of 1969 slipped past. The television showed rock concerts and protest marches, beautiful people being groovy at the climax of the Swinging Sixties, but my life was nothing like that. I went to work in the pub, came home, sat up late reading and listening to music on my headphones, slept all morning, ate my mother's meals. I was half dead, and I half knew it.

One night I watched the Apollo moon landing with my parents, fuzzy pictures of men bouncing about in an arid landscape and unfurling a flag. There was a shot of a boot mark printed clearly in the moondust. The commentator pointed out that without any wind on the moon it would stay there forever.

"Doesn't it make you proud to be a human being?" said my mother.

My father poured a gin and tonic.

I went outside.

It was a warm, clear night. I could see the moon, about a third full, hanging in the east. Somewhere up there some men with a flag were looking down at the Earth. Except that they weren't looking down. They were looking up.

But it didn't make me feel proud. It made me uncomfortable. What were they doing there? Those astronauts added nothing to the moon. They took away the mystery and left behind their rubbish. They must feel pretty good up there, I knew that: a high like nothing else. *That's one small step for man, one giant leap for mankind*, the astronaut had said. But what did it actually mean to "mankind"? It was only an idea. It wouldn't dig a well, or grow a plant of rice.

Was I the only person in the world who felt like this? It made me feel lonely. Why did I have to be different?

I could hear a train on the railway line, at least a mile away, but the night was so still the sound carried. A train in the night, rumbling slowly along. Thousands and thousands of trains all over the planet, moving people, food, mail. I liked trains. Trains were real. They had a function in people's lives. The flag and the boot prints on the moon—they meant nothing at all.

I shivered, and went to bed.

I didn't go to sleep, though. I lay there thinking about Astrid and Spencer. Were they watching the moon landing? They didn't own a television set as far as I knew. Rob would know all about it even if he didn't watch it, and he'd have opinions too, but Astrid and Spencer didn't seem to relate to that bit of the world at all.

"We're very into purity," Astrid had said as she walked with me to the Underground. "Pure food. Pure thoughts. Keeping away from all that commercial rubbish."

"Don't any of you smoke or anything?"

She smiled sweetly.

"You can't stop people doing what they want to do, Stevie. If you repress something, it just comes up another way. Sure, Ray smokes, only not in our house. He smokes a lot of hash actually. He used to be a heroin addict before, so it is like nothing to him. He's got a lot of craziness in his past. Spencer doesn't mind. He doesn't tell people what they should and shouldn't do."

"Spencer—is he some sort of guru?" I asked.

Astrid smiled to herself.

"He doesn't like that word. . . ." She took my arm and leant against me. It was a good feeling to have such a beautiful girl hanging on my arm, and heads were turning to look at us. But although I was attracted, it wasn't the same as before. Her beauty didn't awe me. I was comfortable with her.

"Oh, Stevie, it's so good to see you again. I always knew I would one day. You were so special then, so sweet and young. And you've grown up so good. You'll come back and see us, won't you? And we'll move to the country soon, and you can come and see us there too."

She paused, her face close to mine, looking into my eyes.

"Spencer says you are special too."

We were at the Underground. I kissed her goodbye. I felt a little electric sensation as our lips touched, and then she shut her eyes and held me for a moment.

"Promise you'll come back!"

"Of course I will," I said.

"Promise me!"

"I promise."

But I never had.

The summer continued, meaninglessly. I had my birthday, and my uncle and aunt came over and made pointless conversation, and nobody mentioned my cousin Harriet because she'd become a hippie. My mother was selected as Conservative candidate. I went on working in the pub. Sometimes I drank too much.

One evening Jude came into the pub with Chris, one of the guys in our group. I served them, and they joked a bit about how drunk I'd been the night before, then went over and sat in a corner together. When they went out, Chris put his arm round Jude's shoulder. She glanced back and caught my eye, then she leant against him. I felt jealous, but I couldn't blame her. I was useless. I wanted to explain to her that I couldn't do anything because I couldn't work out what anything meant, or what was the point of it. But I couldn't have said it anyway.

The bar closed. I went home and sat by my window and contemplated my life slipping away towards a business-studies course I wasn't interested in. And even that wouldn't start for another five weeks—five weeks of hanging around at home doing nothing, or of getting drunk and watching Jude flirting with Chris. It seemed like an eternity.

Was this all that life was? I remembered Spencer looking in my eyes and turning my world upside down. I remembered Astrid hugging me, making me promise. Ever since then I'd felt unsettled, as if I had some unfinished business. I should have phoned them, like I promised. Perhaps it wasn't too late after all.

The next morning I got up at about eleven o'clock. The house was empty as usual. I ate some breakfast, then I went over to the phone. I had Astrid's number. I could ring her. There was nothing to lose, nothing to it at all really. It was just like phoning an old friend. Yet I was nervous. I sipped my tea to calm myself and tried to pluck up my courage.

As I looked at it, the phone started to ring. I picked it up, expecting someone from the Conservatives.

"Hello."

"Stevie?"

I couldn't believe it. My heart was thumping, and my mouth was dry. It was Astrid, her voice bright and alive.

"Oh, so good you are there! We are moving to the country. We have found this lovely place—a big house where we can all be together. It will be so nice, Stevie. We will grow our own vegetables and have chickens and goats. Will you help us? We are doing the move on Tuesday. Please come! We need you!"

So that was it. They needed me. Nobody needed me here. It was settled. I'd go down on Tuesday, my day off, and help them move.

And that was how it was that I was the first into "The Hollies," clambering in through a bathroom window, just as later I was the last to leave.

They were going to squat. That was the plan. I'd never seen a squat before and wasn't sure what to expect, but I'd read about it in the papers. Everyone seemed to be doing it.

I'm not sure who found the house, but it was probably Richard. Richard managed most things round Spencer, as I later discovered. He was at the flat when I arrived, along with a couple of other people I hadn't met before, gathered round Spencer, who was sitting with Chinook on a pile of luggage while Astrid wiped surfaces in the kitchen.

"I am so bourgeois," she said apologetically. "I have to leave everything clean when I go. Ray says it's stupid, they will send someone in before the next tenants, and anyway they make so much money out of us, but I have to do it."

There was a roar and a grinding of gears in the street.

"That'll be Ray," said Spencer.

Ray's van had once been white, but Ray had gone for it with pink emulsion paint, already peeling off. The rear doors were tied together with string, and dark fumes pumped from the exhaust. It was big, though, and we piled cardboard boxes, mattresses, furniture and the blue carpet into the back.

As we were doing that, Tim and Louise, the people I'd met the last time, arrived in a bulging Morris Minor. Richard had his own car too, already parked in the street.

We all went upstairs and sat on the bare floorboards in a circle.

"The space has been kind to us," said Spencer. "Let's leave it with our good feelings."

Then everyone was silent, presumably giving their good feelings to the empty flat.

"Right," said Spencer, breaking the silence and beaming round at us all. "Off to the country!"

It looked spooky at first sight: a big Victorian house, lost down country lanes, with gabled windows and half-ruined stables at the back. It obviously hadn't been lived in for years. A clump of holly bushes by the gate gave it its name: The Hollies. Beside it a garden with fruit trees and wild roses ran down to a railway cutting.

Ray parked the van in what had once been a graveled drive and turned off the engine. We all piled out, Chinook stretching his legs and sniffing around for a place to pee.

Only birdsong broke the silence.

And then a rumble grew to a roar, and suddenly a train sped past. It was only a few moments, and then the birdsong was back.

Ray was advancing on the front door with a crowbar, but Spencer stopped him.

"No violence on the house, Ray. There's an easy way, you'll see."

And in fact I'd already spotted it—a small window over the side porch, slightly ajar.

"Look! I can get in there, I'm sure I can," I said, and in a wave of enthusiasm pulled myself onto the roof of the porch, eased open the window and squeezed through.

I found myself in a bathroom, long disused. Half a cracked mirror hung on a wall above a filthy wash-basin. I wiped a patch clean with my sleeve and looked at myself, clean and pink among the grime. The bath had yellow stains, and a big spider lurking by the plug. I tried one of the taps. It turned reluctantly, then gurgled, and rusty water gushed out, sending the spider into a frenzy. I turned it off, opened the door and stepped out onto the landing.

An atmosphere of the past hung heavy and formless about me. Everything was thick with dust and cobwebs, and so quiet, but the stairs were broad and solid, with strong banisters. I stood looking into the stairwell, feeling the emptiness and silence, the beat of my heart. How long had this place lain unused, lost in the English countryside? Well, the waiting was over. Now the house could come back to life, in all its warmth and chaos.

As I leant on the banister, I had a curious feeling that the house was me, dull and dusty, breathing in the silence, waiting to be opened.

I stepped slowly down the stairs, hearing the echo of my footsteps. My shoes left their pattern in the dust, like a moonwalker's. At the front door I paused again, my hand on the Yale lock. This was it: one of those moments when everything is about to change. I clicked back the lock and pulled open the door, letting in fresh air and sunlight and breathing bodies and laughter and pain. Life and life only.

We had a busy afternoon. The house was full of bustle as people ran round exploring it, opening doors and windows, claiming rooms for their own.

Years of dust covered everything, but Richard distributed cleaning equipment and got us organized. Most of us, anyway. Spencer was looking round the garden, while Ray did something in his van. Louise wafted around not doing much until Astrid set her to cleaning windows, and then she polished every pane till it shone. Two other people had come with Richard— a girl called Carla, who had a small baby who she strapped to her back while she mopped the kitchen tiles; and Peter, a South African guy, who helped Richard sort out the electricity and the plumbing.

It was exhilarating to work in a team like that, with the single aim of bringing the house back to life. I found myself liking everyone, and liking myself too, in a way that I hadn't for a long time. And I felt really useful, sorting out the old solid-fuel cooker and then finding a stash of wood in an outhouse, so we had a fire in the kitchen and Astrid could make tea for us all.

I was nervous, though. Surely it could only be a matter of time before the police came with sniffer dogs and vans to chuck us out. My own instinct was to lie low and pretend not to be there, but Ray had different ideas and sat in front of the house smoking a big joint. The others took cups of tea outside and sat around in the afternoon sunshine.

And nothing happened. A couple from one of the neighboring houses came by and said they were glad somebody was moving into the house at last, and offered us some old furniture. A farmer on his tractor stopped and stared, then grinned and waved and drove on.

By evening, most of the house was clean and its windows sparkled. I went into the kitchen, where Astrid was cooking supper on the stove that I'd got going.

"I've got to get back," I said, hoping for a lift to the station.

Astrid looked at me anxiously.

"Oh no, Stevie. You can't go. We're going to eat."

"It's just, I'll miss the last train."

"So stay the night. There's plenty of room. And tomorrow we're having a party. A housewarming. All our friends have promised to come. You're the one who got us in here, Stevie. You have to stay for the party."

"But I haven't got anything with me. I haven't even got a sleeping bag."

She came up close to me, smiling into my eyes.

"We'll find you something. You have to stay. We need you."

She needed me. Well, in that case . . . I'd miss a day's work, but what the hell?

But I had to make a call to my parents or they'd be worried, so Tim drove me in his Morris Minor to the village on the main road, and I rang them from a phone box. Luckily I got my father, who just said, "Oh yes, thanks for telling us." If it had been my mother, she'd have bombarded me with questions.

"Fancy a drink?" said Tim as I came out.

We went into the village pub. The locals all stared at us as we came in, but the barman was friendly enough, and we retreated to a corner with our pints.

"Cheers!" said Tim, taking a big draft of his beer and licking the foam off his lips. He seemed like a nice guy, cheerful and straightforward, with a Manchester accent. He asked me how I knew Astrid, and I told him how she and her boyfriend had given me a lift to India, years before, and how I'd just met her again by chance.

He shook his head.

"Chance? I doubt it."

"What do you mean?"

"You don't really know Spencer yet, do you? Well, I'll tell you how I met him. I was living in London with Louise and a few other people, smoking a load of dope and stuff. We knew Richard. Richard was always a bit straighter than the rest of us, doing this accountancy course, but he took six months out and went to India, and when he came back he was—I don't know— different. It was because he met Spencer there. I realize that now. He'd started meditating and stuff, and I thought he was a bit stuck-up at first. Then Louise had this freak-out on acid and ended up in hospital. I didn't know what to do. Everybody else was too stoned to help, but Richard was brilliant. And then he told me about Spencer, and took me to see him.

"Spencer had just got together with Astrid, and they were both, like, totally radiant. He took both my hands and looked into my eyes and something opened in me and I knew. I just knew. I can't explain it really. It was like seeing the world from inside out, and everything making sense where there'd been no sense before. It changed everything for me. And then he came to visit Louise, and since then she's been getting better all the time. Did you see how she cleaned those windows? She'd never have done that a month ago. She's going to get well here, I know it."

He swigged his beer.

"Spencer's amazing, you know. It's not just what he says, it's what he is. He's not like anyone else. He's been really deep. Deep inside."

"Deep inside—what do you mean?"

"Stick around and you'll find out. Come on, we'd better get back if we want any supper."

We were all tired that night, and we went to bed early. Astrid found me a blanket and a cushion, and I lay down on the blue carpet in the front room along with Richard and Peter, the other single guys. But I couldn't manage to get to sleep. The house still had an empty feeling and the floor was hard, but it wasn't that. It was something that was happening inside me. A layer of fear that had numbed me for years had fallen away, leaving an openness, an expectancy, that was both painful and hopeful at the same time. Life no longer seemed quite so pointless. I lay on my back and listened to one of the guys snoring, and a jumble of memories pounded through my brain: the mountains of Afghanistan; Jude in the pub; sunset in the desert; Astrid on the beach in Greece; my mother jabbering at me over a glass of wine; Mukhtibaba, the sadhu I met in India, touching my forehead and releasing a rush of bliss up my spine.

At about two o'clock in the morning Carla's baby, who had been so quiet all day, started to cry in one of the rooms upstairs, a distant, tiny voice in the night. She cried for a long time.

Chapter 4

I fell in love the next night. Nothing else like it has ever happened to me, and even now when I remember it, I can't quite get ahold of it—the suddenness, the totality of it, like stepping out of an airplane into nothing, the exhilaration of free fall. But no, it wasn't like anything. It was like falling in love, and everybody does that, don't they, at least once in their lives?

All day I'd felt different, my senses awake in a way they hadn't been for years, as I rough-cut the grass with a scythe and collected wood with Tim. I don't know if the others noticed; perhaps they thought I was always like that. Astrid smiled whenever she saw me and Spencer looked serene, but I didn't take much notice of either of them. I was just there, happy, in a beautiful place on a beautiful day.

At one point in the morning I came across Spencer sitting on a rotting bench at the front of the house with Chinook beside him. He motioned me to sit down. I felt shy and couldn't think of anything to say, but I felt him watching me, and when I turned towards him, his face lit up with that extraordinary smile of his.

"So," he said. "It's happened."

"What?"

"An opening. A different way of looking at the world. You'll see." And then: "Whatever comes, it just is. Remember that."

I've no idea where all the people came from for the party, but they came. Friends, and friends of friends, I suppose; people who'd met or heard about Spencer, or just fancied a party in the country. Some of them I saw again later at Spencer's gatherings. We made a fire in the garden, and Richard drove to town to buy food and beer, which we laid out on a folding table we'd found in a shed. I didn't know anybody, but I was caught up in the bubble of enthusiasm and the sense of something new and exciting.

Then the band arrived, a bunch of musicians who lived in a commune in a neighboring village. Somehow they'd heard about us, and they arrived together in an old van with a bunch of friends, all piling out together as the sun set.

"Hey, man, we heard you guys moved in. Too much! What a place! Somebody should've squatted it years ago. Can we join the party?"

We built up the fire to make a big blaze. The moon came up, and a couple of trains roared by, and suddenly the energy was up, the music was lifting off into the night, joints were circulating, and people were dancing on the rough grass that had once been a lawn.

I went to get a beer, and as I came back, I saw Spencer standing away from the fire, watching. I remembered what Astrid had said about being into purity, and I wondered whether he minded, whether things were getting out of hand, so I went up to him.

"Is it okay, what's happening?" I asked.

He smiled.

"Whatever happens is okay. That's the point. Whatever happens is beautiful. Whatever happens couldn't be better. Live now, Stephen. This moment will never come again."

I looked at him. He really meant it.

And I suppose that is half the reason why, later, when a chillum came to me, instead of passing it straight on, I sucked the smoke deep into my lungs, and coughed the terrible cough of the chillum smoker, and was stoned again, properly stoned, for the first time in years.

The other half of the reason was the girl who passed it to me.

I hardly noticed her at first. She was small and dark, with braided hair, wearing a velvet dress. She was pretty, but I didn't really take her in until she held the chillum out to me, looking up at me with a cheeky smile and wide eyes. I smiled back, then shut my eyes as I put the chillum to my lips, and then a few moments later she was patting me on the back, and we were giggling together like old friends although we hadn't exchanged a word.

And then . . .

And then our eyes met, and the giggling stopped, and everything else seemed to stop too, as if we were alone in the universe. We were lost deep in each other's throbbing consciousness, and I have no idea how long that moment lasted. But slowly the world came back—the moon first, then the fire, then the music. . . .

Astrid was singing a Joni Mitchell song. She was high and remote and perfect. I'd never known she could sing like that, and I never heard her again. It was the only time.

Spencer's words echoed in my head: "Live now. Remember: this moment will never come again."

I blinked and was aware of a person attached to the eyes, a girl, her face shining at me with the same experience.

"What's your name?" I asked—as if it mattered!

"Michelle."

She had a slight French accent. I smiled because it reminded me of the Beatles' song, but I didn't say anything, just gazed at her. I had never seen anything so lovely.

"And you?" she asked.

"Stevie."

"Stevie. Like Stevie Wonder. That's nice."

The fire flickered in her pupils, which were growing huge again, and I felt myself falling back into them.

"*Tes yeux sont la citerne ou boivent mes ennuis,*" I mumbled.

"You speak French?" she asked.

"Just some old poems I learned at school."

She smiled, not really understanding, but taking me in, everything about me, as our faces moved towards each other, drawn by a force that neither of us could have resisted.

We kissed.

It wasn't so much passionate. I was too high for passion—stoned from the chillum, exhausted by a sleepless night, all my senses on an edge. But it was extraordinary, electric, perfect. And more than anything, it was easy. Her smell, her taste, the touch of her fingers, all felt so natural, so familiar, as if this was what I had always been looking for, without knowing I was looking for it, as if . . .

No, it wasn't as if. It was. Simply was. Real. Real as a dream.

Astrid had finished singing, and the band was working up an intense rhythm with bongos and guitars. We sat pressed against each other, looking across at happy faces in the firelight, and I felt I was Michelle and Michelle was me, and we loved everyone, everyone.

The dew fell just before daybreak, and I woke feeling damp. The fire was still glowing, and there was a streak of yellow in the eastern sky. As I opened my eyes, a blackbird started up in the rosebush behind us.

Michelle was lying beside me on Astrid's blanket, nuzzled up against me, her arm over me, pulling me to her even in her sleep. I moved gently so as not wake her, and looked at her face. I had never really seen it, I realized, and even now I could only just make out her features in the twilight, so I lay still while the light grew and watched her beauty unfold from the mystery of shadows.

She stirred and opened her eyes and saw me. There was a flicker of surprise as she took in where she was, and then she smiled, reached her arms round my neck, pulled me to her and kissed me.

She was still there. She still wanted me. It was un-believable.

I knew that my life had turned. Nothing would ever be the same again.

Chapter 5

It was Michelle's idea to go to the Isle of Wight. Everything was Michelle's idea, really. After that first night we stayed together, so attached that if I was away from her even for a few minutes, I felt physical pain from the separation. All my own plans had evaporated into nothing, and I would have followed her to the moon. So when she asked me to come with her to this massive festival in the Isle of Wight, with Bob Dylan and The Band, I could never have refused, even though she snuggled up and said she'd stay with me anyway, whatever I did. After all, what was I doing with my life? I thought about my parents and my job in the pub, and it was all meaningless. A distant dream.

I had nothing with me, though, not even a toothbrush.

"What do you need? You have me!" said Michelle. But Astrid found me a shoulder bag and rolled up the blanket she'd lent me.

"You don't have to return it," she said. "But you'll come back soon, won't you?"

We were standing in the drive, saying goodbye. Spencer came from behind Astrid, took my hands and looked in my eyes, and for a moment I felt his power again, like the first time I'd met him.

"You are waking up, Stephen," he said softly. "This is only the beginning." Then louder: "Enjoy yourselves!"

As we got into Tim's Morris to drive to the main road, Ray sauntered across to his van.

"Off to see Dylan, then? Don't need a weatherman to know which way the wind blows!"

And then we were off. Alone and together at last.

We hitched down to London. The lifts came easily, but I didn't care—I was with Michelle and that was all that mattered. We held hands as we drove, and when we stopped, we held each other tight and kissed, oblivious to the world.

In London we went "shopping"—or rather Michelle did, leaving me standing in the street with her rucksack while she went into a department store. Even for that short time I didn't like being away from her, but she was soon back, bringing me a change of clothes stuffed under her jacket: fashionable pre-faded jeans and a new T-shirt. I must have looked shocked because she opened her eyes wide and stroked the fluffy stubble on my chin.

"You are funny—the clothes are there. You need them. Like fruit on a tree. It's not stealing, it's liberating."

All the same, I bought a toothbrush and paid for it.

On the road out of London we met up with a bunch of stranded hitchhikers all heading for the festival. As evening fell, we left the road and camped together in a sort of mock temple in a park, sharing food and joints and watching the sun set. A line of swans flew by with their heavy wings, silhouetted against a purple sky. A boy sang to his guitar: All you need is love. I looked around the faces in the fading light: kind, smiling, open to the world. Michelle was beside me. We held each other tight and it was true: love was all we needed.

A chill came with the dark. We used my blanket for a mattress and squeezed together into Michelle's sleeping bag. Near us, in another sleeping bag, a couple were making love, discreetly enough though you couldn't help but hear. But we simply lay in each other's arms, feeling the love around us. We had time. We had our whole lives.

Next day we arrived at the Isle of Wight, standing on the packed ferry with spray on our faces, then walking down country lanes in a crowd of young people, all infected by the same willingness to share everything: their dope, their food, their love, their dreams—the hope of a new world.

Hope. I had almost forgotten hope. Not the stupid hope of technology—putting a man on the moon and all that stuff—but the hope of living together without struggle and wars, in love and laughter. We could hear the music already, in snatches on the wind. Michelle was beside me, and if I squeezed her hand she squeezed it back, but we weren't looking at each other, we were looking out together at the world, sharing our love with it.

It was quite a long walk, but we got there at last, paid a couple of quid to get in, and lay on the grass in the hazy sunshine with the music flowing around us. I must have fallen asleep because the next thing I knew, it was evening and colder. The music was great, though, full of energy and humor. I stretched, then pulled Michelle's face to mine so that I could speak into her ear.

"Let's dance!"

She jumped up, pulling me up with her, and we picked our way to the front. We couldn't hear each other speak, but we let our bodies talk instead while the sky darkened, and the stage lights came up bright, and the beat pulsed through us. Everything was one.

It was almost dark by the end of the set as we threaded our way back through the growing crowd. Without speaking, we both knew we wanted somewhere we could be alone together.

Next to the arena there was a big tent for people to sleep in, so we wandered over and looked in. It was already crowded, with a stench of old socks and damp sleeping bags. A guy coming out held his nose, smiling at us. Everybody seemed to smile at us. I'd never known the world was so friendly.

"Try the beach," he advised. "It's only ten minutes' walk, down that way."

We took his advice and walked away from the crowds and the noise, down a path through a wood. It was like going into a dark tunnel where we could hardly see where we were stepping, but then suddenly we came

out, and the sea was in front of us, glittering with re-
flected lights from the other side of the strait. We clambered down a bank and found a stretch of dry sand.

Others had come here too, in little huddles, sharing
joints or bottles of wine and lighting campfires. We'd
have been welcome with any of them, but we walked
on past them until the beach narrowed and the bank
behind us was too steep to climb. There we laid down
my blanket.

A half moon and the lights over the water gave just
enough light to see Michelle's face, to see her eyes
searching for mine, to see her lips part as her fingers
reached towards me.

She was so beautiful. Everything about her. Beyond
my dreams, beautiful.

The waves were swishing against the beach. Another
band started in the arena, a soft pulse in the background, not loud enough to drown the sound of laughter from around a neighboring fire.

We opened up Michelle's sleeping bag to give our
bodies some protection, and we touched each other, in
awe of the vastness gathering around us, as if we had
never touched or been touched before.

The vastness opened and swallowed us, and there
was no I or you or this or that. Then it spat us back
out, gasping and clinging to each other in infinite ten-
derness.

All I could say was "I love you."

Michelle nuzzled my neck.

"Oh, Stevie," she murmured.

We ran naked down to the sea and splashed cold water over each other and then, salty and tingling, dried each other with Michelle's towel and put on all the clothes we had to stop our shivering.

Michelle rolled a joint, and we talked.

We had never really talked before—just little bits here and there. We knew so little of each other. It made me happy to think there was still so much of her to know. Because in that moment I was sure we would spend all our lives together. Nothing less seemed possible.

I told her stories from my past—stories I'd hardly told to anyone because they wouldn't understand. I told her how I'd been seduced by my English teacher. She wasn't shocked at all. In fact she laughed.

"What happened to him?" she asked.

"They kicked him out of the school. After that I don't know."

"He sounds an interesting man: sure he screwed you up a bit, but he gave you something too, made you stronger. And you're okay now. I can tell you that."

She nuzzled against me and we kissed again.

I told her about Afghanistan and India, about the light on the mountains, the smells of the bazaar. Then she told me about her life, growing up in Paris.

"My mother is French but my father is English. He is an artist. He left when I was small, and I stayed with my older sister and my mother. Then I argued with my mother, and I came to London, to my father. It was very exciting at first. He is not like my mother at all. He is so rich and successful, and he gave me everything I asked for, but he never talks to me. Or actually, sometimes he is lots of fun and other times he is just somewhere else. So I had a big row with him. I told him he is a capitalist pig and he has too much money. He just laughed and said maybe, but I live off him. So I left, with nothing, just to show him. And I am okay. If your mind is good, you can live without money, no problem. It is a beautiful way to live. Because when you need it, everything is there."

"I did try, once," I said.

"You did?"

"In India. I tore up my passport and threw it in the Ganges. Then I gave all my money away—not that I had much by then. I was trying to lose my past."

"Too much! And you were okay, huh?"

"I didn't starve, but I went a bit mad. I started to think I was like Jesus."

She laughed at that. We both did. I could see how funny it sounded. She put her face close to me.

"But I think you were," she whispered. "I think you still are."

For a moment I almost believed her, and felt the madness welling up in me, that sense of personal power, that I could control other people, that I could do and be anything. But I pushed it away.

"No," I said. "I wasn't. I'm not," and I kissed her before she could say anything back.

* * *

51

Looking back, that was the best, that night on the beach, cold but so together, just the two of us and our lives stretching before us. I wanted nothing more, ever. We slept in the end. The moon went down and the stars shone out brightly above us, then in the rosy dawn we woke in each other's arms, still lost in our love for each other and for the world that we saw fresh through each other's eyes.

As the sun rose, we packed up our few possessions and wandered back through the woods. The arena was empty now, apart from the rubbish, but in the tent cities people were beginning to wake up. A smell of frying bacon came from a few food stands selling breakfast. We queued at one of them.

And then a girl was rushing towards us, and Michelle's face was alive with pleasure—or was it alarm?—as the girl threw her arms around her, talking in rapid French. After a while, Michelle disengaged herself and turned to me.

"This is my sister, Suzanne. Isn't that amazing?"

Suzanne looked like Michelle, but not so pretty. Next to her Michelle looked suddenly young. She pecked me on both cheeks.

"Pleased to meet you," she said formally, with a strong French accent. Behind her, her boyfriend, Jean-Claude, was smoking a Gauloise and trying to look cool. I felt a shiver of anxiety. Why were these people invading our perfection? But I pushed it away. We were strong enough, Michelle and I. We had love to share.

They took us to their tent, where they made good

coffee and gave us bread and jam, and Michelle and Suzanne talked nonstop, too fast for me to understand. I felt a little lonely at first, but I was so tired I could hardly keep awake, so after a while I went inside the tent and lay down on an air bed, warm and dry. After all, it was amazing meeting Suzanne like that, an amazing coincidence. Soon Michelle joined me, and we both fell deep asleep.

We woke at the same moment. I opened my eyes and looked at Michelle. It was strange not to feel her body against mine, but her face was only inches away. And she opened her eyes at once and smiled at me sleepily, and I knew everything was okay, we were still together. We were warm and dry and rested, and we made love again, gently, silently. The vastness was still there.

Bob Dylan was coming! That was the buzz. He hadn't played live for three years, but he was going to play for *us*! Sunday, the big day, and Bob Dylan was coming!

We sat in a vast crowd of eager faces, listening to one band after another. The music was too loud for talking, but I didn't mind. Real communication is beyond words, and I would have been happy anywhere. I was with Michelle, and all things were the same to me as long as we were together.

Suzanne was nice, and she seemed to like me. Jean-Claude sat the other side of her, silent and cool, nodding in time to the music while Michelle leant against me, squeezing my hand and smiling up into my eyes when I passed her a joint. Nobody cared that the weather had got worse, low clouds with a light English drizzle that made everything damp. Anyway, after a while the clouds lifted and some sunshine burst through. A girl took off all her clothes, and the crowd raised her over their heads, and she walked naked towards the stage as if dancing in the air while everyone cheered.

I held Michelle, and our love was part of something enormous, something that would change the world.

One thing I never thought about was home. My parents' house, the pub, Jude and my other friends—all that was a dream, another reality that had no meaning anymore.

As darkness fell, people made bonfires with the rubbish, lighting up the night.

"You are the Blessed Generation! You are the Body Beautiful! Thank you—keep it that way!" enthused the disembodied voice of the MC over the loudspeakers. Even at the time it sounded pompous, but I believed him.

At last Dylan came on, a small white figure in the distance. He glanced around nervously and burst straight into "She Belongs To Me." I looked at Michelle, and we were lost again in each other's eyes. For a little while longer everything was perfect.

Chapter 6

It was over. The small white figure left the stage, and the MC's voice informed us that that was it. Finished.

Obediently the kids around us started to move, back to their tents or the long trek to the ferries. The drizzle had stopped, but the paths had already turned to mud.

I nudged Michelle. I wanted to be alone with her.

"Let's go back to the beach for a bit."

She came with me, but it wasn't the same. The sand was wet, and a mist was rising from the sea. We held hands and walked down to the pebbly foreshore, but she was miles away.

"What are you thinking about?"

"Oh, nothing."

She slipped on a patch of mud and swore in French.

"What's the matter?" I asked dopily as I helped her up.

"What do you think's the matter? I hurt myself."

She was so sharp it was like a physical shock. I let go of her hand and stood, all my nerves jarred. Suddenly I was shivering from the cold.

"Oh, look at this! I ruined my skirt."

She tried to examine the mud stain, which was

hardly visible in the dark. I didn't understand. How could a little mud come between us?

"I'm going back to the tent," she said abruptly. "I've had enough of this."

The way she said it made it sound as if it was me she'd had enough of. I was stunned and didn't know how to answer. Perhaps she had a point, though. We'd been together so much, maybe we needed some space from each other.

"I . . . I think I'll take a walk. I'll join you later. That is, if you want me."

She softened.

"Of course I want you." She squeezed my hand and brushed my cheek with her lips. Then she turned and disappeared into the night.

I missed her immediately, with an ache of anxiety that I'd never see her again. But I was being stupid, and besides she was right: the beach was damp, and the mist was gathering, tinged orange from the lights across the water and smelling of old fish. I waited a couple of minutes, then followed her into the tunnel through the trees.

There was no music from the arena anymore, but I could hear a sort of hum—a hundred thousand people getting ready to leave or sleep or make love or party.

It was dark in the tunnel, and it was strange not to feel the warmth of Michelle's body next to me. I had got so used to her. But my own body was still there, pumping and pulsing and tingling. A light wind breathed through the treetops, and I thought I heard small creatures rustling in the undergrowth.

I shivered again. The night was growing colder. I came out of the trees and turned towards the hill, looking for a campfire where I could warm myself.

"C'mon, man, take a seat."

It was the biggest fire on the hill, beside a makeshift hut that looked as if it had been there for weeks. The people sitting round the fire looked like that too.

"Hey, yeah, don't stand there getting cold! Come on and join us."

"Thanks," I said, and stepped into the circle lit by the fire. The guy who had called me over threw on some more wood, from what looked like a chopped-up piano. I sat down on a bit of cardboard next to him and stretched out my hands to warm them.

"I'm Jonno," he said. "Been here a week. We got so settled in, I don't really want to leave. Beautiful, huh? What a scene!"

"Hi," I said, "I'm Stephen."

"Hi, Stephen. You're welcome."

We sat in silence for a while. I didn't feel any need to say anything. I was just there, with good people who accepted me, not knowing what I was, not caring. The fire warmed me and the night was alive.

I couldn't quite distinguish most of the dark figures huddled in the flickering shadows, but a blond girl's face caught the firelight as she leant forward, rolling a joint. Between us a tall guy with a quiet face sat absolutely still.

"Did you come for Dylan, or for the scene?" asked Jonno.

"I just came," I said. "With a friend. She wanted to come, so I came with her. But I wanted to see Dylan too."

"Yeah, everybody wants to see Dylan. Everybody saw him too. Like, some of us don't have the bread for the arena, but by the time he played, they'd knocked down all the fences, so we just walked in. Except for Matthew." He pointed to the tall, immobile boy the other side of me. "Matthew never went nowhere, the whole time. I mean, the rest of us, we've been busy all week, getting firewood, building the hut, listening to the music. We even built the stage when we first got here. I don't know how they'd have done it without us. But Matthew, he just stays right here by the fire, and he never misses nothing. That right, Matthew?"

I turned to Matthew, and he moved his head—just his head—so that he was looking at me. He had big eyes that seemed to look straight through me, huge pupils reflecting the firelight.

"It isn't real," he whispered, as if taking me into a confidence. "It doesn't exist. Can't you see? Nothing is real. Not you. Not me. Not the fire, or the hills or the sky. Nothing . . ."

"What about Bob Dylan?" I asked. "Didn't you want to see him?"

His eyes narrowed. "Bob Dylan, Bob Dylan, Bob

Dylan . . . Don't you understand? Bob Dylan doesn't exist. We just imagine him. That's all there is: what we imagine. That's all there is. . . . Nothing . . ." His eyes left mine and wandered back towards the fire.

"You can't argue with him, can you? When you think about it, he's right," said Jonno. He shut his eyes and took a deep breath. "Matthew just rolled up by the fire a few nights back. Guess he took an acid trip and can't come down. Only question is, what's he gonna do tomorrow, when we all split and there's nobody to feed him except the cows? And they're not real either."

The blond girl finished rolling her joint and leant over in front of the unmoving Matthew, offering it to me.

"Here! You light!" she said with a Scandinavian accent. Her hair was hanging down round her face, and her nipples made little tight points on her T-shirt. I couldn't have refused her even if I'd wanted to. She got up and squatted in front of me, holding a match, and I smelled the sweat from her armpits. A few days before I'd have been attracted, but now there was only Michelle for me. I blew out most of the smoke before it got into my lungs, then I passed the joint back to her. She gave a throaty, ironical laugh and stroked my cheek, then stood up and took a deep drag herself, looking out into the night.

"This is the world as it could be, man," said Jonno beside me. "This is peace and love in practice. This is looking after each other, and looking after the planet and having a ball. It's the future, man, we're the future, never forget it."

On the other side of the campfire a boy started strumming a guitar and singing:

"Blackbird singing at the dead of night . . ."

Jonno tapped out the rhythm on an old saucepan. On the other side of me, Matthew sat immobile, staring into the unreality of the fire.

"All your life you were only waiting for this moment to arrive."

I must have sat a long time with Jonno and Matthew and the beautiful blond girl and the others who came and went, sharing their joints and their talk and their music, because fingers of light were showing in the east by the time I crawled into the tent and snuggled down beside Michelle. There was just room for the four of us, lying in line. She didn't wake but threw an arm over me as I nuzzled up to her and drifted into sleep, smelling her smell that was now so familiar, listening to the rooks announcing the dawn.

When I woke, the others were already up and packing. I could hear Michelle and her sister arguing, their French too fast for me to pick up. They stopped when I came out. Suzanne, brisk and efficient, flashed me a smile and asked me if I'd slept well. Michelle looked at me moodily. Her face was young in the morning light.

"Where were you?" she asked. "Where did you go all night?"

"Just a campfire," I said.

She grunted, but then she smiled.

"Come on, we have to go. These guys ate all the bread this morning before I even woke, so there's nothing to eat. Maybe we can get some breakfast on the ferry."

I looked around at a desolate scene. Most of the tents had already gone, leaving mud and litter blown in spirals by the wind. It wasn't raining yet, but black clouds were gathering in the west.

We packed the tent and trudged towards the ferry in a line of thousands, all tired, dirty and hungry. Suzanne and Jean-Claude both had big rucksacks, so I carried the tent for them, feeling cool for traveling so light. Suzanne had a car parked in Southampton, so we wouldn't have to hitch back to London. Or so I thought.

It was a long walk on empty bellies, until Michelle spotted a bakery van with the back door left open and liberated a tray of doughnuts. Everyone laughed at her audacity, and she shared them round. I glanced back and saw the driver glaring at us, but there was nothing he could do, faced with such a crowd. I felt a pang of guilt, and then I felt ashamed of being so uncool. Because I was part of something huge now, a movement that would change the world. What was it Jonno had said? "We're the future. Never forget it."

The ferry was packed, and we were all so dirty we must have made quite a pong, though I couldn't really smell it because I was part of it. Suzanne pushed ahead and grabbed some seats, and then I queued for plastic cups of gray tea. Suzanne and Jean-Claude turned up their noses, but Michelle sighed with pleasure at the hot liquid.

She turned to me, squeezing my hand.

"What do you want, Stevie?"

The question took me aback. What did I want? For the last three days I'd thought about nothing but the moment I was in, the bliss of being with Michelle, of loving and being loved in return. I didn't think about what would happen next. There would always be something.

"Nothing. I don't want anything."

"You must do. Everybody wants something."

"To be with you," I said. "That's all. Just to be with you."

I felt her response. Her pupils dilated, and she leant into me and kissed me softly. Then she sighed.

"You don't know me. It will not be always like this. I want so many things. You are too good for me. Too good."

"No, I'm not," I said quickly, but there was a thump in my chest. Southampton was approaching. What would happen when we got off the ferry?

"Michelle . . . we're going with your sister to London, right?"

"I don't know," she said. "I don't know. . . . Why don't we go to your parents?" she suddenly asked brightly.

My parents! The thought was so absurd that I laughed.

"Why do you laugh? Won't they like me?"

"I just can't imagine it." I started to explain, but Michelle interrupted me.

"Suzanne wants me to come back with her to my father, but I won't go, ever. He's shit."

There was bitterness in her voice. I squeezed her hand.

"She also said she can't fit you in the car. It's shit, I tell you. It's just she doesn't like you. . . ."

My heart missed a beat. I was amazed. I was sure Suzanne liked me. She'd smiled, flirted almost. What had I done or said?

"Or maybe she likes you too much. She is jealous. She is always jealous of my boyfriends. Because Jean-Claude is such a bore."

Boyfriends? She hadn't told me about other boyfriends, and the thought had never occurred to me. I knew so little about her still. We needed to talk again; we needed somewhere where we could be together quietly.

"Why don't we go back to The Hollies?" I said. "We could stay there for a while."

She looked at me curiously, and shook her head.

"No, I don't like. That guy Spencer, he's on some weird trip."

The ship was docking. Suzanne and Jean-Claude shouldered their rucksacks. Suzanne smiled at me as if I was her best friend, and then called out something to Michelle over the hubbub. People were milling past us, towards the exits, and I got separated from Michelle, who had worked her way close to Suzanne. Suddenly they were shouting at each other angrily. The crowd pulled back from them, and a moment later I was back at Michelle's side. Suzanne tossed her head and muttered something to Jean-Claude. Then she turned back and looked at me.

"You be careful," she called in her strong accent. "It is not like you think!"

Michelle grabbed my arm.

"You want to be with me. Then come!"

She pulled me to one side, and we watched Suzanne and Jean-Claude carried away from us in the crowd of young faces—so many lives crossing for a moment, never to see each other again.

Michelle put her arm around me. She had already softened.

"Let them go," she said. "We don't need them."

"Where shall we go, then?" I asked.

She smiled and hugged me.

"Trust in the universe. It is big."

Chapter 7

Michelle: did I ever know her? Did I even have the slightest idea what she was really like, or did we only ever see our own reflections in each other?

Spencer once said that when people fall in love, they think it's about the other person, but it's not. What they really love is their own dreams, their own desires. I've thought about that a lot, and I'm still not sure. I still want to believe that there was something else when I was with Michelle, something more like a loss of individual self, a merging together of our souls. While we were in that state, making love was easy, perfect, but it was also unnecessary, because we had the union anyway. Once we fell out of it, physical love became impossible.

Yet it's true: I didn't know her. I think back, and I can remember things she said, the way she looked at me, in love and later in anger, the way she ate, the way she half closed one eye when she smiled at me. I can remember her smell, her laugh, her face when she slept—but mostly I remember the tingles of joy that went through me at her touch, I remember the sense of completion that her presence gave me, I remember seeing, hearing, feeling, more vividly than I ever had since I was a child. I remember how *I* was with *her*.

Even on the ferry I already knew deep down what was going to happen. Michelle was already moving on, and the dream was over. I couldn't admit it, but subconsciously I knew it, and my knowing made things happen the way they did. It was my fault. All of it.

We didn't know where we were going. We trusted in the universe, and the universe sent us a battered Mercedes that cruised the long row of hitchhikers and picked us out deliberately.

The people in the Mercedes had been at the festival and were as dirty as we were. As we got in, the rain started, lashing the windscreen. The driver grinned, and passed Michelle a joint.

"Where are you heading?"

"Don't know," said Michelle. "Wherever we get to."

"Come back to our place, then. You'll like it."

So we did.

At first sight it looked like a great place—a half-derelict hotel on an island in the Thames, with overgrown lawns and a ballroom where the Rolling Stones had once played, now housing a haphazard community of artists and dope dealers. The guy who had given us a lift showed us a pokey little room the size of a broom cupboard, and told us we were in luck because the previous occupant had just gone. Then he left us to it.

We found a bathroom with a huge, ancient bath with legs like lion's paws. For hot water we boiled up saucepans in the kitchen, and then got in together, soaping

66

each other and rubbing off layers of dirt. Then we lay for a long while in the warm water. It relaxed me and I wanted to make love, but Michelle gently detached herself.

"Let's eat first. I'm so starving I could eat a bus. Maybe I'll eat you!"

She laughed, and her eyes flashed, but she didn't try to eat me, just stepped out of the bath, patting my wet hair.

We headed back out across the rickety footbridge that was the only access to the island, and found a transport café on the main road where we ordered the full works: eggs, chips, sausages, beans. I paid of course. Michelle didn't have any money—not that that mattered; my money was hers too. The first few mouthfuls tasted okay, but then a wave of exhaustion hit me, and suddenly it all seemed heavy and greasy. Opposite me Michelle grinned, a red trickle of tomato sauce on her chin.

"You know, when I first came to England, I thought the food was disgusting. But now I am used to it. When you are hungry, everything tastes good."

I leant forward and dabbed a paper napkin at her chin. Then I looked down. On my own plate, yellow yolk was flowing slowly into gray chips. I watched it, repelled and attracted at the same time. The yolk looked alive.

Two guys came over and started chatting, but I didn't take much notice. I hadn't realized how tired I was. Nights of snatched, uncomfortable sleep were catching up with me. After a while I closed my eyes, cut out the sounds and watched little flickering lights—blue, green, orange—on the inside of my eyelids.

I opened my eyes. Michelle was rolling a cigarette. One of the guys was grinning at her flirtatiously, and she was smiling back at him, one eye half closed, the way she looked at me. . . .

I stood up abruptly.

"Let's go."

She was surprised, but she came.

"Are you all right?" she asked, puzzled more than anything.

"Just tired, I think. Sorry!"

We lay down on the grass by the river. The showers had passed, and the afternoon sun felt steamy. Michelle made me roll over onto my front and gave me a massage.

"It's a good place. Nice people. We are lucky. We should stay here."

She was kneading a point in my back that was incredibly painful. I could only groan.

"You should be careful. You are very tense," she said. "But beautiful," she added, almost as an afterthought, stroking my thighs.

I don't remember much about the afternoon except that Michelle kept talking to people and I didn't like it. I wanted her all to myself. I stayed with her, though, feeling glazed and not saying much; sometimes I felt her irritation with me, though she never said anything.

Then as night fell, people gathered in the old ballroom, smoking joints and playing music. When the joint reached me, I took a token puff and passed it on. I was too tired to cope with being stoned. I turned to Michelle.

"Let's go to bed."

She wanted to stay. I knew she did. She must have been tired too, but she was intrigued by the place and the people and ready to keep going, while I'd just had enough. All the same, she gave a wry look and came with me.

In our little room she lit a candle, and then she took off her clothes, slowly, trying to be seductive. I sat on the mattress watching her. She was smiling at me, but she wasn't there. I knew her mind was downstairs, with the scene. But I took my clothes off too, and we lay down, and she touched me gently.

I wanted her so badly, but it wasn't right. Something had changed between us. Something was slipping away. I knew it, and there was nothing I could do.

She brushed her nipples against my chest and kissed me with a show of passion, rubbing against me.

I looked at her—her big dark eyes and her skin glowing orange in the candlelight. She was as beautiful to me as ever, but she wasn't real. We had had reality, and this was only acting. We had known perfection, and I wouldn't settle for less. A cold shadow seemed to pass into me.

She felt the coldness.

"What's the matter?" she whispered.

"It has to be real," I said. "I can't fake it. Not with you. I love you too much."

I was afraid she might be angry, but she wasn't. I felt her soften, and she lay down next to me and pulled the sleeping bag over us.

She turned to me and buried her head in my shoulder, kneading the skin on my chest with her fingers and trembling slightly.

I held her gently. Was she upset? I wasn't even sure. I wasn't sure of anything anymore.

After a while her breath slowed and she fell asleep, but I didn't. I couldn't. The shadow had turned to a tight ball in my chest, and the tension had returned in my shoulders and my back. I lay still, though, so as not to wake her, and listened to the muted music from downstairs and the melancholy horns of the boats on the Thames. Much later, a couple came into the room next door and had sex with a great deal of humping and gasping.

It had to be perfect, I kept thinking. It had to be perfect, or nothing.

That held out so little hope.

I twitched. A shudder that started in the small of my back twisted my spine and flicked my legs into the air.

Michelle stirred and rolled over, away from me.

I got up, stepped over to the little window and watched the mist in the moonlight, shapes that formed and dispersed, like ghosts. I stayed there a long time, and when I finally lay down again, I fell into a light sleep and dreamed I was being chased endlessly down city streets by nameless forces, never quite being caught, but with no hope of escape.

When I opened my eyes, light was coming in through the window, and Michelle was sitting up and brushing her hair, which glistened sleek under the brushstrokes. She smiled at me brightly.

Too brightly, I thought.

"Hi there! You coming down the café? You like some breakfast?"

Her friendliness seemed put on and distant.

I stretched and sat up. The café? The memory of the egg yolk came back to me. I couldn't face all that, not yet.

"Couldn't we get some stuff and make our own breakfast here—muesli and things?" I suggested.

"Aren't you meant to be English? Don't you like an English breakfast?" She sounded annoyed. "Okay then, I'll go on my own."

And then suddenly she turned to me and she was different, there with me, and I felt myself melt into her eyes again. She sat down and leant her head on my shoulder, touching my lips with her fingers.

"Oh, Stevie," she murmured. "You are too good for me."

It hardly lasted a moment, then she jumped up.

"But I'm starving. I can't live on air like you do. See you later."

* * *

I went down to the kitchen, made myself a cup of tea and took it back upstairs. In the morning light I could see all the smears on the wall and the stains on the mattress. I had a stomachache too, but that wasn't the problem. Last night, when the cold shadow entered me, it had woken a dreadful certainty: Michelle was going to leave me.

In a way she already had.

I sat there for a long time with the tight ball of anxiety in my chest and thoughts running in circles in my head: memories of that first night under the rosebush, so short a time ago and yet an eternity . . . dancing at the festival . . . making love on the beach. . . .

No, I was wrong. Nothing was over. Michelle was coming back to me. She loved me. The future stretched in front of us.

What future? I wanted to see it, I wanted it so badly, but there was nothing there.

At last a bunch of people came in through the front door, and I heard her laugh. I waited for her to come up to me. If she loved me, she would come up. She had to come. She had to.

She didn't come. They all went together into the kitchen.

After a while I went down.

They were sitting round the table. I knew one of them, the guy who'd given us a lift. He was sitting next to Michelle, rolling a joint. On the other side of her was an older guy with thinning hair tied back in a bun, a bushy beard and little round glasses, and an air of authority. Next to him a girl in a brightly colored sweater was crocheting.

The window was open. Sunlight shone on the grass outside, and you could smell the river.

They all looked round as I came in. The older guy raised his hand.

"You're Stevie, huh? Greetings!"

Michelle smiled vaguely, but she didn't move up to make a space. I sat down opposite her.

"Guess what?" she said. "I met an old friend—Stu. He's living here."

Stu nodded wisely.

"We been here six months, me and my old lady." He gestured at the crocheting girl, who didn't look up. "Welcome! You are obviously a destined person, to have got here. This is one of the focus points of the New Age." He looked at me intently. "We're living the future here, man."

I hesitated. I didn't feel quite up to living the future at that moment. And I wanted to know when Michelle had met this guy, what she might have done with him. Or maybe I didn't want to know.

"We've been hearing a lot about you," Stu continued. "You've been on a Journey to the East, Michelle says."

I didn't want to talk about it. I didn't like Michelle talking about me behind my back either.

"I suppose so. It was a long time ago."

"Well, isn't that great?" said Stu. "Who'd have thought it?" He turned to Michelle with a conspiratorial smirk, which she returned.

I felt intensely uncomfortable, but I didn't show it. I tried to look cool.

"We were just talking," said Stu. "We have a little ritual here, Tuesday afternoons. I think it's a Tuesday, isn't it?" He chuckled. "Yeah, those of us who are here, we like to drop acid on Tuesday afternoons because it's quiet and it's really cool by the river, and it's a group thing. Good vibes."

Acid? LSD? I'd never taken it before. Suddenly my heart was throbbing. I glanced at Stu, making sure I was too quick to make eye contact. Could I trust him? Michelle did, but then . . . I remembered Matthew by the campfire, fixed in a paralyzing perception of unreality. No, it wasn't a matter of trusting Stu. It was a matter of trusting my own mind. And I didn't.

"It's good acid, man. Totally pure. Never had a bad trip with this lot. Michelle's up for it. What do you say?"

I was aware that Michelle was trying to catch my eye, but I kept my gaze firmly on the table. What did she want to do to me? Drive me mad? I remembered Suzanne's last shouted words to me: "You be careful. It is not like you think!"

So how was it? How was it?

In the end I didn't care. The choice was simple. I knew I wasn't seeing things quite right, that my body was getting ill, and I was already oversensitive. I knew it was dangerous to take acid in my present state. But it was that or Michelle. She was up for it, and I couldn't be left behind. If I took it, I might lose my mind, but if I didn't, I would lose her, to Stu or one of the other guys that flocked round her.

There was no competition.

"Yeah, okay," I said.

"Good one, Stevie," said Stu. "You won't regret it."

But I never did drop acid. I didn't even get that far. And I still don't understand why I did what I did.

Michelle was trying to catch my eye, but I wouldn't look her way. I didn't understand anything about how I felt, or why the ball in my chest was throbbing so painfully. I only knew I wanted her more than ever, but all to myself, alone. I couldn't cope with the rest of the world coming into our lives. I wouldn't be able to keep her, but I couldn't let her go. And the acid was like a coming death.

Without saying anything, I got up and went outside. Down by the riverbank some moorhens were busy in the rushes. I sat down and watched them. It was a peaceful scene, but it didn't calm me. My breath was rasping.

After a while I heard Michelle. She came up behind me and passed her fingers over my shoulders, then sat down, a couple of feet away.

Yesterday she would have been beside me.

"You okay?" she asked.

"Yeah, I'm okay."

I spoke clearly, with a pretense of normality. I could still do that. But I didn't look up. I was afraid of what I might see in her eyes, or not see.

"You don't seem very okay. You need to eat, you know. And calm down a bit. You're driving yourself crazy like this."

She was matter-of-fact and detached, like an advice columnist.

"I don't feel hungry," I replied, still trying to be normal. I could play that game too. "Maybe I picked up a bug on the Isle of Wight."

"You know, I don't think you should take acid. Not now."

I could feel her looking at me, but I still didn't look back.

"You're only taking it because I take it. It's not a good reason. You can take it another time, when you're better."

I looked up then, straight into her eyes. She didn't look away, but she didn't melt into me either. She was there, but separate, holding her most important part aloof.

"Where do you know Stu from?" I asked.

"Oh, I met him last year. He's a nice guy. Wise. He doesn't get attached."

"He's a prick," I said.

I don't know why I said that. I didn't have any opinions about Stu, really. He was just another face in the crowd that was not me or her. She bristled, suddenly angry.

"What's your problem, man?"

I winced. She spoke like a stranger, hard and hostile.

"Us," I said. For a last time I would try to be open, as we should be. "You're not like you used to be. I . . . I just want you . . . to be with you, like before. . . ."

She snorted and tossed her hair.

"Get your head together, man. You're not my dog."

She got up and walked angrily back towards the house. I watched her go, seeing the tension in her spine.

I turned back to the river, inhaling in tight gasps, as if I'd forgotten how to breathe. How could she do this to me? How could she betray what had been between us?

Yet, she'd done nothing.

Yet, she'd gone.

The tight ball in my chest was growing, throbbing with anger and sorrow. It wouldn't let me sit still. I had to do something, anything. I got up and followed her.

She was sitting on the mattress in our room, head in her hands. She looked up and started to smile, then stopped herself.

She stood up and faced me, hands on hips. "Shall we talk?" I said.

"Oh, Stevie, just stop hanging on to me, will you? Let go. It's been great, but can't you see? Things have to change."

What was she saying? Only yesterday she'd said she would stay with me forever. Except that she hadn't said that. She had said, trust in the universe. But I didn't. Not anymore.

"What do you mean?"

"The Isle of Wight. All that. It was beautiful, but it's over."

Over. Over.

Blood pulsed into my head and my eyes dimmed. I understood. Over. It had to be perfect or it was nothing. . . . Over . . . It must be, and finally and forever and no going back. Anger, shame, despair . . . The ball in my chest exploded into my arm, and my arm went back, and swung, and with a cry of rage and pain I hit her with the flat of my hand across her cheek.

She gasped, in surprise more than pain, and for a moment our eyes met in the mutual terror of two animals falling into an abyss.

A red patch was spreading on her cheek. She gave a little scream and stepped back, picking up her hairbrush and brandishing it as if to defend herself.

"Don't you come near me," she snarled. "Don't you dare!"

"I'm sorry," I said. "Sorry . . ."

I turned and walked out of the room, down the stairs, out of the hotel, across the rickety bridge, onto the main road with its roar of cars and smell of exhaust. I saw nobody and nothing. I didn't look back. It was over. Over. My mind was clear, but a terrible emptiness had settled in my heart.

For each man kills the thing he loves.

That's what Oscar Wilde said. I'd never believed it. And yet that was what I'd done.

I went into a phone booth and rang my parents. My mother answered, and I held the phone away from my ear while she ranted about how worried they'd been.

"I'm all right, Mum," I lied as the pips went. "I'm coming home."

Chapter 8

I thought it might be better to be back in my own room. I thought I might feel some security. But I was wrong. There was no security for me anymore. I'd only been gone a week, but in that time everything had changed, and when I shut the door to my room, that was when it really hit me: a torrent of shame, regret, loss and loneliness. If loneliness can describe that sense of total isolation in a hostile universe.

It convulsed me, sending shudders up my spine and twisting my body. Soon I came to think of it as a physical presence—demons that I fled from, hiding under my blanket or behind a wall of sound from my headphones. But there was no hiding. They always found me, flattening my chest and squeezing out sobs of grief and rage.

One word throbbed through me: Michelle. How could I have lost her, so soon, so suddenly? How could something so good, so true, have had so bitter an end?

I made mad plans to win her back, and rushed down the stairs to put them into immediate action. But by the time I reached the front door, my schemes had turned to dust. Even if I found her, she'd only spit at me.

I tried to read, but words jumbled up and made no sense. Then I picked up a volume of poems by Gerard

Manley Hopkins, opened it at random, and the words leapt off the page at me:

. . . a rack where . . . thoughts against thoughts in groans grind.

Thoughts grinding against thoughts—that was exactly how my mind was too, torturing itself. I flipped back to the introduction and read that Hopkins was a celibate Jesuit priest. It wasn't a girl who had left him to terrible isolation in a friendless world. It was God.

I struggled on for a while. The book list came for my course. I got the books from the library and sat reading the same sentence over and over, trying to make the jargon come to some sort of meaning, then gave up and let my chaos overwhelm me. I played loud music through my headphones to drown my thoughts, but anything like a love song reduced me to a blob of longing. I had tasted something and I'd lost it, and I couldn't bear to go on living without it because without it nothing had any point at all.

Nights were the worst. I lay awake for hours, then when I finally got to sleep, I dreamed I was being chased down city streets, or trying to catch railway trains that accelerated away from me in hoots of steam as I ran down the platform searching windows for a face.

Yet I wasn't mad. My thoughts were only thoughts. The loneliness and desolation that crowded in on me through those endless nights, that was what I was. But it wasn't all that I was. I didn't know how to explain this. I had no words for it, but I knew it all the same, and the knowledge kept me going.

One day I met Jude in the street.

"Hi, Stephen, where've you been?"

She was genuinely pleased to see me. It took me aback.

"I . . . I went to the Isle of Wight."

"Isle of Wight?" She looked awestruck. "You saw Dylan? Fantastic! I wish I'd gone."

"I didn't know you were interested in . . . that sort of thing."

She looked at me quizzically. She was probably thinking that I didn't know much about her at all, and she was right. We walked on down the street together, silently. I couldn't think of anything else to say.

"I'm going out with Chris," she said after a while. "It's not that serious, but it's kind of easy."

Kind of easy? What could I say?

"Good," I managed.

"By the way, how were your results?"

"B for English and French and D for History. How about you?"

"Oh, mine were terrible. But who cares? I can always be a hairdresser."

She looked at me with a face full of freshness and laughter. Then she swiveled away and was gone.

I stood where she'd left me. The street was crowded, and people pushed around me, taking no notice of me, as if I didn't exist. Perhaps I didn't. But one thing was certain: there was no life for me here, and there would be no course in reading either. Whether I liked it or not, I had left this reality behind. I was wasting everybody's time by pretending.

I had to go.

By the time my mother got home, I'd already packed an old sleeping bag and the few things I wanted into my rucksack.

"I'm going," I said.

She was cleaning up the tiny amount of mess I'd made, and hardly seemed to hear.

"Where?" she asked without much interest.

"To London. I'm leaving, Mum. I'm leaving home. I just wanted to tell you."

"Well, I suppose that's all right. You are nineteen after all. You should be able to look after yourself for a couple of weeks. You'll come back here of course, before you go to university."

"I'm not going to university."

"But you've got a place. Your father took a lot of trouble to get it for you."

"I'm not going there, Mum. I'm not interested in business studies."

She put her hands on her hips and faced me.

"Then perhaps you'd like to tell me what you are going to do?"

"I don't know. I'll get a job in London. I thought I might stay with Rob for a bit. . . ."

She snorted.

"I might have known Rob would come into this somewhere."

She turned away from me and started scrubbing at some invisible grease on the counter.

"Well, wait until your father comes home, at least."

"I was going to, Mum."

Yet I didn't feel she cared that much after all. Her heart was elsewhere.

My father came home from work, tired. I told him, and he glanced at me, and then looked away, off into the distance. His lip was twitching.

"Yes," he said. "Yes." And then: "I'm sorry."

He looked at me again, his eyes big, and I felt a wave of sadness.

"Well, you must do as you think. It's your own life. I'm sure you know better than I do. . . ."

Again he looked away.

"I haven't been much of a father to you, I'm afraid."

I didn't know what to say. I wanted to say, yes, he was a great father, but I couldn't find any words, so I just stood there.

"Anyway, I'm glad you'll be with Rob. Your mother will find that a great comfort."

"I'd better go," I said. "Or it'll be getting dark."

"I'll run you to the station."

"No, I was going to hitch."

He raised his eyebrows.

"Let me buy you a train ticket. You'll let me do that for you, won't you?"

I couldn't really refuse.

*   *   *

My mother had another meeting to get ready for, so she pecked me on the cheek at the door. She didn't think I was really leaving. She thought I'd be back in a few weeks with a more sensible attitude. In a way she was right.

"Tell Rob he should come up and see us. There'll always be a dinner on the table for him here. And for you too," she added.

As I got on the train, my father pressed a wad of notes into my hand. I tried to refuse. I didn't want his money. I wanted to make my own way in life. But he insisted.

"Take it. Take it. It's the best I can do."

He was still standing on the platform, waving self-consciously as the train turned a corner, and he disappeared from sight.

Chapter 9

Rob didn't know I was coming. I couldn't tell him because although he had a phone, he'd never given my parents his number. But he was there, fortunately, when I arrived, and made me welcome in his own way. He gave me a place to sleep on the floor behind the sofa and introduced me to his friends, who took no further notice of me. He worked at a bookshop in Camden Town, but he didn't seem to have any regular hours and often stayed up all night writing or talking, fueled by dope and coffee, then slept all morning.

Arriving in London made me feel a bit better at first. For a few days I even went out looking for jobs, but I got no offers so I gave up. I still had most of my father's money anyway, and I could live cheaply because Rob shared everything. I smoked Rob's dope, which kept me in a numbed haze, and passed the days reading and listening to music, walking in the park and hanging round the boutiques.

The girl I'd met in Rob's flat the last time, Melanie, came round a lot at the beginning. I liked her. She looked spaced-out, but she was actually pretty sensible. Most of Rob's friends were left-wing poets or political radicals too absorbed in themselves to notice me, but

Melanie was different, and the three of us often sat around, stoned and relaxed, making parodies of polite conversation. She did the washing-up and kept the place nice too, burning incense to disguise the damp. I wasn't sure about her relationship with Rob, though. It was all meant to be free and easy and no commitments, but they had rows sometimes in the bedroom. I pulled my sleeping bag round my head and tried not to hear.

Melanie worked at the Roundhouse, which was the hip place to hang out, and she got free tickets for us to come to concerts there. I liked that: grooving and dancing, part of a big friendly crowd. I thought I was getting better, that I might even meet someone.

And then I saw Michelle.

I spotted her heading towards the Underground station. I only saw the back of her head and a glimpse of a cheekbone, but I was certain it was her. I tried to run, but the street was crowded and I couldn't make much headway. I yelled, "Michelle!" at the top of my voice and everyone looked round at me, wondering who this madman was, except for her. She quickened her pace and a moment later had disappeared down the steps. I ran after her. I even searched the platforms, but she'd gone.

From that moment the demons returned. I smoked more dope, hoping to ward them off, but that only led to a blurring of my dream and waking states, with the aching longing of lost love pulsing through both. In my dreams I glimpsed her face in trains that sped away from me as I tried to catch them, and by day I'd hang around the entrance to the Underground, or pound the streets, scanning faces. Sometimes I thought I saw her, sure from the curve of the neck, from the way she walked, only to retreat in embarrassment when a head turned and the face wasn't hers.

I doubt Rob noticed anything, but Melanie did.

"You should get yourself together, Stevie. I'll try and get you a job up the Roundhouse if you like."

"No, it's okay," I said quickly. "I'm not quite ready."

"Suit yourself," she said from behind her hair. "Only I think you could do with having a bit more purpose."

She was right of course. I had no purpose. I never had done anyway, even before I met Michelle, but now my life was more meaningless than ever. I was just wrapped up in my own morbid thoughts, disappearing up my own arse, as Rob would have put it.

And Rob always had a purpose. Like my mother, he was always focused outside of himself. Just then it was the Vietnam War. I'd never thought about it much. Nobody in my parents' world ever questioned it. It was a necessary part of the great "Fight against Communism." I'd winced at pictures of a Buddhist monk setting himself on fire, but it wasn't our war, it was America's.

"What do you mean it isn't our war?" Rob snarled when I said something of the sort to him. "Because we're not sending English kids to get killed there? This is Capitalism's war, and we're in that up to our necks. You can't wash your hands of it, Stevie. It's our society making the bombs, making the guns, making the whole flatulent stew of lies and corruption—and it's killing people, it's ripping their skins off and skewering them and frying them and blowing them to small bits, real people, and it's doing it now. People are doing that to people. How are you going to stop it, Stevie? Are you just going to let it go on?"

"I . . . I don't feel there's much I can do," I said lamely.

Rob snorted.

"Well, you could at least try."

"Maybe we should take Stevie to the demo next week," suggested Melanie.

"A lot of good that'll do," said Rob scornfully.

"Demo? What do you mean?" I asked.

Rob looked at me, puzzled more than anything.

"Don't you know about the Vietnam marches?"

"Sort of. I mean, I heard about them, but I didn't pay much attention."

Rob shook his head.

"Where have you been, Stevie? Where have you been?"

I knew he was right. I knew it was too easy to close your eyes to all the wrong things in the world and worry about your own stupid love affair. So for the next week I read everything I could about the war. Rob had loads of books and articles. I saw photos of Vietnamese children running screaming in wreaths of flames as their bodies burned with napalm. I learned statistics: six hundred thousand tons of bombs dropped in two years; over 2 million people killed, including forty thousand Americans. I read about kids of my age being drafted and sent out to kill and be killed in a country the other side of the world of which they knew nothing, and protesters being violently beaten up on American campuses. Why? Why? Why? It was hell on earth and it made no sense at all.

Yet along with the horror I felt a curious elation. Because here was something that could take me out of myself and give me a cause to believe in, something that could give my life back the meaning that it seemed to have lost forever. Perhaps I could join an antiwar group, though Rob was rude about most of them. I was looking forward to the demo.

We picked up the march in Piccadilly. It was a good feeling, people greeting old friends and laughing as we headed up towards the American Embassy. Then, as we turned into Grosvenor Square, Rob muttered, "Christ! There's nobody here!" I didn't know what he meant. There were loads of people—a couple of thousand at least—carrying banners with slogans like STORM THE REALITY STUDIOS: RETAKE THE UNIVERSE, and chanting, "Ho! Ho! Ho Chi Minh!"

There were a lot more police than demonstrators, though. Rows and rows of them lined up in front of the embassy and ready to charge if we came too close. Some of the demonstrators at the front were trying to provoke them. A tall girl was yelling, "We are all Vietcong! We are all Vietcong!" and for a while a chant got going, but no one quite seemed to believe in it.

Rob pushed his way through, and Mel and I followed until suddenly we found ourselves in the front line. A girl next to me was yelling insults, and the cops had linked arms, grim-faced, trying not to react. A surge came from behind, pushing us forwards, and one of the cops raised his baton, eyeing the shouting girl as if he wanted to swat her. Without thinking, I reached out and grabbed his wrist, stopping the blow. The cop was as surprised as I was. He turned to me, and I saw the excitement in his eyes. He made a grab, but Rob was beside me, pulling me away, and at the same time the police line retreated.

That was it really, the height of the action, at least from where we were. After that, both sides kept a distance and gradually the energy went down and people started to drift away. We ended up in a café in Soho.

"What a waste of time," said Rob.

"At least we tried," I said.

Rob gave me one of his rare smiles.

"You should have been here last year, Stevie. Last year it was practically a revolution. A quarter of a million of us marching down the Strand, then on to the American Embassy, and in their face the whole way. Shit, Stevie, you don't know what you missed! We had a will and an anger that time. We were going to do it, we were going to get into that embassy, and pull out that rat who calls himself an ambassador, and make him feel what it's like for the Vietnamese. We had those bastards scared too. The cops charged us on their horses, and we threw marbles on the road so that they were slithering around. The pigs on the ground were going crazy, smashing at people with their batons. We pulled one of them out of his line and gave him a kicking. He curled up crying, and a guy started running round with his helmet on, which got the rest of them even more fired up. But there were too many of them in the end. They came at us in a big surge and we all ran. . . ."

He stopped and sipped his coffee.

"We thought it was the start of the revolution, like in Paris, but it wasn't. It was just a one-off. Then the next time, last March, there were millions of people, but it was tame. We were all good little lambs and did what we were told and trooped down to Hyde Park and listened to speeches. And a fat lot of good that did. The politicians told us what proper citizens we'd all been and gave us a pat on the back, but it made no difference. They just ignore it. The killing goes on."

"Maybe if people keep up the pressure . . ."

"Don't kid yourself," said Rob. "Anyway, how many people were there? Two or three thousand, that's all. It's back down to the Campaign for Nuclear Disarmament oldies who never give up because they're too stupid to see they're never going to change anything by shouting slogans. . . . It's time to wise up, Stevie, time to try a different tack."

"Like what?"

Rob grinned.

"I don't know yet. But I'll think of something."

I felt deflated. As usual I should have been there last

year, but I wasn't. Somehow Rob always made me feel I'd missed out on something, come too late.

We went to someone's place and watched it on television. Rob was right. The London demo was a fizzle. But then they showed the footage from the rest of the world. Everywhere else there had been huge marches. In New York and Washington they just came and came and came, the same in Chicago, Boston, Philadelphia, Seattle, even in Paris and Bonn. Forty million people taking to the streets in one day.

"They can't ignore this, can they?" I asked naïvely.

Rob laughed sarcastically.

"You watch what happens, Stevie. Whatever the bombing now, they'll double it. It'll be nastier than ever. Nixon, Kissinger, they don't give a shit for marches. They despise us because we won't buy into their greed."

"I've got to be going," said Melanie. "I'm on duty for the gig this evening."

"See you, then," said Rob casually. He didn't even look at her as she left.

It was late when we got back to Rob's flat. The lights were on, and three people were sitting in a circle on the floor.

"Hi!" said Rob, not really surprised. Half London knew where to find his key.

There were two girls and a guy. One of the girls, Suzie, worked with Rob in the bookshop. She had a perfect, doll-like face, but stern and a bit scary. The other girl had a clever, intense face and short blond hair and glasses, and the guy was stocky, with cropped hair like a soldier's. All three wore very ordinary clothes, the kind of stuff you buy from Marks and Spencer.

They didn't greet us, or make any apology for being in the flat, just looked up as we came in.

"Did you see anyone outside?" asked Suzie.

Rob shrugged.

"It's late. Why should I?"

"Just checking. You've been at the demo, right? How was it?"

"Waste of time. That VSC shit's dead," said Rob. He set about rolling a joint.

"Who's this?" said the guy, gesturing at me.

"My brother, Stevie. He's cool."

"You sure?"

Rob stared back.

"He's my brother. What's the deal?"

Everyone was exchanging glances, but no one said anything. It was as if they were waiting for some sign. You could feel the tension.

Rob made coffee, lit a couple of candles and turned out the lights.

"So what's the shit? Come on, what's up with you guys? You haven't just looked by for a smoke, have you, Gail?" Rob got out his tin and started to roll a joint, looking across at the blond girl. She smiled briefly, then stopped herself. The candlelight made all their faces softer.

"The question is this, Rob. Who makes the rules? Are you going to stay with your gesture politics, or are you going to do something real?" said Gail.

"Real?"

Nobody said anything. They waited.

"You've done something heavy, huh?" said Rob. He was sitting up, alert and excited.

"You like the idea?" asked Gail.

"Depends what," said Rob.

There was a silence. Gail looked at her watch, then leant forward towards Rob, almost whispering.

"Somebody might have planted a bomb in the Imperial War Museum. If so, it should be going off just about now."

"A bomb? Holy shit!"

Gail leant back with a look of satisfaction, lit a cigarette and passed the packet round.

"It's just the beginning, like a visiting card. Demos are dead. You know that, don't you? All they do is let off the steam of the people's anger, and the bosses are laughing in our faces. Those Vietnam Solidarity Committee creeps play along with the government, and the pigs beat up a few hippies. What does that achieve? They take photos of every single person who goes on a march. They'll have taken photos of you today so that they can get you on their files. Well, we're not going to let them make the rules any more. They think they're untouchable, but they're not. We're going to hit them where it hurts. Top pigs. Politicians. Judges. Those arseholes. But they're soft, Rob, they're soft, and they think they're safe. They think they can kill and oppress all they want, and nothing will touch them, but it can. It will." She dropped her voice. "Because they've got houses, nice houses in nice streets, full of expensive stuff they like, paid for by the sweat of the poor, the blood of the oppressed. Well, they've got a surprise coming. It's time for them to taste a bit of their own medicine."

She sat back with an air of satisfaction.

"Christ!" Rob muttered. I'd never seen him shocked like this before. And he was enjoying it.

There was a long silence. Rob lit his joint and the smoke curled up. The smell of it gave me a little shiver.

"What do you say, Rob?" asked Suzie. "Are you with us?"

"Yeah," said Rob. "Yeah, sure. I'm with you."

They went on talking deep into the night as the air thickened with smoke and conspiracy. Most of the time it sounded like riddles: "political contradictions," "revolutionary class movement." It was no good, I'd never be able to understand. Not that I wanted to. After a while I stretched out my sleeping bag and went to sleep listening to Gail's intense voice sounding like she was speaking with capital letters: "The Contradictions of Capitalism can only be Resolved by a Dictatorship of the Proletariat. . . ." I didn't know what it meant, but I knew I didn't want anything to do with it. All my enthusiasm at joining a cause had popped like a balloon. My political fervor was already dead.

By morning they'd gone, leaving dirty mugs and full ashtrays. I cleaned up and made a cup of tea, then I went out for a newspaper. On the front page there was a photo of a policeman hitting a demonstrator outside the American Embassy, but I couldn't find anything about the Imperial War Museum. Perhaps none of it was true. But it left me with a bad feeling in my chest.

I walked on to the park. It was a fine autumn morning. The sky was blue and the leaves were turning. It was beautiful, I could see that, but I couldn't feel it. My life was more pointless than ever. In Vietnam, kids were dying and there was nothing whatsoever I could do to stop it. Nothing Rob could do either. What were his friends talking about? Bombing politicians? I wasn't clever like them, but I could see one thing: you never end cruelty with cruelty, you never end bombing with bombing. I didn't like those people. I didn't much like any of Rob's friends except for Melanie. I was in the wrong place.

I sat on a bench and mechanically opened my tobacco tin. I'd started smoking roll-ups. They gave me a sore throat, but they were a connection with Michelle.

"You shouldn't smoke that stuff, you know. Haven't you heard? It ruins your aura. Not to mention your lungs."

A guy was sitting next me. I was so wrapped up in myself I hadn't even noticed him. I looked round, surprised, and he laughed. A gentle laugh, with a sense of his own absurdity.

"Hi!" he said. "Come here often?"

"No, my first time on this particular bench." I smiled back. "How about you?"

"Oh, yeah, sometimes. I'm a bird of passage. Aren't we all?"

He was called Chet, and he was American, on his way back to New York, he told me. He wore a greatcoat over a T-shirt, and he had a rubbery face that creased into surprising expressions. Just the sight of him cheered me up. We strolled across the park together, chatting easily. Dads were playing with their kids, old ladies out with their dogs, lovers holding hands. Ordinary people doing ordinary things. Normal.

"Where are you staying?" he asked.

"With my brother."

"Okay?"

"Sort of. A bit too much heavy politics at the moment."

He nodded. "I know what you mean. Same at my place. Thinking we can set the world straight."

"But we ought to try." I still half believed it.

"Yeah," he said. "We ought to try. Only you know, maybe we ought to start by setting ourselves straight."

It sounded obvious, but it wasn't shallow. I glanced at him. There was pain in him as well as humor.

"I'm staying in a place round the corner here," he went on. "Come and take a look if you like. It was empty for years, then some political guys moved in and set up something called a "street commune," and they had great ideas about creating a new way of living. Only problem is, it's filled up with squatters and people who want to fight the cops and no-hopers like me.

What the hell! That's the way the dream ends. It suits me actually. It's a place to lay my head, and it's free. You'll hear it in a minute."

I did. On the other side of Park Lane was a crumbling mansion with the ground-floor windows boarded up like a fort, and in front of it a group of skinheads held back by a row of police were yelling things like "Kill the bastards!" and "Filthy hippie scum!"

Chet shook his head.

"Sad, huh? Can't they think of any better slogans?"

He led me adroitly past the police and up a sort of drawbridge made of an old plank, to the ground floor window that was the only entrance.

"I brought a friend back," said Chet to the Hell's Angel standing guard.

The Angel grinned.

"Great, mate. More the better!"

Inside, we went up a grand marble staircase to a big room with stuccoed cherubs on the ceiling. A group of hippies was sitting on the carpet, sharing a joint with a couple of Hell's Angels. At the other end of the room a tramp was snoring with an empty bottle beside him, and a guy was painting a slogan on the wall. He wasn't very good at painting, but I remember the words:

NO!
We don't give a shit
For labels and lies
We're not selling any alibis
We just want to live our lives

We can't wait until your old world
sickens
and
DIES.

We are the writing on your wall

Chet rolled his eyes, then led me over to the window, and we stepped out onto a balcony.

Below us, the crowds were being pushed back by the police. I could hear the shouts:

"Make 'em jump!"

"Dirty squatters!"

From the next balcony, a couple of guys were responding by throwing colored plastic balls. One hit a policeman's helmet, and they laughed.

A girl burst into the room behind us, eyes glowing with excitement, wearing a combat jacket and radiating enthusiasm.

"The pigs are planning an attack. War council upstairs. Come on!" she commanded with a public-school accent.

"Hey, what's the point?" a guy called back. "That's their game."

The girl rounded on him.

"Don't be so bloody defeatist. We're going to fight, man! They'll get a few surprises, I can tell you."

Chet looked at me ironically.

"Council meeting, Stephen?"

I shrugged. "You didn't tell me this was a war zone."

100

He narrowed his eyes. "If you think this is a war, Stephen, you're kind of wrong."

We sat at the back and listened to some talk about the ideals of the "street commune" and the need to uphold these ideals against the forces of repression, or capitalism, or whatever. It didn't make much sense, because as far as I could see, the cops were actually protecting them from the skinheads. Then a girl came in with a huge bunch of roses that had been delivered to the door, a present from a rock star, and handed them round. Someone suggested we use them to fight with. It was the best laugh of the day.

And then, as if it was the end of a school assembly, the girl who'd summoned us announced that food was ready.

I turned to Chet.

"I think I'd better go."

"Better at your brother's, eh?" He smiled with his eyes.

"For now."

"It's only ever for now."

He walked me back out, past the Angels.

"See you again," he said. "Same bench, right?"

Back at the flat, Rob had gone out. He came back late, with Gail. They were both excited and went straight into the bedroom, where they made love noisily.

The next day I noticed my shadow.

I thought I saw Michelle. I did this the whole time,

and I knew I was chasing phantoms, but I couldn't help myself. I ran after her into the Underground. Her head was bobbing on the escalator ahead of me, but I held back because when we met it would have to look accidental. And then suddenly she started running for a train, and I ran behind her. We both leapt in, just in time, and another man jumped in too as the doors shut.

As soon as I was on the train, I knew I'd made a mistake. She was nothing like Michelle. So I jumped out at the next station.

The man behind me did the same. He was there too when I went back up the escalator, face hidden behind a newspaper, like in a film.

Back at the flat I told Rob. He was typing and didn't look up.

"Yeah, that'll be Special Branch. They tap the phone too. You're a danger to society, Stevie. They've got their little piggy eyes on you."

"Aren't you worried?"

"Not much. They're stupid. They get everything wrong. Make me a cup of coffee, will you?"

I made the coffee. Rob might not be worried, but I was unnerved. Rob was getting into all this heavy stuff, and the police were watching us. I'd be guilty just for living in the same house. Maybe it was time to move on. Maybe I should pack up and move to Chet's squat, if I could bear it. What was I doing here anyway? Melanie had stopped coming, and the flat was a dump. Gail and Suzie and their friends scared me. Rob never hassled me or asked for rent, but I was just a drain on him. All I did was lie around in the basement, or walk the streets of London scanning the crowds for Michelle while Rob went off with Gail and plotted the revolution.

That night I dreamed of Astrid, her eyes looking calmly into mine. I hadn't thought of her and Spencer for weeks, but I woke remembering Spencer's words: "Whatever happens is beautiful. Whatever happens couldn't be better. Live now. This moment will never come again."

Live now? All I had was fears and regrets. Spencer and Astrid seemed very far away.

The next morning I got up early, drank some coffee and wandered out to the park. My plan was to walk across to Piccadilly and find Chet, but I didn't have to go that far. I found him sitting on the same bench where we'd met before. He had a bag with him.

"Hi!" He grinned. "Told you I'd see you again. How's it going?"

"Not so good."

"Me neither. The cops are massing. I don't even leave my bag there these days in case the whole thing's been flushed while I'm out."

"So you're leaving?"

"Looks like it."

"Where are you going?"

"Well, I've got a friend, and she's pretty sussed, and she says there's all these empty houses, somewhere, you know, that way." He pointed vaguely. "So I guess I'll head down there for the time being."

"Can I come with you?" I asked. "I've kind of run out here."

He grinned.

"Sure. Why not?"

We went back to the flat to get my rucksack and leave a note for Rob. Then we walked across the park to meet up with Chet's friend Vicky and catch a bus to Brixton. As we left the flat, and then again on the bus, I had the feeling that a man in a raincoat was following us. I couldn't be sure. Perhaps he just happened to be going in the same direction. But it made me nervous. Why me? I hadn't done anything. Was I guilty just for knowing people? Still, as Rob said, the pigs always got everything wrong.

Chapter 10

It looked pleasant enough in the late October sunshine: a run-down Victorian terrace in Brixton, waiting for "development" that never came, with cast-iron fireplaces in the bedrooms and space for all of us.

Vicky took the attic room, and Chet and I were on the floor below. Sue and Greg, who had opened up the house, occupied the first floor. They'd already got the electricity turned on, then bypassed the meter so that we didn't even have to pay for it. We went out looking for old furniture in skips, and came back with mattresses, tables and armchairs. I enjoyed that. It was good to be using my body again.

Sue and Greg were a gentle couple who'd dropped out of art school. They made their room nice with a sari hung along the wall, and I often sat there with them, getting mildly stoned and listening to music. Sue was pregnant, and Greg dealt dope, so they had a string of visitors. We had a communal kitchen in the basement, and one of the ground-floor rooms was meant to be a group sitting room, though we hardly ever used it. A quiet German guy called Rudi lived in the other downstairs room, but he was usually out.

Vicky took me down to the benefits office. I'd never

signed on before, and I was nervous about it, but it was simple enough. I gave the address of the squat, filled in a load of forms, and had an interview on the spot with a nice woman who was impressed by my A-levels and said they'd post me a check. Afterwards Vicky nipped into John Lewis and came out with some new clothes under her coat, which made me think of Michelle. She was nothing like Michelle otherwise, though. She was big and round-faced, with a brooding look that said, "Don't mess with me!" I was worried about her shoplifting; I thought she was too obvious and she'd get caught, though I'd never have dared say anything.

I started to enjoy life. This was far better than being at Rob's—I had my own room and my own friends. The dole checks gave me a sense of independence, and we lived well on vegetables left behind in the street in Brixton market, cakes baked by Sue and fancy cheese and chocolates liberated by Vicky. I scored quid deals of dope from Greg; as long as I didn't smoke too much, it kept me mellow.

The only thing I missed about Rob's was the books. I thought of nicking some, but somehow I couldn't bring myself to. Anyway, I could always sit by my window watching the foxes that had made their home in the overgrown wilderness of demolished houses opposite, living like us without permission in the unused fringes of the city.

Chet had black days when he shut himself in his room or went off on his own, and times when his pupils were tight and he seemed to look at me from a long way away. I put it down to mood swings. But when he was on form, I enjoyed his company like no one else's. He suggested we explore London together, and we went off into town on the bus. The first time we went in the National Gallery, he looked round at the marbled grandeur and the paintings worth millions of pounds, spread his arms and said, "Wow! And all this is free? You Brits don't know your luck!"

Later we sat on the steps in Trafalgar Square and ate fish and chips. It was sunny but the wind was cold, and Chet had his greatcoat buttoned up to the neck.

"You know, you've not got a bad little country here. Sometimes I think you guys don't really appreciate it. Free health care. Free art. Free money. Even friendly policemen."

He waved at a couple of helmeted "bobbies" who were weaving through the crowd, doing their bit for the tourist industry.

"Make the best of it. You don't know what you've got till it's gone." He grinned. Then he asked casually, "You been in the East?"

"Yes," I said. "I went overland to India, a couple of years ago. I got ill and had to fly home. I don't think about it much now."

"Lucky you," said Chet.

I didn't know what he was referring to—the traveling, or the not thinking about it, so I didn't say anything. We both ate our fish.

"I was in Vietnam," he said suddenly. "I came back

the slow way. You know, through the desert. I loved the desert. I loved the stillness and the steel in people's eyes. It gives you strength, the desert. It made me want to live again. I wasn't so sure after Nam."

I glanced at his profile. His face had lost its rubberiness and he looked stern. Some lines of Shelley came into my head and I quoted them to him:

> *"I love all waste*
> *And solitary places; where we taste*
> *The pleasure of believing what we see*
> *Is boundless, as we wish our souls to be."*

"Yeah," he said. "Boundless. It's a good word. And it's what we wish. But we're all bound, aren't we? We're all bound to something."

He stood up.

"Better head back."

On the bus, I asked him what it was like in Vietnam.

"It was war," he said. "Don't even ask me about it. You wouldn't want to know."

"Do you go on demos, anything like that?" I asked.

He paused. I glanced over my shoulder. There was a man in a raincoat sitting two seats behind us who I thought I recognized.

"You know, if I could stop the war, I would," said Chet with a bitterness I hadn't heard in him before. "Believe me, I'd die happily to stop that war. Maybe I'd even kill, if I could get the right people. But I wouldn't go on a demo. What's happening over there, it's worse than anything you can imagine, but those guys were my buddies. . . ."

He lapsed into silence. He was getting withdrawn and slightly twitchy, in a way he often did in the afternoons. I thought how painful it must be for him, and felt embarrassed by my antiwar enthusiasm. What did I know about it? Nothing was easy. I let him be, and instead turned and stared at the man two seats behind us, who was looking fixedly out of the window. I couldn't be sure it was the same guy who had followed us across the park, but it looked like him. Surely the cops weren't still following me? Could they be that stupid? Or were they staking us out for a drugs bust? I didn't say anything to Chet, who had retreated into himself, but when I got home I told Greg.

Greg looked solemn.

"Why would they follow you?" he asked.

"I don't know. My brother was into some heavy politics."

"Politics!" Greg snorted the word. I'd never seen him so animated. "Politics messes everything up, doesn't it? Still, as long as they're Special Branch and not the Drugs Squad, that doesn't matter. They're wasting their time as usual. We mustn't get paranoid. Once you allow yourself to be paranoid, they've won. Don't think about it any more, Stephen, that's my advice."

I did think about it, though, of course, and from then on I lived in fear of a drugs raid at dawn. Whenever I went out, I kept turning round to check for shadows, but I saw no more of the man in the raincoat. Greg was worried too, whatever he said. He took a lot more care about hiding his stash, and from that time on he and Sue started talking about moving.

It was getting colder. I found an electric fire on a skip and hung an old blanket in front of the cracked panes in my window, but it didn't make much difference. My sleeping bag was cheap and thin, so I slept in all my clothes, with my coat over the top for extra weight. Chet had the idea of collecting wood from the skips to make fires in the open grates. Even if some of it gave off a bad smell, an open fire was friendly on the dark evenings. Yet the house was still cold, as if it was dying and nothing could warm it.

It was still friendly, though, to hang out in the basement kitchen, where Sue baked cakes and we cooked up shared meals. We left the cooker on the whole time with the oven door open, and huddled around it drinking tea and smoking roll-ups. I was heading down there one evening when I heard Sue scream. It was a terrified, blood-curdling scream, and I raced downstairs to find her standing petrified opposite a big rat. I grabbed a broom and whacked at it. It scuttled off under the door.

Sue was shaking. She put an arm on my shoulder to steady herself.

"It was in the cupboard. I opened the door and there it was. It didn't even run away. It just sat there and grinned at me."

Greg appeared.

"What's up?"

Sue told him, and he put his arms around her protectively.

"Bloody rats!" He shook his head. "We can't live with this. Don't worry, Sue, it won't be long."

They left the next week. With rats in the kitchen, who could blame them? I'd only started to get to know them, but I was sorry to see them go. It felt like the soul was going out of the house.

"It's no good here for Sue, not with the baby coming," Greg explained. "We've found a place in Herefordshire, with friends of ours from art school. It sounds like a great place too. Back to the land. Goats and chickens, home-brewed beer, all that sort of thing. The good life, Stephen. The *real* good life. You should come down and see us there."

"I'd like to," I said.

But I never did.

Chet and I went to Paddington station to see them off. Greg gave me a piece of hash as a goodbye present.

"Good people," said Chet as their train left. "Fine, upstanding drug dealers. A credit to their profession."

Two Irish guys moved into their rooms. They couldn't have been more different. They were longhaired and scruffy, but they went out to work somewhere, and they got drunk every night. They noticed me and Chet lighting fires in our rooms, and one day I came home to find them chopping up the banisters.

"What are you doing?" I protested.

"We want a fire," said one of them.

"But those are our banisters."

The other one looked at me, red-eyed and uncomprehending.

"It's only a fokkin squat!"

November turned to December. It rained day after day, with gusts of wind that rattled the windows and made my candle flicker. I hardly went out anymore, and the foxes had disappeared too. I got a bad cold, which went onto my chest.

The shops were full of Christmas, but it meant nothing to me. I was lost in myself again. The illusion of a home had gone with Greg and Sue, and my demons were back to torment me through the long, cold nights—not with the same intensity, but a steady, damp depression like the weather, a hopeless longing for a bliss I would never taste again.

I wanted to talk to Chet about it, but I couldn't. He had his own demons, a darkness that came into his eyes and drove him back into secret places to which I was not admitted. Besides, I was working steadily through Greg's hash, despite my cough, and Chet didn't smoke.

One afternoon, Vicky came down. She had her own life up in the attic, with her own visitors, but she was always friendly. This time she came in and sat down on my mattress, kicking off her shoes.

"I brought you a book," she said. "You like books, don't you?"

It was a science fiction novel. I didn't usually read science fiction, but it might pass the time.

"Been feeling down, haven't you?"

I couldn't deny it. I started rolling a joint, but she put her fingers on my hand to stop me.

"Tell you what, Stephen, you try some of my stuff. It'll cheer you up. You could do with a lift."

She put some tobacco in a single skin. Then she sprinkled white powder through it.

"What's that?"

"Heroin," she said. She looked at me cheekily. "Don't worry, it doesn't addict you if you only smoke it. That's the latest thing now."

I knew I shouldn't take it. It was like supping with the devil. But I didn't care anymore.

I smoked the joint as if it was a cigarette.

A warm, tender rush enveloped me, banishing the demons. This was much better than hash, and it didn't even make me cough. The rush passed, and I felt ordinary and present, no shame, no anxiety, no longings; just here, calm and happy and wanting nothing.

Vicky smiled at me.

"That better?"

"Yes. Yes, it is. Thanks . . ."

"Don't mention it!"

She smiled enigmatically, caught my eyes for a moment and looked away. Then she leant forward and unzipped my fly.

"Ohh," she whispered huskily. "It's a big one!"

Uncertainly, because I still wasn't sure what I wanted, I reached out and touched her neck. She unbuttoned her blouse and took my hand and placed it on her breast.

"You're cold," she said. "Never mind, soon warm you up!"

She did, and I enjoyed it—her big body, her good heart. I knew it was the sex she loved, not me, so it never felt personal—but it wasn't totally impersonal either. We never forgot who each other was.

And that was the best of it—she wasn't Michelle. Apart from the shoplifting, she wasn't anything like her at all. And she gave me release, for a while, from all those longings.

She came back the next day, and the next, till I expected it. Sometimes I went up to her room, amazed by the number of shoes she had that she never wore, all liberated.

"Don't you worry you'll get caught?" I asked.

She shrugged.

"Not really. They'd just give me probation, and anyway I only go lifting when the *I Ching* is favorable."

I thought she said "itching," and I didn't understand. We laughed about that, and then she got out her book and the special coins she used.

"It's ancient Chinese, the oldest book in the world. It's like an oracle. It tells you the best thing to do. Why don't you try it? Ask it a question."

"What sort of question?"

"Anything you like."

I couldn't think of anything.

"What happens next?" I asked vaguely.

She threw the coins repeatedly, drawing lines as she

114

did so until she had six, a hexagram. Then she looked it up in the back of the book.

"Oh dear," she said. "You've got Number 23. '*Splitting apart: It does not further one to go anywhere.*' There's a moving line too. Let's see. '*The bed is split at the edge. Those who persevere are destroyed. Misfortune.*'"

She closed the book.

"Oh well, it doesn't look like you ought to be going anywhere for now. Never mind, you can try again tomorrow. It might be better then."

She kept on with her own life. I'd hear other guys sometimes coming up and down from her room, but I never met them, and she kept the afternoons for me. At night the demons still gathered, but the afternoons with Vicky were something I could look forward to.

One afternoon Vicky had just passed me the joint when Chet came in. I didn't think he'd realize what we were smoking—after all, it looked like a normal roll-up— but he took one look at my eyes and he knew.

"What's that?" he asked, sniffing. "It's smack, isn't it? You're smoking smack, aren't you?"

"So what if we are? We're grown up. We can do what we like," said Vicky.

Chet took no notice of her.

"Don't you start on that, Stephen. Don't do it!"

He came over and grabbed the joint from my fingers, opened the window and threw it out.

"Hey, what did you do that for?" asked Vicky. She

was angry, and she stood up, bigger than Chet. I thought she was terrifying, but Chet was stronger.

"Get out!" he said quietly. "I'm talking to Stephen."

Vicky opened her mouth to say something, then thought better of it and flounced out of the room, slamming the door.

I hadn't smoked enough to get a rush, but the whole scene had become unreal, like something from a play. I was annoyed with Chet too.

"You've got no right to do that, Chet. And who are you to talk, anyway?"

Chet looked out of the window.

"I'm nobody to talk, Stephen. Nobody. But if I don't, who will? I know what that stuff does. . . ."

He turned to me, smiling ironically.

"Come into my room. I'll show you."

I'd hardly been in his room before. He kept it private. It was bare, but neat and tidy, his bag packed, as if he might leave at any moment. I half knew what he was going to show me. It was obvious really: his mood swings, his occasional twitchiness. But in another way he was so discreet that I'd never have believed it until he took out his syringe and his needles and his little ampoules of heroin that the doctor gave him on prescription, and showed me the marks in his thigh where he injected himself.

"I'm a junkie, Stephen. Didn't you guess? If I don't get my fix, I turn into a chimpanzee . . . maybe that's unkind to chimps. You don't want to go this way, Stephen. I'm telling you. I know! Don't do it. That stuff

116

feels so nice, but it'll take hold of you and take you over so you can't quit. Look at me!"

I looked at him. He looked all right. He looked normal.

"I'm stable now since I came to England. That means regular. I never up the dose. I just take exactly what the doctor gives me. I don't get high. I don't even get pain release. It just makes me feel okay, so I can function. And I'm one of the good ones, Stephen. I don't lie or cheat or steal or humiliate myself to get supplies. I don't do any other drugs. You know, when I get back to New York and quit, I'm not going to take anything. No hash, no pills, no alcohol, no tobacco. I'll be so clean, I'll get high on air. It's the only way. You don't need this stuff. You don't know how lucky you are."

I felt shaky. I rolled a cigarette.

"Okay," I said. "So what makes you so different from me? Why should it be all right for you?"

"It isn't all right for me."

"Then why did you start?"

Chet didn't answer immediately. He opened the window to let the smoke out and repositioned the electric fire. The rain clouds had moved in again, darkening the afternoon, and he lit a candle against the gloom.

"Yeah," he said. "Why did I? All right, I'll tell you. If you want to know, I'll tell you."

He sat down on his mattress, and I sat with him.

"You know . . . ," he started, then stopped, disappearing into his thoughts.

"I was in Vietnam," he started again. "Fighting for

117

my country." He laughed ironically. "Opium, morphine, heroin—they're painkillers, that's all. You know how it is, you still feel everything, but it's not you, and your mind is at peace, no paranoia, no fear, no regret. You know, at the beginning when I'd had my fix, I used to think I could look at pain from outside, see it for what it was, and it didn't swallow me. But when you're in it, it sort of becomes you. You can't handle it, you can't grow from it, it just goes on and on, worse and worse, so there's no bottom of worse. It's not physical pain I'm talking about now."

I nodded. I thought I understood.

Chet got up to shut the window. He stayed there, looking out, his back hunched, speaking softly.

"I never talk about Vietnam. I can't tell anybody what it was like. I wouldn't want to. Don't try and understand, because you won't."

He stopped, still staring out of the window. I could hear his breathing.

"But I'll tell you. All right, I'll tell you. . . ."

Suddenly he turned round and faced me, his eyes fierce.

"I killed a little girl. I shot her through the stomach and she died in front of me. There wasn't a reason. We were in a village, tense as hell and the adrenaline pumping. Then the Cong started firing from the trees, and I thought, 'Holy shit, it's an ambush,' and threw myself down and held my gun over my head, shooting at random. That's what we did. The little girl, about nine, very pretty, she stepped out of a hut. I don't know why. Perhaps she wanted her mother. She stepped out of a hut, and she died, she died in front of me in a pool of her own blood with her stomach full of my bullets. . . ."

He was looking at me but he wasn't seeing me. His fists were bunched tight and his face was rigid.

"I could take all the heroin in Afghanistan, and I could take it all my life, I could obliterate all my thoughts . . . and that little girl, she'd be the last thing to go. And there's nothing I could ever do that could make it right."

He sat back down on the mattress.

"I didn't feel anything at first. I was wounded and they got me out. The wound healed, but I guess they gave me morphine, and I've been giving it to myself, or something like it, ever since. You could get anything over there, any drug you wanted. Half my platoon were junkies. Who cares? Half my platoon are dead. You die, you kill, you die inside. What for?"

He sighed.

"You know, I was in this kind of dream state at first, but then I woke up a few days later sweating and terrified. Not of anybody else. Of myself. Because I'd remembered. And I could never forget her, that little body crumpling meaninglessly in the dust. She's there now. She's always there. . . ."

He paused again, his eyes half closed.

"I tried to talk to one of the guys in my platoon, and he said it didn't happen like that and she was just a gook anyway. So I shut up about it. But you know what you know. I got a medical discharge, but I couldn't face going home, so I came back overland, hanging around in the deserts of Iran where the smack's cheap, wondering if I had any reason to go on living. And somewhere it came to me: she is my reason to live. Otherwise I'd die easy, and be glad of it."

He looked up, taking in my presence again.

"There. That's it. I've told you. No more secrets."

He shrugged and managed a smile.

"You know, when I was a kid I used to dream of being an actor or a baseball player. I never thought I'd grow up to be a child murderer and a drug addict."

We went out together to eat. The nearest place was a Kentucky Fried Chicken, newly opened on the Brixton Road. We got our boxes of greasy chicken legs and sat on stools in the window.

"Why don't you go back home?" I asked. "What's the point in putting it off? You could be there for Christmas. I bet your family miss you."

He shook his head.

"I can't go back like this. I'd be too ashamed. And we don't have friendly doctors giving legal prescriptions in the U.S."

"Then get yourself off it. There's detox places, aren't there?"

"Yeah. Yeah, you're right. I've talked about it with my doctor. But you have to wait. There's always a waiting list."

We munched on our chicken. The truth was, I

didn't want him to go. He and Vicky were my only friends, and I couldn't imagine going on living in the squat without him.

"Stephen, you'll quit with the smack, huh?" he said suddenly.

"Yeah. I'll talk to Vicky about it too."

"Then so will I."

"What?"

"I'll stop. Just stop. In my room."

"But don't you need detox, doctors, all that?"

He shrugged.

"What can they do? It's cold turkey, that's all. I've been cutting down already. I don't fix into my veins, just into the muscles, and I'm on half the dose I was."

I was alarmed.

"I don't think you should. You might die."

He smiled and licked the grease off his fingers.

"Yeah, and . . . ? It's only pain. My pain, that I've brought on myself. You know, I think it might be kind of interesting. They say you feel things crawling all over you, up the walls, everywhere. Maybe I'll see pink elephants. Yeah, there won't be a better time. I'll do it now. I'll do it for my little girl."

I went up to see Vicky when we got back. I thought she'd be annoyed, but she was fine.

"No, no, Chet's right," she said. "You can't go on too long with that stuff or it takes you over. It's time we stopped. Anyway, the supply's run out. The guy giving it to me's disappeared. Just as well really."

121

I didn't ask further. She came up to me and put her arms on my shoulders.

"We don't have to stop the other thing as well, do we?"

So I lost myself for a while in her big body.

As I came down, Chet called me from his room.

He was sitting on his mattress staring at his needles and some ampoules of heroin. He was already several hours past his time.

"Take them!" he said. "I can't have them in here."

"Chet, are you sure?"

"Just take them!" He almost shouted. I'd never heard him so agitated.

"Where?"

"Out of here . . . anywhere! Don't argue with me, Stephen. Please."

I wrapped them up and went down to the late night chemist's in Brixton. I bought a pile of vitamin pills for Chet, which I thought might help, then put my package on the counter and walked out before they had a chance to look.

When I got back, Chet was lying down. His face was gray and withdrawn. I put the pills next to him, and he managed a flickering smile.

"Leave me to it. There's nothing you can do. Don't think there is," he whispered.

I heard him through the wall off and on through the night, pacing around. At one point he was throwing up—the fried chicken presumably. Then retching and

122

breathing deeply with little groans. I didn't sleep much.

Early next morning the doorbell rang. I went downstairs. An enormous lady in a leopard-skin coat with a matching handbag was standing on the steps. A Jaguar was parked in the road behind her.

"Victoria! She's here!"

"What do you want her for?" I started to ask, but she shoved past me into the house.

"Where is she?"

She pushed open the door to our unused sitting room, and then to Rudi's room, which was also empty. I hadn't even realized he'd left. I was worried she'd barge into Chet's room, and I was trying to block her way to the stairs, now banisterless, but Vicky appeared above me.

"Oh, hello, Mum!"

"So there you are, you little minx. Did you think I wouldn't find you in this hovel?"

"Look, Mum, come up to my room. It's really nice. I've got a kettle. I can make you a cup of tea."

"Your father's waiting in the car. I'm getting you out of here, Victoria. Now!"

She charged up the stairs. Vicky led her on, up to the attic. I went back into my room and listened to muffled shouts and occasional thumps on the floor above me. God knows what Chet made of it.

Half an hour later, Vicky appeared at my door, her face flushed.

"It's my mum. I've got to go," she said apologetically. "I don't know how they found me, but you can't argue with her. Here, look, I've got something for you. Something to remember me."

She held out the *I Ching,* complete with its cloth wrapping and its coins.

"It might help you."

I was touched.

"Are you sure? I mean, you'll need it, won't you?"

"I'll get another."

"Victoria!" her mother shouted threateningly.

"I'll miss you," I said.

"I'll miss you too, Stephen. Look after yourself. You're nice."

She blew me a kiss from the door.

A minute later I watched from my window as the Jaguar drew away. Another person disappearing out of my life forever.

I picked up the *I Ching*. It smelled of Vicky.

Two days before Christmas I saw Chet off to New York. He wouldn't let me go to the airport with him, so we had a coffee together at the terminus.

Chet had been clean for a week. As soon as he could, he'd rung his parents in New York, and they'd wired him the money for a ticket. He was pale and his hands shook sometimes, but otherwise he didn't seem much different. It was as if the important part of him wasn't affected by the junk anyway. I asked him about that.

"Yeah," he said thoughtfully. "I guess I'd kind of

given it up already, you know, inside. I didn't want it. I didn't want the needles and the visits to the doctor. I didn't want the rush. I didn't want to not feel anymore. So all I had to quit was the habit. I needed a little push and you gave it me."

He sipped his coffee and chided me gently about my roll-ups.

"I'm gonna be a first-class, pain-in-the-ass, ex-junkie Mr. Righteous now," he joked, then sat back, smiling. "I'm looking forward to Christmas. My mom's cooking, wow! *Hot* turkey! Wish you could come and share it with us. And I'll be seeing my little sister. She's only nine. I haven't seen her for a year and a half."

I was startled. A little sister? He'd talked about his parents, but he'd never mentioned a sister before. I thought I knew why.

"What are you going to do now?" he asked. "Stay on at the squat?"

"I don't know. The squat's not the same anymore. I don't know what I'll do, really."

"You could go to your parents' for Christmas. They'll want to see you. It's no defeat."

I shrugged. Chet let it hang.

"You know what I'm gonna do?" he said finally. "I've got it figured out. I'm gonna be a clown. I'm gonna make little children laugh. There is no better thing I could do in the whole world than make little children laugh. My life's work, Stephen."

His coach was leaving. We walked over to it, and the driver flung Chet's bag into the luggage compartment.

"Hey, come and see me in New York. It's only over the water. I'll do a clown show for you. That's a promise."

He embraced me quickly. The engine was revving.

"See ya, Stephen."

"See ya, Chet."

He smiled back at me, his crooked ironic smile. Then he was gone.

I went back to the squat. A thin sunshine lit the wet streets, but it gave no warmth.

A couple of girls from Manchester had moved into the ground-floor rooms. They looked nice enough, and normally I'd have talked to them, but now I couldn't be bothered. A Japanese student had taken over Vicky's room. Someone would take Chet's room soon. Everything was changing, too fast for me.

In the bareness of my room I pulled my sleeping bag round me against the cold. I was alone again. Alone with my own emptiness.

I rolled a joint and smoked a bit of it, then slumped down and fell into a light sleep.

I woke up feeling worse. Every bit of me was an aching longing. What for? For Michelle? For Chet? For the false peace of heroin? I didn't know anymore.

Flurries of hail crackled against the window. I shivered and moved closer to the electric fire. It reddened my face but left my back chilly.

With cold hands I picked up the *I Ching* and sniffed it for the smell of Vicky. I missed her big body, her appetites. I found the coins in their silk purse tucked inside the book, took them out and threw them, marking the lines. Then I looked up the tables at the back of the book to find the hexagram for Number 24:

Return.

Return. Success.

Going out and coming in without error.

It furthers one to have somewhere to go.

Somewhere to go . . . In the end there was only one place to return to at Christmas. I'd swallow my pride and go back to my parents. Chet was right. It was no defeat. I packed my rucksack and walked out into the hail.

Return. Success.

Well, maybe.

Chapter 11

Home.

If I could call it home.

The sterile comfort brought back my demons with the same old mixture of loneliness, loss and shame. Nothing had changed.

I spoke to my parents in bland formalities. Their world seemed empty and cruel—the world that had sent Chet out to slaughter others and ruin his own life in a war that had no meaning.

But it was Christmas, after all. I found a refuge in politeness.

Rob came for Christmas lunch. I was surprised. He hadn't been for the last two years, and he certainly hadn't come out of duty. Perhaps he wanted to see how I was after my sudden departure from his flat, though he'd never have said so. More likely he just fancied a good dinner.

After the pudding, my parents took coffee through to the drawing room to watch the Queen's speech on television. Rob rolled up his eyes.

"Let's get out of here. Come on, Stevie!"

My parents made no protest. I expect they were only

too happy to do without Rob's sarcastic comments on the monarchy. We walked down the road until we were well out of town, then cut across the fields and down to the river.

We sat on the bank and Rob rolled a joint. It was a grim, overcast day, but a yellow light was breaking through the clouds in the west. The stream moved slowly through the flat land, full and brown from the recent rain. On the other bank a stand of poplars was home to a colony of rooks, who cawed and quarreled, swooping out on missions into the corn stubble and returning noisily.

"Looks like Mum's going to be a Tory MP," said Rob.

"Oh yeah." I knew she was trying, but I'd never taken much interest.

"It's a sure thing. Couldn't get a much safer seat, and there'll be a general election soon. Very soon, maybe."

I made a noise to show I was listening.

"Christ, why is it always the worst people that get the positions of power?"

"I suppose they're the ones who believe in it. Does it make any difference?"

"Yeah," said Rob. "Sure it makes a difference. Labor are bad enough, but if the Tories get in, they'll make things a fuck of a lot worse. You'd be surprised."

He lit the joint.

"Have you been writing any poetry?" I asked, to change the subject.

He inhaled and blew the smoke out slowly.

"Poetry's dead. A few years ago it had a little flicker

129

of movement with the poetry circuses and that stuff, but now . . . Nah, it's a waste of time. Who reads it or listens to it? Old guys with bellies and bad breath, and spotty students with tin ears. Song lyrics, that's where the real poetry is now."

"So are you writing songs, then?"

He grinned. The dope was taking effect and mellowing him. He passed me the joint.

"I try. Only problem is, I can't sing."

"Does it matter? I mean, Dylan can't sing either— not in the usual sense."

"Yeah, but Dylan's a one-off. Nah, Stevie, I've tried with the music. I've taught myself guitar, sitar, I understand it all, but basically I'm crap. I need someone to work with."

We watched the rooks quarreling. A pair of swans gliding up by the far bank stopped to pull at some weed.

"I wish Melanie would show up again," Rob said suddenly.

"She hasn't been, since . . . ?"

"Since you left, no. Guess she didn't like me sleeping with Gail. But she's no one to get all righteous about fidelity. I miss her though. I didn't think I would, but I do. And the flat's a dump."

"Perhaps she didn't like the politics. I mean, Gail and Suzie, they're a bit heavy, aren't they?"

Rob grinned again.

"Yeah, you could say that. But I like my politics

heavy, she knows that. We had a row about you actually. She liked you, you know. She reckoned I wasn't looking after you. I told her that was bloody condescending. So maybe it's all your fault."

"Go and see her," I said urgently. "Ask her to come back. Say you're sorry. Anything. She's more important than politics."

He looked at the river for a while.

"Yeah, maybe you're right," he said finally. "But it don't come easy. And then there's Gail to think about. She fucks, that woman! And she's serious about politics in a way Melanie can't be. But she's got a temper too. She'd never admit to being possessive, but she is."

I laughed.

"She's got you right under her thumb. She's just like Mum!"

Rob looked startled. For a moment I thought I'd said too much, and that he was going to shout at me. But then he started to laugh too.

"My God, you're right, Stevie! And it's what I deserve. Just what I deserve."

It was already getting dark. We headed back up through the wheat stubble, the rooks cawing in triumph at our departure.

"Year's turned," said Rob. "End of the sixties. So what do you reckon the seventies'll bring?"

"More of the same, probably. I haven't thought about it."

"Tell you what I think—I think it'll be the decade of women, when they finally take over the controls. How about Mum in the cabinet, for a start?"

I laughed.

"I'm serious. Want a bet on it? Never underestimate the Mouth of Darkness."

We walked back down the road in the gathering gloom, towards a log fire and Christmas cake.

"What about you, Stevie? What are you going to do now?"

"I don't know yet."

"You can come back to my place if you want."

"Thanks," I said. I appreciated the offer. "But I don't think so."

"What are you going to do now?" "What are you going to do now?" Between Christmas and New Year's it was a chorus that followed me everywhere. My mother asked me of course, incessantly. Even my father did, in his hesitant way. And if I went into town, I'd meet old friends, and they all said the same thing:

"So what are you going to do now, Stephen?"

The person who asked it most insistently, though, was myself.

I met Jude in the street. She took me to the new coffee shop that had just opened on the High Street, where we perched uncomfortably on high stools looking out at the traffic and drinking cappuccinos. I'd never had one before, and licked curiously at the froth.

"I got a job," she said almost apologetically. "I'm working for the Steiner Community, looking after handicapped people. They have Down syndrome and things like that. They're really sweet. I spent Christmas Day there, and it was lovely, much better than being at home. They were all so excited, and kept coming up and giving me big hugs. We've sort of grown out of Christmas, haven't we? I mean, my parents want to keep all the rituals going, but we're just pretending."

I agreed, but I couldn't say anything. Everything she'd been doing sounded so worthwhile, and everything I'd been doing was self-indulgent rubbish.

"We're having a party on New Year's Eve. Me and Chris. His parents have gone to Spain. Why don't you come along?"

"Thanks," I said. "Are you still going out with Chris, then?"

"Yeah." She gave me an awkward smile and held up her hand, showing a diamond ring. "We're sort of engaged. Well . . . you know . . ."

But I didn't know. I didn't know at all. I didn't know anything.

I started to plan my future. The details changed every time I thought about it, but the essence was simple: I would do something worthwhile. Probably I'd be a care worker, like Jude, or perhaps a social worker helping drug addicts. At least I knew something about that. I'd stop smoking (I hadn't had a joint since the one with Rob at Christmas) and save money to go and visit Chet in New York for my holidays. I'd rent a flat in town and meet a girl to become "sort of engaged" to.

It seemed a sensible way to a fulfilling life. By day I could believe in it completely. But the nights still belonged to the demons and the sense they brought of total isolation in an indifferent universe. I'd pace around my room, fighting them, till I couldn't stand it anymore, then put on my coat and go outside to smoke a roll-up in the mysterious country of the night that made lonely into lonesome, made me feel for a while that the night was my friend.

On New Year's Eve, I had supper with my parents before I went to Jude and Chris's party. My mother was in high spirits. She and my father were going to see in the New Year in the Conservative Club. Over pudding, she looked at me, pointing with her spoon.

"You mark my words, there'll be an election this year, and WE WILL WIN!"

"Oh yeah," I said, obviously not very interested.

"And what about you, Stephen? It will be your first chance to vote. How are you going to cast it?"

I looked from her to my dad, bewildered.

"Well . . . er . . . I suppose I'll vote for you, Mum."

"I don't mind about that," she said, though she looked pleased. "But I do mind that you do vote. Young people are much too inclined to take these things for granted. It's your democratic right. People died for it. Make sure you exercise it."

I stopped chewing midmouthful. Was that what people

died for? Chet's friends in Vietnam? Chet's little girl? Some of Dad's friends probably too . . . Had they all died so that I could put a cross against my mother's name on a piece of paper, and send her to play games in Parliament? I felt the blood rush to my face and a surge of anger. . . . It was so meaningless, so stupid, so utterly trivial.

"Are you all right?" asked my father, concerned.

"I . . . I swallowed something . . . do you mind?"

I went upstairs.

But it was nothing. I realized that as soon as I calmed down. It was just the way she talked. I should know that by now. I shouldn't take it so seriously.

I put on a clean pair of jeans and a waistcoat and brushed my hair. It was getting quite long now. I thought I looked good. Then I put on my thick winter coat and went out.

"Happy New Year!" I shouted to my parents as I left.

I'd been looking forward to this party, but I was nervous. So instead of going straight there, I walked a roundabout way past the station. The lights were on on the platforms, but it was pretty deserted. A train came in and half a dozen passengers got out. I listened to it rumble off into the distance, wishing I was on it, going nowhere.

The party was in a big terraced house. The front door was open, with light and music coming from it, but I couldn't bring myself to go in. I carried on walking round the block. The empty streets felt safe—

nobody asked me what I was going to do. The second time, though, I steeled myself and, before I could change my mind, ran up the steps towards the light.

"Hi-i-i! Stephen!"

A girl flung her arms round me. Katie. She was slightly drunk.

"So where've you been? What've you been up to?"

Behind her was that party clamor of people shouting over music, the smell of alcohol and cigarette smoke, young people dressed up and looking slightly silly.

"Hello, Stephen."

It was Chris with his arm round Jude. He had grown a mustache. Jude smiled at me unconvincingly.

As if to prove something, Chris bent over and kissed her.

In that moment all my plans for the future dissolved back into the dust of dreams. There was nothing here I could belong to.

"Oh shit," I said. "I forgot something."

I detached myself from Katie, put down my bottle of wine, grinned apologetically, and fled back out into the anonymity of the streets, the darkness at the edge of town.

Eventually I made my way back to my parents' house. At least it was warm. I turned on the television and watched Elvis Presley's comeback concert. He was fat, and the heartbreak of the songs sounded phoney. I turned it off and put on some rock music, but I couldn't concentrate and it only irritated me.

So I sat in silence and listened to the clock and the beat of my heart: my life ticking away into a new decade.

What was the point?

I opened the French windows and stood half in, half out, smoking yet another roll-up. I'd had too many, and it made me feel sick. Behind me was all the meaningless comfort of a bourgeois life. In front, the wildness of the night. Where did I belong?

Nowhere, that was the answer. Everyone else tonight was at some party, celebrating the end of a decade, the beginning of another. Everyone else was getting drunk together in congenial groups—even my parents. But not me. I belonged nowhere. I thought of that scene round the campfire at the Isle of Wight—Jonno and Matthew and the beautiful blond girl. It had been good for a moment, and then we were all scattered by winds that blew us in never-ending circles, in my case always ending up back at my parents' house.

I couldn't stay here, and I wouldn't. There must be something else. There *must* be . . .

And then I remembered Astrid: "You'll come back soon, won't you?" The last thing she said. And I realized that there was something else—as Spencer had put it, a different way of looking at things. Maybe like Michelle said, Spencer was "kind of weird," but who wasn't? Maybe he was the only one who was sane.

Still, I needed confirmation.

I fetched Vicky's *I Ching* from my room, sat cross-legged on the carpet of my parents' living room and threw the coins.

The first throw was all heads. The next was two heads and a tail. Then all heads, all heads, all heads, all heads . . . so many heads!

The hexagram was Number 1: *The Creative*. It sounded promising. Vicky had told me that the first two hexagrams were the strongest in the book.

The Creative works sublime success.

Furthering through perseverance.

So far so good. I looked up the explanation.

When an individual draws this oracle, it means that success will come to him from the primal depths of the universe, and that everything depends upon his seeking his happiness and that of others in one way only, that is by perseverance in what is right.

There was one moving line, the second:

Dragon appearing in the field.

It furthers one to see the Great Man.

There was one more hexagram to look up, the one that grew out of the moving line. According to Vicky, this one indicated the long-term future.

It was Number 13: *Fellowship with Men.*

I shut the book. My mind was made up.

The clock struck midnight.

1970.

PART TWO

If you seek God with your whole heart,
then you may be assured
that the Grace of God
is also seeking you.

SRI RAMANA MAHARSHI

Chapter 12

Spencer was a good listener. To begin with, he spent a lot of time with me, asking me about a past that I'd almost forgotten myself. There was one incident that he kept coming back to. When I was sixteen, I went to India and met a sadhu—a wandering ascetic—called Mukhtibaba. He took me up into the mountains, and made me sit at the back of a cave for a long time. Then he touched my forehead, and a rush of power rose from the base of my spine to the top of my head. It felt as if I'd touched the energy source of the universe.

"And that was it," I told Spencer. "After that, he told me to go. Sent me off on my own to sink or swim. I went mad after that, so I suppose I sank."

"I wouldn't assume that," said Spencer carefully. "Anyway, I'm not sure that would be part of how he saw the world."

"What do you mean?"

"I mean that madness and sanity only exist within duality. Did you trust him?"

"I didn't trust or not trust him. I just went along with him."

"Then that's okay. Keep going along with whatever

comes from it. He gave you something. It's still there, right?"

"Yes. I forgot about it for ages, but it came back in the Isle of Wight—the beauty and unreality. But the madness is there too, not far away, like demons. I'm afraid . . ."

I broke off. We were walking by the river, with Chinook bounding ahead, sometimes looking as if he was going to leap into the freezing water, then pulling back comically at the last minute. Spencer stopped and I felt his eyes probing me.

"What are you afraid of, Stephen?"

"I'm afraid of losing myself."

"Yeah, sure. Only, you know, in the end there isn't anyone to lose, is there?"

He paused. I met his eyes.

"You fell in love and it opened you, because you were ready to open. Sure, it's shaken you up a bit, but that's good. Now your work is this: be still. Something's hatching in you. Give it space. Stay in your room or sit quietly somewhere. Watch your breathing and your body. Do your jobs in the house, but keep coming back to yourself. Your breathing will help. It keeps on coming in and going out through your nose, gentle or rough, whatever is. Don't take too much notice of what's going on around you—things happen, they're bound to, but stay in yourself. Remember, your thoughts are only thoughts, and the feelings in your body never stop changing. And don't worry about the demons. They're your friends, they're helping you. Oh, and one other thing: keep away from sex. Sexual union is powerful. It has its place, but it's already blown you wide open. You are Brahmacharya, living in Brahman, the absolute. You don't need sex."

My breath felt gentle in my nose and my heartbeat had slowed. We walked on over the frozen ground in bright sunshine. The world was full of beauty.

A week earlier Astrid had welcomed me back to The Hollies with a big hug, and everyone had treated me as an old friend. Richard's friend Peter, who'd helped us move in, had just left to go back to his family in South Africa, so I took over his room. Something had changed since August. They had done amazing work on the house, painting, cleaning and furnishing it, but it wasn't just that. It was the sense of purpose.

Richard took me aside and explained things. I hardly recognized him, he looked so straight and smart, with a short haircut and a turtleneck pullover. He had a job with insurance brokers in Colchester, but his appearance was also making a point. It was saying: "We are not hippies!"

"It's good to see you again, Stephen," he said. "We've been expecting you. Stay as long as you like. Just bear in mind what we're about here."

"What's that?" I asked innocently.

"Spencer," he said seriously. "We're here for Spencer. Nothing else. We're here to help Spencer with his work. There won't be many such beings in our lifetime, and we're very privileged to be with him. At the moment we have him to ourselves, but it won't always be like that.

The work has to spread, and we'll all have our part to play. My part is looking after the practical side. We've done quite well so far, I think. We're not a squat anymore. I've made an agreement with the hospital, and we pay them rent, so we're legal. That doesn't matter to Spencer, but it does matter for the work. We live in a clean and ordered way, and we need money coming in. Do you have a skill?"

"Not really."

"Well, you can sign on. Tim will take you into town tomorrow."

I gave my dole straight to Richard. I didn't need it. I was a bit worried by what he'd said about Spencer and "the work," though. I wasn't sure about being part of some cult. Yet Spencer was special. I knew that. It was he who gave the place purpose, and that purpose, as I was finding out, was an inner inquiry. He used Hindu terms that I was beginning to understand, and we all sat silently together in the sitting room every morning and evening.

Usually as we sat, I only experienced my normal chaos of thoughts and emotions, so it was hard even to stay on my cushion. But sometimes in the mornings when we gathered in the dark with blankets round our shoulders against the cold, and the light rose with the birdsong from the garden, I felt a deep peace hanging in the room. Occasionally I looked at Spencer. He sat with his eyes half closed and a ghost of a smile playing round his lips, utterly still, as if he wasn't there.

Guests came to the evening sittings, and afterwards

they'd stay and talk. They sometimes asked Spencer about his background. He answered them briefly and humorously, with the sense that it wasn't important. He'd been a merchant seaman and traveled all over the Far East, stopping off in Burma, where he'd become interested in Buddhism. Then in Calcutta he met a sadhu, much as I had met Mukhtibaba. The sadhu took him to Nepal, where he received Tantric teachings from a Tibetan lama. After that he wandered randomly through India until he ended up at the ashram of Ramana Maharshi.

"It was the place I'd been looking for all my life. Ramana had been dead for fifteen years, but his spirit was so present, his silence. I read books of his sayings and they were words I already knew. *Advaita Vedanta*—that's what it's called, the oldest religion in the world: *Advaita,* meaning not-two. No this and that. No me and not-me. No outside and inside. Because everything is Brahman, the One, the indivisible. It's very simple and very vibrant."

He looked round us. Some of us nodded wisely, but I doubt if we really understood.

"What happened? You must have had some Experience?"

It was the question we all wanted to ask but didn't dare. Spencer paused before answering.

"Nothing happened. Nothing," he said softly at last. "Unless you mean the full moon rising over the trees. Unless you mean the rumble of the train, or the crackle of the logs, or a smile."

He closed his eyes and went back inside himself.

"Whatever you are looking for, stop looking," he said into the silence. "You are already it. It is already there."

The cold weather continued, and the trees sparkled white with frost in the early morning. I did as Spencer had told me, staying quietly in my room and observing the patterns of my thoughts and my breath.

The demons hadn't gone away. They'd wait till my mind was quiet, and then storm in in rushes before falling back, leaving me panting with exhaustion, waiting for the next attack, but knowing, somewhere: it is not real, it is only thoughts.

Yet if thoughts aren't real, then what is? I couldn't have answered that—still can't, but the question took me deeper into myself, to places where images swarmed like fishes, where figures leapt into vivid life and as suddenly disappeared, where strange voices made incomprehensible babble, where my body felt like a drum skin collecting and reflecting every vibration of the universe, a place of dark shadows and brilliant lights, the source of dreams, where the demons rose and dissolved back into the abyss that formed them.

I had no guide to these lower regions of the mind, not even Spencer. There was only me, and I was nothing. But sometimes I'd catch Spencer's eye, and I knew he understood.

That was my real work. My jobs in the house were more like relaxation. I went daily with Tim to fetch firewood. It was a bit like scouring the Brixton skips with Chet, only with fresh air and nature, and Chinook sniffing around for rabbits. We'd go up through a field to the copse, pull out a big log and carry it back between us. Or we'd gather piles of sticks and tie them into bundles and lug them home on our backs. Chopped and sawn, the wood was making a pleasing pile in one of the outhouses.

"It's brilliant here," Tim told me. "Everybody's been great. Astrid's amazing, isn't she? She's really changed. I used to think she was a bit of a princess, but she's been getting stuck into things. And have you noticed Louise? She's almost back to normal again."

It was true. When I'd met her before, Louise had had a vacant look as if something wasn't quite working in her brain, but this had given way to a calm serenity. She and Astrid often sat in the window of the sitting room where the light was good, spinning wool from a fleece. With their long dresses and contrasting beauty—Louise tall and dark, and Astrid slight and fair—they looked like something out of a fairy tale.

But the person I got on with best at that time was Carla. She had a thin face with a slight squint that made her look streetwise, and a down-to-earth way of talking that eased my sense of unreality. Her baby, Ruby, had just learned to crawl and was great friends with Chinook, climbing all over him and pulling at his ears while he lay floppy and loving it.

"How did you meet Spencer and Astrid?" I asked her. We were washing up together.

147

"Spencer. I met Spencer. I was pregnant and my boyfriend left me—the bastard! Then I got kicked out of my flat. I didn't know where to go. I couldn't have gone home, my dad would've killed me, so I was sort of mooching about by the river thinking about throwing myself in—just stupid really, I wouldn't have had the nerve—when this huge dog came bounding up and almost knocked me over, and then there was Spencer, smiling like he does, you know? I said something to him, I don't even know what, and then he took my hands and looked into my eyes and I felt this—I dunno—I felt so special in a way. The next thing I knew, I was crying on his shoulder. So I ended up going back to his place, and Astrid was there, and Richard, and we did this sort of meditation, and it made me see things differently. It wasn't like anything I'd ever known. And then in the middle of it, I felt the baby move for the first time. It was magic I tell you, just magic."

She went on washing up in silence for a bit.

"Between you and me, though, Stephen, I owe a lot to Spencer, but I'm not sure about him. I just don't know where he's coming from. I've never worked it out—have you? I mean, look at Astrid. She's his partner, right? Or meant to be. And she tries so bloody hard, but half the time he doesn't even give her the time of day. I don't know how she puts up with it—I wouldn't. Yeah, Spencer's got the power, but sometimes I think he's kind of weird."

Kind of weird? That was what Michelle had said. It made me uneasy.

"I don't know him that well," I said quickly. "I came here because I knew Astrid."

"Yeah?" said Carla. "Well, you should look after her a bit, then. I reckon she could do with it."

At the time I didn't know what she was talking about. Astrid was perfect. She needed no help, least of all from me.

Ray was away when I arrived, off on some business. But one day towards the end of January he arrived back in his pink van. And the next day it snowed.

I woke up knowing immediately that something was different. It was so quiet. It wasn't properly light yet, but I jumped out of bed and looked out at a white world, with big snowflakes still falling.

Everyone was bubbling over at breakfast. No cars or trains had passed, and the snow lay deep in the road. We crowded into the kitchen, where the stove was already hot and Louise and Astrid were making porridge and toast. Richard stretched and smiled amiably.

"No work for me today, anyway. Think I'll go back to bed."

Ray trudged in from his van, his head and shoulders white, his footsteps disappearing behind him.

"Got here just in time, didn't I? Yeah, Astrid, gissa bit more of that porridge. It's bloody cold in my van, I'll tell you that. I'm not staying there another night."

"I can't wait to get out there," said Carla. "Ruby'll love it!"

Soon we were outside, gleefully chucking snow around or quietly watching it fall. A special train came up to clear the lines and plowed white waves to the edge of the track. After that, the trains started to run again, but more slowly than usual. We built a snowman, complete with red scarf and hat and carrot nose, while Chinook ran in big circles, snapping at snowflakes, and Ruby, strapped to Carla's back, held out mittened hands in wonder.

Ray stuck a joint in the snowman's mouth.

"Oh, come off it, Ray," said Carla. "What are people going to think? You might as well put up a big sign saying Here Be Drugs! for the narcs." But she was laughing, and when Ray took the joint back from the snowman, lit it and passed it to her, she accepted it.

We had a big soup for lunch, with homemade bread. Then in the afternoon Spencer suggested walking through the snow to the village to stock up on food supplies. Astrid and Tim and Richard were all keen, and Chinook was bouncing everywhere. I thought I'd go too, but at the last minute I changed my mind. The snow was still falling thinly, with small flakes, and it felt cold. I wanted to be inside looking out at it. So I built up the fire in the sitting room, and Ray produced a Monopoly set.

"How about a game, then?" he asked Carla.

Carla was interested. She looked at me.

"What about you, Stephen?"

I played, but my mind kept being distracted by the fire, or the snow, or Ruby, who crawled onto my knee and tried to grab the little green houses. To my relief I soon went bankrupt, leaving it to Carla and Ray to fight it out for domination of the London property market. I built up the fire, and then I could play undistractedly with Ruby, which was much more fun.

Already the light was fading. Ray had taken over most of the board. He seemed an unlikely property magnate with his wild beard and dirty clothes, but there was fire in his eyes, and a half-comic frustration as Carla kept landing on the spaces between his hotels. Louise sat serenely in the window, using the last light to knit a jumper with her homespun wool. I lay on my back on the carpet and bounced Ruby on my stomach. She squealed with delight.

No demons. No regrets. No desires. I was just there.

Ray moved into a little room in the attic. He wasn't easy to live with. He complained about the food, smoked dope in the house, smelled bad, and did nothing to help. He was devoted to Spencer, though. He'd take orders from no one else, but if Spencer half suggested something, that was it. For his part, Spencer was understanding, almost tender with him. I remembered what Astrid had told me, that he'd known Ray longer than anyone. They had a lot of history together.

We had plenty to do for the next few days, digging out the cars, clearing the drive and just mucking about in the snow.

As we cleared the drive, Ray sat in the open back of his van smoking a joint.

"How d'yer find Dylan then, Steve?" he asked.

"Yeah, great. A long way off, but great."

He grinned.

"The sky cracked its poems in naked wonder! How do I know? I was there. Didn't see me, did you? And what happened to that little French bit you picked up? She was tasty!"

I turned my back. I had my own work to do.

All the same, I couldn't help noticing something was going on between Ray and Carla. It was obvious he fancied her, and perhaps she liked the attention. In any case she couldn't really avoid him, as the snow held us in even tighter isolation than usual. One of the few things Ray did around the place was to help Carla bring in wood from the shed. One day Tim and I were coming back with logs when we saw him lean over and whisper something in her ear. She blushed and pushed him away, and he laughed.

Tim caught my eye and shrugged.

"You going to help us saw up this lot, then, Ray?" he called over.

Ray shook his head.

"It ain't me, babe!" He cackled and wandered away.

"What did he say to you?" Tim asked Carla.

"It doesn't matter. He's just Ray, isn't he?"

That night Ray went to Carla's room. I knew because I had the room next door. I could hear muffled talking through the wall, then silence for a while, then Ray left.

It happened the next night too. I didn't think much about it. Probably they just smoked a joint together.

A warmer wind blew in showers of rain, and we were stamping around in slush. We needed more wood. We'd gone through our pile in the snow, and what we were bringing down now was sodden. Tim suggested using Ray's van to fetch a load of offcuts from a joinery, but Ray put it off, hanging around in the kitchen watching Carla wash nappies and making sarcastic comments about Astrid.

Then a couple of nights later I woke up because Ruby was crying—a high insistent wail from the other side of my wall. I heard Carla trying to comfort her. And then Ray's voice.

Suddenly Carla was shouting.

"Get out! Get out of my room! Now!"

Ray said something, but I couldn't hear what. Ruby had gone quiet. I hoped it would all settle down so that I could go back to sleep. But a moment later Carla started screaming.

"Take your fucking hands off me and get out or I'll kill you."

And Ray shouted back, "You've got a lot of nerve!"

There was a thud, and a gasp from Carla, and then Ruby was screaming again.

I jumped out of bed and ran onto the landing. Richard was coming from the other direction.

"What's happening?"

Carla's door opened and Ray sauntered out, grinning.

"Just like a woman!"

He went up to the attic. Richard pushed past me, into Carla's room.

"Are you all right?"

Carla was holding Ruby over her shoulder and pacing up and down. Ruby's face was red and distressed, and she was whimpering but closing her eyes, going back to sleep.

"I'm all right, Richard," Carla said softly, still pacing. "Just gonna get a bloody padlock to put on my door from now on to keep that arsehole out."

The next morning, Carla knocked on my door and asked me to look after Ruby. I was only too happy. I loved looking after Ruby. She reminded me of what Chet had said about making little children laugh. Ruby laughed at a look or a funny noise or a tickle—anything really.

Carla gave her to me, but she didn't leave immediately.

"God, I need a smoke."

"Have one, then," I said. "Open the window. It's too wet to go outside today anyway."

"Smoking in the house? I'm surprised at you, Stephen. You're a bit of a secret rebel, aren't you?"

She leant against the sill, looking out at the rain washing away the last traces of snow while she lit her cigarette. She didn't offer me one, and I wouldn't have taken it. I'd given up when I came to The Hollies.

"Shit!" said Carla quietly. "Shit!"

She looked over at me and Ruby.

"I know—I'm falling to pieces, aren't I? But it's not easy, man. It's not easy."

"You mean, because of Ruby?"

"No. Ruby keeps me going. No. Me. It's me. All my chaos."

She lit her cigarette and drew on it heavily.

"Sorry about last night."

"Why?"

"We woke you up, didn't we?"

"That was nothing. Were you all right?"

She shook her head.

"No. No, I wasn't. I wasn't all right, whatever that is. But it was my own fault, letting that thing into my room. I should've known better, right from the start. Some of us don't ever learn."

"What did he do?"

She stopped and gave me a squinty look.

"You're so innocent, aren't you? That thing had better keep away from now on. If it touches me again, I'll kill it. And I mean that. I'm not soft like you. I wish I was."

She looked back out into the rain.

"I don't belong here, really."

"You do!" I meant it. I really liked her, and suddenly I was worried that she and Ruby would leave. The house would be empty without them.

"Nah. I've just been pretending. Because I like some people and because of Ruby. I'm going to see Spencer now, tell him what that shit-arse is. And you know what he'll do about it? Nothing. And you know why? Because he isn't there. And nothing's real. Well, I'm here, and I'm real. And so's Ruby. And so are you, two days a week. And by the way, there is such a thing as right and wrong. Sorry."

I reacted badly when they left. It was my first crisis in the house, the first time I had to deal with something outside, rather than the strange mists of my inner world. If there's a difference.

It wasn't that Carla minded going. She'd rung up an old friend who happened to have a room free in her flat, and she'd jumped at it.

"You know what, Stephen, when I first realized it was us that was going to have to leave and not that creep, I was really pissed off, but I don't care now. I'm glad actually. I want to do something with my life, not sit around dreaming of enlightenment or something. It's been nice here for Ruby, but I've been kind of rotting. Come and look by sometime. Ruby'll miss you."

And I would miss Ruby—but it wasn't just that. I had a sense of injustice, and with it a great surge of doubt. What was I doing here? What was anyone doing? "A dream of enlightenment"—Carla had hit the nail on the head. I'd come here in a sort of dream, and because people were a little bit friendly, I'd bought the whole package.

Richard drove them away. I stood in the drive after they'd gone, my thoughts dark. Then I felt Astrid's hand on my arm.

"Hey, don't worry. Carla's doing the best thing. They'll be happy."

"How do you know?" I said, shaking my arm free.

She looked at me, startled by my anger, and I met her eyes. They were as beautiful as ever, but for the first time I was seeing through them to something else: doubt, anxiety, the desire to please and the fear of rejection. Since I'd been in the house, I'd been too caught up with myself to think much about her. She was just there: Astrid. Beautiful, charming, warm, and Spencer's partner. Perfection. But that wasn't her, not really. Underneath she was pain and confusion just like me.

"Are you okay?" she asked. I could hear the hurt in her voice, but I couldn't respond to it.

"I don't understand why Carla's leaving and Ray's staying. But it doesn't matter. I'm going for a walk."

I strode out of the gate into the lane.

Walking calmed me, but only a little. I felt the strength in my legs, and I saw a fox by the wood, but my thoughts were raging. I made no attempt to stop them.

When I got back, Tim and Astrid were making bread in the kitchen with a forced jollity. I leant against the stove.

"Where's Louise?" I asked, for something to say. I didn't really care where she was. I hardly ever spoke to her.

"She's upstairs with Spencer," said Tim. "Receiving teachings."

He tried to say it straight, but he winced. I didn't

know why, and I didn't understand. Receiving teachings? It didn't make sense. Spencer was always saying that there was no path to spiritual awakening, no technique.

"Spencer says there are no teachings," I objected. But even as I said it, I realized Spencer did give teachings, or at least instructions. He had given them to me, so he must have given them in some form to everyone else too.

"Maybe initiation is a better word," said Astrid. She stopped kneading the bread and tried to catch my eye. I looked away, but I could feel that she wasn't quite right either. None of us were. We were all pretending, more or less.

"Look," Astrid continued. "Spencer has so much knowledge—secret stuff, not for everybody who walks in the door. He knows when we are ready, and then, you know, it takes the master to show you what you already are. There's a new energy coming into the house now. Everything will be purer and more powerful. It will spread out in waves. . . ."

It sounded as if she was repeating something Spencer had said, or more likely Richard, and not getting it quite right. She broke off, though, because Ray came in. He sauntered over to the table, cut a thick slice of bread and smeared it with margarine.

"Yeah, Steve. Didn't you know? The times they are a-changin'."

I could never work out whether Ray disliked me or was trying to be friendly, but I felt a bristle of hostility towards him, which spread over to Tim and Astrid, who had let Carla and Ruby go and said nothing.

"So that's why you kicked out Carla and Ruby. Because they weren't pure enough," I accused them.

"We didn't kick them out," said Tim defensively. "It was their choice—"

"Oh, come on!" I interrupted. "Come on!"

I was standing with my legs apart and a hand on my hip. It was how Rob stood when he argued. My voice had become like Rob's too, cutting, sarcastic.

Everyone seemed to be becoming someone else. Who was I? What the hell was I doing here?

They were all staring at me. Astrid's face held an anxiety that frightened me. I turned and almost ran from the room.

In the security of my own room, I drew breath. I was panting. I didn't know why. What was I so worked up about?

There was a pile of books on the floor, all to do with meditation in some way. I picked up the top one, a book about Zen by Alan Watts. Yesterday I'd thought it made sense, but now it seemed like a jumble of words.

Who was I? Who was this person with this desperate need to belong?

It was all nonsense . . . the wind in the trees.

A train juddered past in the cutting. People thinking they were getting somewhere, but they were all fools, going nowhere, in endless meaningless circles, like me.

There wasn't anything to belong to. Nothing but dreams and delusions. Suddenly I remembered Matthew in the Isle of Wight. Was I going to end up like him, mumbling that nothing is real?

I lay down. Another train passed outside, and then a thrush started its cheerful song. Maybe it knew something I didn't. Because I was nothing. A hollow egg.

A tap on the door. I sat up. It would be Astrid or Tim. Probably Astrid, worried about me, but I couldn't talk to her. I'd pretend to be reading and she'd go away.

I opened the door, and there stood Spencer.

"Hi, Stephen!"

He smiled. Spencer's smile. It was irresistible. All my resentment melted like mist, and I smiled back.

He went past me into my room, sat down and picked up my book. I sat hesitantly at the other end of the mattress.

"Alan Watts. Yeah, he's got it, at least theoretically. Funny, huh, how you can understand everything and still be lost in your head?"

"We're all lost in our head, aren't we?"

"If you mean that, Stephen, then you're getting found. Don't be afraid of conflict. If you try to avoid things, that's a sort of death of the spirit. Conflict, doubt, fear, that's what you go through, that's what life is."

He stopped himself as if he'd already said too much.

"Were you thinking of leaving?"

I nodded.

"You're right," he agreed. "It's time to decide. Not that there's really a choice. When you look at it straight, you know what you have to do. Do you want to talk about what's worrying you?"

I looked at him. The great guru—sitting neatly cross-legged on the end of my mattress. With his eyes turned away, he looked so ordinary. Yet I could say anything to him and he wouldn't judge, or get defensive, or react in any personal way at all. Was that a good thing or a bad thing?

"Ray and Carla," I said. "You know Ray was in the wrong, don't you? Why should it have been Carla and Ruby who left?"

Spencer paused for a while, weighing my words.

"Wrong, right, right, wrong, it's only ideas. . . . But yeah, it's true in a way. It wasn't my decision, though. There wasn't even a decision to make. You can say what you like about Ray, and there's plenty, but he wants to be here right now. He's committed. Carla isn't. She wants to be in a world of doing and becoming, and maybe that's better for Ruby too. This isn't a great place for a baby. Nobody made them leave. Carla saw what she had to do, what was necessary, that's all. They'll be fine."

I couldn't accept it. I could hear Carla in my head saying: "And by the way, there is such a thing as right and wrong." An injustice had been done. I knew it, and looked away.

Spencer touched my hand, speaking with sudden intensity.

"Stephen, everything is as it is, that's all. You can't divide yourself from what's happening and try to order it around. You are not separate. Do you understand what I'm saying?"

"Sort of." It was what Spencer always said. It was just words, though. A blackbird was tugging at a worm on the lawn.

Suddenly his voice changed.

"Look, let's get real. You're not worried about Carla and Ruby, are you? You're worried about yourself, your own sufferings, your own longings. Like everyone else."

I turned back in and looked at him. Was he right? His eyes were huge. . . . I sank into them, and as I did so, I felt as if they were Michelle's eyes, and a wave of longing rose inside me.

"What *are* your longings, Stephen?" Spencer was asking. "Can you see them, touch them? Are they real?"

My longings? I thought I knew the "right" answer, that they were only shadows in the mind—but the right answer was wrong.

"Yes," I said, my voice cracking with sudden intensity. "They *are* real. As much as anything. As much as the garden, or you. More. They are me."

I blinked and looked down. Spencer waited for me to continue.

"I was in love. You know that. It was like another world, another way of being that opened—something I'd lost and forgotten and found again. It was truth. It was beauty. It was everything really. And I blew it."

"The love—whose was it? Yours or Michelle's?"

The question slowed me, made me think.

"It was neither. We hardly knew each other. It was like, we saw through each other to something beyond. An immensity. Something so good I never believed we could lose it. I thought I loved *her*, but it was more that she was a gateway to something. . . . I don't know . . ."

I broke off, struggling with emotion I still didn't understand.

"I still want her, though," I mumbled. "I want her so much. I've woken every night since, and there's a blank beside me where she ought to be. She made me whole, and she was the only one who could do that. I still hope she might turn up here one day, say hello, and we'll start again."

I looked pleadingly at him. His eyes were so big, so kind. He could do anything. He could bring us back together, me and Michelle, if he chose.

"Cut the crap, Stephen! She's gone. Let go!"

Spencer's voice was hard, and his eyes seemed to freeze over.

I felt a rush of anger. How dare he talk like that? Then in the next breath I could see it: the clinging, the holding on that had started even while we were still together, that had pushed us apart. I could see it for what it was in all its destructiveness, and I knew too that I could walk away and leave it.

"But not the love," he continued, his voice soft again. "The love's still there, not yours or hers or mine or anybody's, but always there. Everywhere. Lose yourself and it will find you."

"How?" I asked.

Spencer let his breath slowly out through his nose.

"Can you commit yourself?"

"Commit? What to—to you?"

"Not to me. I'm not anybody. No, to truth, to love, to the immensity, as you called it. Are you staying or going, Stephen? Have you decided that?"

I sat back and for a moment surveyed my life. It was suddenly obvious. There was nothing for me anywhere else, nothing for me to do or become, nothing else worth living for.

"I'm staying."

Spencer smiled.

He took me to his room—his private room, not the bedroom he shared with Astrid. I'd never been in there before. It looked over the railway cutting to the woods, and it was almost luxurious, with the blue carpet, a big stereo, a desk, even a leather sofa.

He told me to sit on the carpet and be aware of my breathing while he sat cross-legged opposite me, sometimes in silence, sometimes speaking softly: "Nothing is done by you. Everything just happens. Watch it happening, know it to be unreal." And later: "You are a conjuror of dreams."

My breath came slowly while a flow of words and images formed and dissolved in my brain with extreme rapidity: my consciousness, that was all, day and night, on and on. Conjuring dreams was all I'd ever done.

I don't know how long I sat there absorbed in this

fractured dream world, but then without any warning the flow stopped. Just stopped. Leaving nothing. No content, no commentary, nothing. Which was also the immensity: vast, nameless, whole.

I opened my eyes. I was alone. I stood up, stretched, walked to the window. The sky had cleared and the low sun burned in an orange haze. A train sped through the cutting.

The immensity was always there, immutable, all around and through me and through the world. I and the world were one.

Chapter 13

No more doubts. Although my mind soon restarted its commentary, I knew it now for what it was: a conjuror of dreams. The demons had lost their power because I knew, *knew*, beyond all certainty, that woven through all my so-called reality the immensity was everywhere, and everything was of it.

I was contented and alive, and blissfully unaware of anything that didn't immediately affect me. Like my body, the world went on of its own accord. I was in it and it was in me and the immensity was everywhere, eclipsing my sense of my own importance. I had found a love that was not dependent on anything or anybody, not even on Spencer, a love that would never go away.

Spencer asked me to take charge of the garden. He wanted it productive as well as beautiful. It was an important responsibility, and I bought a few tools and set to work. The Hollies had more than an acre of land in a long strip between the railway and the road, as well as several outbuildings. Tim and I converted a shed into a chicken house, then went to the local market and came back with six brown hens that gave us instant eggs. I was worried Chinook would chase the hens, but he sniffed at them amiably and made friends.

Minkie the goat was a gift from a middle-aged lady called Penelope who lived on her own with goats and cats, knew about Eastern religions and visited Spencer sometimes. She brought Minkie over and showed us how to milk her. I liked feeling the warm milk spurt from her udders into the pail, but I was suddenly busy with many projects, so I passed the job on to Louise. The white, tangy milk wasn't to everyone's taste—Ray wouldn't touch it—but Astrid made little fresh cheeses from the surplus that were delicious.

The land at the front of the house had once been a vegetable garden, so I set about reclaiming it, slashing and digging all day till my muscles ached and calluses grew on the pads of my hands. I made friends with a robin, and knew the rhythms of the sun and moon and the times of the passing trains. I mended a half-ruined greenhouse, set out little trays of seeds and waited hopefully for the seedlings to poke through the soil. I pruned the bushes and tethered Minkie on the over-grown lawn so that she grazed the grass tight and smooth. Under the rosebush where I had lain with Michelle, I planted primroses and anemones as a little shrine, and as the weather improved, I often sat there hearing the birds chorus the sunset and feeling the great flow of change.

New people had moved into the house: Anneke and Brigit had taken over Carla's room—two Swedish girls who sat in front of Spencer at the evening sittings with rapt expressions on their faces and followed him around devotedly. To everyone's relief Ray went off in his van, and an old friend of Tim's called Graham moved into the attic. Graham was a big, amiable guy who'd been a hash dealer and then changed his mind and become very antidrugs; he worked with Tim, converting the stables to make accommodation for visitors. Slowly but surely, The Hollies was becoming a Center.

In all this activity, I more or less ignored Astrid. She was there, always there in the background, Spencer's partner, smiling and friendly, but somehow unattainable.

Then one afternoon in April I came into the kitchen for a cup of tea. Astrid was on her own there, hand washing clothes.

I picked up the kettle—we had an electric one by now, though we still cooked on the range—but she took it off me.

"Sit down. I'll make you tea, Stevie. You are working so hard."

It was nice, the way she said that. Anyone else would have said, "Make one for me too." I let her take the kettle, noticing how her fingers were raw from the washing. I looked at her, and for once I took her in. She was no longer the glamorous hippie who had found me that day in Notting Hill. Her dress was worn and faded, and she wore a shapeless home-knitted jumper over it. Her hair was unwashed and tied back casually, and there were lines of tension round her mouth. Why hadn't I noticed before?

I sat down and she turned towards me.

"You want herb tea?"

She had a row of little jars of herbs, and was always trying to get everyone to drink her infusions instead of the thick brown brews that Tim and Graham favored.

"Yes, please," I said.

"What sort?"

"Whatever you think. Something to give me some energy."

She selected a mix for the teapot, then went back to wringing out Spencer's trousers.

"You know, Stevie, I've been thinking. I would like to plant a herb garden."

"There's the remains of one already," I said. "Overgrown sage and rosemary bushes. We could get it back."

"Yes?" She looked pleased.

"Yes," I said. "Let's do that. We can do it together."

That was when Astrid started working with me. We soon sorted the herbs, sowing seeds and taking cuttings, and from then on she came out and joined me in the garden whenever she had the time, helping with the weeding and planting while I dug. I loved watching her plant seedlings. Her hands were reddened with eczema, but she touched the plants with such delicacy.

Sometimes we worked in silence, and sometimes we chatted. She told me things about her childhood in Germany; about her grandfather, who grew sweet peas and strawberries in his garden in the hungry time after the war; about her mother, who died when she was young and she remembered only as a presence, a security that suddenly went away; about her older brother, who disapproved of her; and about her father, a successful industrialist, who she loved and hated with equal intensity.

"Do you feel like that, about your father?" she asked me.

I thought about it.

"No, not like that. I sort of envy you in a way. With my father, everything's half smothered. It's like one of those dreams where you can see someone and you wave at them and they wave back; but there's always a gulf you can't cross, and all you're left with is a sense of yearning. Do you know what I mean?"

Astrid touched my arm, her eyes soft.

"I don't have those dreams, Stevie," she said.

"What dreams do you have?"

She half closed her eyes, her head on one side, her lips slightly parted, showing her teeth. Her fingers held a weed she'd just pulled up. A thrush was singing.

"Last night I dreamed I had two lovers. I wanted them both, but I couldn't keep both happy! It was impossible!" She laughed and turned away.

We talked about other things too, about the past we had shared, Jerry, Afghanistan. I told her about Chet and the squat in London. The one person we never talked about was Spencer.

That is, until we crossed the railway line.

The trains were so much part of life at The Hollies: long, rumbling goods trains, expresses, local diesels, always in the background of our lives. The railway line was in a cutting, past a fence of concrete posts and strands of wire, then down a steep bank that was burned twice a year to control the brambles. From the garden we could see the tops of the carriages, and from some places the heads of the passengers. Richard hated the trains and was always complaining about how they spoiled the place, but I liked them. They were part of the rhythm of my day. Spencer probably had no feelings about them either way, but he was nervous about Chinook wandering onto the lines, so there was a sort of taboo about crossing the track. On the far side, woods of ash and oak stretched away invitingly, but we never went there.

I was trimming dead wood from an old apple tree near the fence when Astrid came out with mugs of herb tea. I put down my saw, and we sat under the blossom as a train passed, and then there was the wonderful midday stillness of the English countryside, the sun on our backs and the canopy of the trees opposite us breaking into green. From where we were, we could glimpse a shimmering carpet of bluebells.

"Why don't we ever go over there?" asked Astrid.

"I don't know. It sort of feels dangerous."

"We can go," she said. "Who's stopping us? Let's do it!"

She jumped up and pulled my hand to lift me, smiling. She looked lovely, soft and alive.

We climbed through the fence and half slid down a steep bank to the track. There we paused for a moment.

171

The line curved out of sight, but I thought we'd hear any trains coming. Then, as we stood, I heard a faint vibration from the rails. It only took a moment to run up the other side, and by the time the train passed, we were in the woods.

Bluebells. Nothing but bluebells, and the trees whispering above us, and the sharp tang of a fox. I must make sure I locked up the chickens at night. We followed a track up the slope until we were back level with the house, which was just visible through the emerging leaves. Someone had made a rough shelter there with branches and corrugated iron, and a log in front of it, which we sat on.

"Looks like they've been spying on us," I said.

"They?"

"Oh, you know, Special Branch, the CIA."

Astrid looked at me in alarm.

"Don't worry. I'm only joking. I was followed though, a couple of times, in London. It was when I was staying with Rob. He was mixed up with all sorts of weird people."

The memory of Rob made me feel suddenly queasy. I never thought about him anymore—all that gray world of politics and negativity.

"Rob, yes," said Astrid with a sigh. She had her memories of him too. "You are so . . . different, you two. Who would have guessed?"

I looked round at her, sitting on the log beside me. Even in her old clothes she was as beautiful as ever; more so in a way because she was more real to me, because I saw her now as she was—her mood swings, her desire to please, her kindness, her vulnerability.

"Thank you," I said.

"What for?" she asked, puzzled.

"You brought me here. Without you, I'd never have met Spencer. I'd still be lost in . . . I don't know where . . . unreality."

"Oh that." Her lip trembled. "But don't you see? I was so glad to find you. Without you, I don't know . . . Sometimes I think you're the only person who cares about me here."

She was studying the rough skin on her hands intently and I couldn't read her face, but I was astounded. Nobody care for her? Surely everybody loved Astrid. Who could help it?

"But you're with Spencer," I said.

"Am I?"

My heart missed a beat, and I felt a sadness in her that I had never guessed. There was nothing to say. She leant against me and put her head on my shoulders; I took her hand and waited.

"It used to be so perfect," she continued at last. "When we first met. It was just the two of us, and there was so much love, Stevie, so much love. . . . But now . . . He's so high up, it's like he's flown away, beyond me, where I can't reach. He doesn't come to our bed anymore. He hardly speaks to me really. He stays in his room, and Anneke and Brigit go to him there. Louise too sometimes. He gives them Tantric teachings. That's what they call it."

I was amazed. I hadn't realized any of this. I thought of Spencer and Astrid as a couple forever, almost like my parents.

She looked up at me, her voice pitched slightly too high.

"I shouldn't care, should I? I mean, we're all meant to be above that sort of thing, aren't we?"

"What sort of thing?"

"You know—possessiveness. Jealousy. It's stupid and I'm ashamed of myself."

We sat together in silence. I could feel the distress in her, the tears that were welling in her eyes. I knew that I could take her in my arms, and she would cry and let me comfort her, and in a way that was what I wanted to do. But what she had said was news to me. I'd been too busy in the garden, too absorbed in my newfound peace, to notice what might be going on between people in the house. I needed to consider it.

I could smell the earth, that rich mulch of old leaves that fed the bluebells. The breeze touched my cheek. A pair of thrushes chased each other round a holly bush. I was breathing, pulsating, alive, and so was Astrid beside me. It was enough. More than enough. It was everything.

I thought I knew what she meant by "Tantric teachings." Spencer said they released psychic power through the mystical union of male and female energies. Which meant sex, basically. Perhaps that was what Anneke and Brigit needed, and if that was a way that Spencer could help them to develop, then that was fine. It had to be.

I squeezed Astrid's shoulder.

"Everything is just as it is."

I said it gently, meaning to comfort her with the truth that seemed to me so all-embracing, but she pulled away.

"You sound just like him," she said almost fiercely. Then she turned back to me and softened.

"Sorry, Stevie. I don't know why I'm like this. He's given us so much, hasn't he? I mean, look what's happened to you. You are so calm these days. You don't seem to need anything. You should tell me how it's done."

She stood up, looking out into the woods. A train passed.

"I'm not good enough really. That's my problem. Not for Spencer. Sometimes I think back to Jerry, how selfish, how deluded, how impossible he was, and I think maybe that was more right for me. More like I am. I can keep up a good appearance. I learnt it as a child. But it's killing me, this having to be perfect. I can't keep it up much longer."

"Nobody has to be perfect. Nobody is. That's not the point. . . ."

I stopped. So what was the point? I hadn't thought it through. Astrid trying to be perfect—that was all right too. And if it was killing her, that must be all right as well.

She turned and looked at me. Her eyes were pleading for something, but I didn't know what it was. And just then, I didn't want to know.

175

Before we left, I poked around the hide and found cigarette butts and boot marks. Somebody had been there, not that long ago. I felt a pang of unease, remembering the mysterious man in the raincoat in London, but I put it aside. It was probably only a local farmer shooting rabbits.

That evening at supper I looked around the table with new eyes. Astrid looked composed enough as she laid out a big flan made from our own eggs. Graham watched her appreciatively, but Brigit and Anneke ignored her. Their attention was all on Spencer.

And he liked it. I could see that immediately, now that I was paying attention to it. These two blond girls dressed in white were his angels, feeding him energy. Not that he talked to them or took any obvious notice. He chatted to Richard about cars for most of the meal. Spencer didn't have a car, of course, but Richard wanted to get him one so that he could drive around the country giving talks.

"There's a whole network of spiritually aware people that's developing," Richard held forth. "They're hungry to hear what Spencer can tell them. The West is ready to wake from its materialist dreams. We have the Truth. We can't just keep it to ourselves."

"You could use the Morris," offered Tim.

No one said anything. It was obvious: the message that Spencer brought could not be delivered from a Morris Minor.

"I think Richard has in mind more like a Porsche," Spencer joked. Everybody laughed, including Tim.

Tim had taken a job as a hospital porter. He worked night shifts, and he always looked knackered. I wondered about him and Louise. They still shared a room, but Louise had lost her dependence on him. She said little, watching Spencer with big eyes.

After supper I went to the gathering—*satsang* we called it now. It was an open evening, which we had twice a week, part of a new system that tried to regulate the flow of visitors. It was amazing how word had spread. A journalist visited for a weekend, then wrote an article about Spencer in a magazine, and now all kinds of people were coming to see him and get the blessing that we had just from being around him.

The sitting room was hardly big enough to contain everybody. Spencer sat on an armchair at the front, the rest of us cross-legged on the floor. Brigit and Anneke and Louise and Richard were right in front of Spencer, very still and absorbed. Astrid and Graham came in late after clearing up and slipped in beside me at the back. Tim had gone to work.

Spencer talked more than he used to, and his method had changed too. He would pick someone out and have a dialogue with them. Then he would look them in the eyes and sometimes touch their forehead, and ask us all to sit in silence.

The silence had changed. I know that sounds strange, but it had. Before, the silence had been deep and peaceful; now, as soon as I shut my eyes, I was aware of something like an electric current in the room, almost tangible.

People left at the end visibly moved. They would come back.

There were exceptions, of course. As Spencer said, where there is a positive there must be a negative. The people from the commune where Michelle had stayed, for example, never came near, and we heard they'd been spreading tales that we were a cult. I was disappointed at first because I'd have liked to hear news of Michelle, but I soon realized how far all our lives had come. Not everyone could understand.

After the *satsang* I went up to my room and read from *The Tibetan Book of the Dead,* which Tim had lent me. It made me wonder about reincarnation, and other realms of being. It wouldn't be any use asking Spencer about that, though. He'd say now is all that counts.

That was the thing: I always knew what Spencer would say. I didn't have to ask him anymore.

I put out the light and lay for a few minutes feeling the immensity flow around and through me, then quickly went to sleep.

I couldn't have been asleep long when I woke abruptly. Astrid was framed in the doorway, a finger to her lips. She shut the door behind her and sat down on the end of my mattress, hunched over her knees. She sat there silently, just visible in the moonlight.

I sat up and moved towards her.

"Astrid?"

"Don't say anything!"

I was kneeling behind her. I put my hands on her shoulders and massaged them gently. She sighed, and then she turned towards me.

"Lie down!"

I did as she told me. She took off her clothes and slid in under the blankets next to me. I put my arms round her and she squeezed against me, but there was no passion in her. It was like holding a child. She buried her head in my shoulder, and I stroked her back in the dark. Her hair smelled of apricots. I could feel the soft vibration of her, her warmth, the light, fluttering movements of her breath. She was still the most beautiful woman in the world, and to hold her like this was beyond my dreams, but I had no desire, just a deep sense of gentleness as her breathing steadied and she slipped into sleep beside me.

I lay awake for a long time with Astrid in my arms, wondering about her and Spencer. It was strange to me, but it was all right. It had to be.

When I woke in the morning, she had gone.

I wish now that I'd asked Astrid why she came to me, but neither of us ever raised the subject during the day, and at night we didn't speak. I told myself that some emotions are beyond words, that it was enough for me to be there for her. I never doubted Spencer, that he knew what he was doing, that his only aim, his only reason for living, was to help us all.

And I was there for her. I was there in the garden, where we worked together, sometimes in an easy silence, sometimes chatting. And I was there for her at night, when perhaps her demons came for her, as mine had once come for me. When she lay in my arms, I loved her as much as I'd loved Michelle, but without thought of possession. If I had feelings of desire, I pushed them away. We had a trust too precious to spoil.

After a while she stopped coming at night. I thought she was better, that she didn't need me anymore. And I was happy for her. She had regained her serenity.

It was spring. Rows of lettuce and cabbage seedlings appeared in the vegetable patch, the daffodils faded and the roses bloomed.

Richard got the phone connected, and I rang my parents regularly to stop them worrying. Not that they seemed worried. My mother was preoccupied with politics, and when my father answered, neither of us had much to say.

"This place you're staying—is it some sort of cult?" he managed on one occasion.

"Oh no, Dad. It's nothing like that. Just a sort of community. Most people go out to work. I'll probably get a job soon."

Which wasn't quite true, though Richard had recently had a word with me.

"You know, Stephen, we can't run this place on nothing. What you're doing in the garden is great stuff, but we need more cash. Why don't you get a job at the

180

hospital with Tim? And by the way, you could do with a haircut. We don't want people thinking we're hippies."

I didn't like either idea. Tim was always tired now, and the joy seemed to have gone out of him. I happened to come across Spencer on his own in the kitchen that afternoon, so I mentioned it to him.

He put a hand on my arm.

"No worries, Stephen. You're fine as you are."

All the same, I felt uneasy with Richard, as if he had his eye on me, so I avoided him. I didn't need to talk to him anyway. If Spencer said I was fine as I was, then that was it as far as I was concerned. As for the haircut—it made me notice for the first time how we all looked a bit the same, the girls with long hair and long dresses, the boys with short hair and loose cotton clothes. Ray, of course, was completely different, but Ray wasn't around. I didn't cut my hair, though. I liked it how it was.

The weather was getting warmer. I proudly brought in my first crops: radishes, lettuces, sugar peas and little new potatoes. One of the hens went broody and produced a clutch of fluffy chicks that followed her round the backyard. Graham had nearly finished converting the stables, and there was talk of starting courses, but I didn't pay too much attention.

Then Tim left.

It happened suddenly. One evening he came up to my room and said, "I'm going tomorrow."

"Going where?" I asked, not understanding.

"Just going. Leaving. I've got a flat in Colchester. It's nearer to my work. It'll be easier."

I was taken aback.

"What about Louise?"

"She's staying here. We haven't really been together recently anyway. She doesn't need me like she used to. It's good."

But it didn't sound good, the way he said it.

"But why . . . ?" I started.

"I'll still come over in the evenings. It'll be better. I'm not doing much here, in the house or anything, and . . . well, I'll miss you, but . . ."

He tailed off.

"Did Spencer say—" I started.

"It's nothing to do with Spencer," he interrupted. "It's my fault. I've got all these issues. I need my own space to work it out."

He looked forlornly out of the window.

"You've done a good job on the garden, Stephen. Remember how we used to get the wood together in the winter?"

"It's Richard, isn't it?" I blurted out. "Richard's making you go."

Tim shrugged.

"Nobody's making me go. Richard only pointed out the obvious. It's just Louise really."

Suddenly his voice was clogged with emotion.

"She doesn't want me anymore, Stephen. She doesn't want me. . . ."

I gave him a hug. It was all I could do. I'd miss him, but not that much. People came and went in one's life. They had to. I was beyond that kind of attachment.

He never came back. Tim had been a good friend to me, and I felt bad about him for a while, but I heard he'd met a Tibetan lama and gone with him to Scotland to build a monastery there. I could see Tim doing that. So things worked out for the best.

A party for Astrid's birthday! Spencer suggested it, and it sounded a great idea. We could open up the house and invite all the regulars at *satsang*. We'd make fresh, wholesome food, and have a fire outside and play music.

I was pleased too for Astrid. Spencer was taking notice of her.

The morning of the party, I crossed the railway line again. I was out early, and looked across at the thick new leaves and the deep shadows, and suddenly wanted to go back there. There was no one about except Chinook, who'd followed me out. At the fence I sent him back. He hung his head. He wanted to come with me. He knew there were exciting new smells over there, but he was an obedient dog, and he slunk back to the house.

It felt strange to be over there, as if I'd stepped out of a magic circle. Apart from the odd trip to town virtually all my time was spent at The Hollies now. It was my work, my social life, my world. Without being aware of it, I was caught in its assumptions. But on the other side of the tracks I belonged to nobody. I was free. Perhaps I should come more often. The bluebells had died back, and everything was green, deep green, with the smell of summer.

I walked up to the log where I had sat with Astrid. The foliage had closed around it, so you couldn't see the house anymore, but a track led back towards the railway line at a higher point on the cutting. I followed it to the edge of the trees and found a hollow where the plants had been recently crushed down. I could see the back of the house and the hen run, close and clear. There was a cigarette butt, pushed into the earth.

It looked like somebody had been spying on us after all. I remembered the man in the raincoat again, and shivered. They couldn't still be watching me, could they? Or watching the house? Surely that was impossible. We had no politics, didn't even take any drugs now Ray had gone. Everything we did was completely innocent. No, it must have been some idiot from the village, hoping to pick up gossip.

All the same, it made me uneasy. I'd have to tell somebody—Richard probably.

I collected up some firewood to carry back. It gave me a justification for going over in the first place.

As I went into the house, I met Astrid in the hall. I was about to give her a hug and wish her a happy birthday, but she stepped back, rigid with emotion.

"What's the matter?" I asked.

"You look, Stevie!"

She held out a card that had just arrived in the post.

It was a German birthday card, with a picture of a candle, expensive but conventional. Inside there were some printed words in German, then in pen "Von Papa."

"From your father?"

She nodded.

"Well, at least he remembered."

"He remembered me, yes, and that's all he can say: 'Von Papa.' No message, nothing. He did it like a machine. No, he did it to get back at me, make me feel bad. He's been like this since I got together with Spencer. He cut me off then. He won't speak to me. He thinks Spencer is . . . I don't know! He knows nothing!"

I'd never seen Astrid angry like this, and I was surprised as much as anything.

"Perhaps he's trying. Perhaps he doesn't know how to do better." I was thinking of my own father.

Astrid sighed. The anger was leaving her.

"My father and I were very close. He knows how to hurt me. And he always knows what he is doing."

Spencer was coming downstairs with Brigit and Anneke in tow. He went straight up to Astrid, taking over.

"From your father? Let's see."

She handed him the card dumbly and looked away.

I went into the kitchen and made tea.

By the time the party started, Astrid had recovered her poise. She wore a blue Moroccan dress, her present from Spencer; her hair shone and she looked stunning. The house looked pretty good too, freshly painted, with new carpets and so clean—what a change since

185

last summer! We all felt proud of what we'd achieved. Food was laid out in the kitchen—flans, salads, goat cheese—much of it from the garden. Spencer had done most of the cooking, as he did on special occasions.

I knew most of the guests from the *satsangs*—at least their faces. There were some middle-aged ladies, showing their husbands that we were harmless, but mostly they were young people like me with fresh, keen faces. What I did find strange was that wherever Spencer went, a crowd formed round him, hanging on his words. He'd acquired a following, people who looked at him as a teacher, not as a friend.

I caught his eye, and he raised an eyebrow. I imagined him saying: "It's how it is!"

Later, we sat round the fire. There were no joints or chillums this time, but we did have a crate of beer. I took a can, but it tasted insipid, so I left it and settled down by the rosebush, a yard from where I'd spent my first night with Michelle, and absorbed the atmosphere.

Compared with the previous party, it was a subdued scene. No band arrived to drive up the energy, no one smoked hash, or danced, and even the fire was restrained. There was music, though: a couple of guys could play guitar, and Anneke and Brigit had a nice sense of harmony. With Venus shining in the sunset and the scent of roses, it was enough—more than enough— because surrounding us now was the immensity, the mystery, unfathomable and beyond words.

A girl sat down beside me. I knew her face from *satsangs*.

"Hi! You're Stephen, right?"

I was.

"I'm Ruth. Hey, you live in the house, that's so cool!"

She talked. I listened half to her and half to the music, watching the flames lick round the logs. She was nice-looking, but I didn't feel any sexual attraction. I'd gone beyond that. Instead, without thinking, I knew everything about her, what she felt, what she wanted. She was talking to me because I lived in the house, and was close to Spencer and had absorbed some of his magic. That was fine by me.

The sun was setting. Bats emerged from the shadows of the wood and circled in the twilight.

"Have you seen Chinook?"

It was Spencer, momentarily escaped from his attendants.

"He was around earlier. I saw him . . ."

"Me too. But he should be here now. Hope he hasn't wandered off."

He glanced towards the railway line.

I got up.

"I'll look out for him. I've got to do the chickens now anyway."

I walked round to the back of the house, following the railway cutting. The wood was in deep shadow by now. Chinook might have gone over, but I didn't think it was likely. I'd sent him back that morning, and he'd gone. He knew he wasn't allowed there.

Chinook liked to sit by the hen run watching the

hens scratching and taking dust baths. He never chased them, but there must have been a rich landscape of smells for a dog, and maybe rats and mice after the grain. That was where I found him.

Something was wrong. Even in the half-light, I could see that immediately. He was half sitting, half lying, making a low whine and stabbing at the ground with his head. He collapsed onto his side as I ran over, shuddered and looked up at me with a clouded eye, still trying to get up but hardly able to raise his head. His mouth was foaming. For a moment I thought he had rabies, and started back.

"What's happened? Stevie, what's the matter?"

It was Astrid, coming out of the house.

"I just found him. He's ill."

Astrid didn't hesitate. She knelt down in the dust in her new dress and put her arms round Chinook. He made a pathetic effort to wag his tail and looked at her through all his pain with the pure love that dogs have. She bent over and hugged him, her hair falling around his twitching body.

"Get Spencer, quick!"

I turned, but Spencer was already coming, running out of the back door, his face wide and blank in the fading light as he took us in. A little posse of followers hovered in the background.

He knelt down opposite Astrid, stroking Chinook's head and whispering his name. I could hear the dog's rasping breathing as he battled for life.

"Shall I ring the vet?" I asked, wanting to be of use.

Spencer looked up.

"It's too late for that."

He glanced at the ring of faces behind me.

"Tell them all to go home."

He took Chinook from Astrid and lifted the dying dog's head onto his knees, speaking to him softly. Chinook shuddered, and then he was still. Spencer knelt there for a long while, with the last purple of the sunset behind him.

The party was over.

Chapter 14

We buried Chinook under an apple tree, persistent drizzle falling as Spencer shoveled the red soil onto the stiff body. He patted down the earth, then stood back and read from the Heart Sutra:

"In the void there are no Forms
No Feelings, perceptions, volitions or
*   consciousness*
No eye, ear, nose, tongue, body or mind
No form, sound, smell, taste, touch or mind object.
No realm of consciousness
No ignorance and also no ending of ignorance
No old age and death and
No ending of old age and death.
There is no wisdom, and there is no Attainment
*   whatsoever.*

Gone, gone, gone beyond. Gone completely beyond.
Oh, what an awakening! All hail!"

I was angry. I accepted my anger, watching it ebb and flow through the pattern of my thoughts. It was so hard to accept that that lovely big dog was dead—poisoned, we knew that much. But why? Did somebody hate us enough to poison our dog? Or had Chinook crossed the railway line and taken some bait meant for foxes?

That must have been it. It was the only explanation. Who could possibly have anything against us? We weren't even squatting now. We were law-abiding people, popular with the neighbors.

And yet, we never saw any of our neighbors anymore. The farmer still grinned when he came past on his tractor, but that could mean anything. The couple who'd been friendly when we first arrived never came near. We didn't go to the pub, and hardly talked to anyone in the village. We were in our own little bubble. And then there was the hollow by the edge of the wood, the sense that somebody had been spying on us.

I told Richard about that. He looked serious.

"You mean you went over the railway line, Stephen? That is well out of order, as you know."

"Yes," I said, "but what about the hollow? I mean, if people think we're some kind of sect and they're spying on us . . ."

He looked at me coldly.

"We are not a sect. Nobody's spying."

It was easily said, but from that time on I think we all felt a slight paranoia. What was next?

For two days Spencer stayed in his room. Only Anneke and Brigit were allowed in to him.

"How's Spencer? Is he all right?" I asked.

They exchanged looks.

"Yeah, Spencer. How is he, huh? How is the moon?"
They both giggled. I felt irritated.

When Spencer finally came down, he was full of energy, and there was an intent about him that I hadn't seen before. He gathered us together round the kitchen table.

"Okay, it's time to get things moving. No looking back, the world's waiting. How's it going with the stables, Graham? We need them ready very soon. Richard says there's already a waiting list."

"A waiting list?" Obviously I hadn't been keeping up with things.

"We're starting courses in two weeks—don't worry, Stephen, it's cool. It's what people want. Astrid, you'd better plan out some menus. We'll use as much homegrown stuff as possible."

I shouldn't have been surprised. They'd been planning this all along. And when I thought about it, it seemed right to share Spencer's insight with the world. Besides, it would bring in money and give the house more focus.

But I was in no way prepared for what followed.

"It's only for the summer, though," Spencer continued. "We're not staying."

"What?" asked Graham. He sounded as shocked as I was.

"It's time to move on, or it will be by the fall. This place is too small, and the vibrations aren't good. We'll find somewhere better. Richard's already looking."

"To rent—or squat?" I asked naïvely.

"To buy. We're going upmarket, Stephen. And don't worry about the money. The money will be there."

I went out into the garden, my refuge. I needed to slow my breathing. The truth was, I didn't want to move. I'd grown fond of The Hollies. I looked proudly at my rows of brussels sprouts, but they wouldn't be ready till winter, and where would we be then? My work would come to nothing.

I hoed around the potatoes, without enthusiasm.

After a while Astrid came out to join me. I knew she would. There was an understanding between us now that we didn't need to talk about. I leant on my hoe and watched her approach. She was wearing her new dress with her hair loose, not dressed for gardening.

"Did you know about this plan?" I asked.

She shook her head.

"No, I think it's new, since Chinook died."

"Is that why?"

"Probably." She smiled uncomfortably. "It's no good asking me, Stevie. I'm the last one to know these days."

We stared at the potatoes.

"They're coming up well," Astrid said.

"Yeah. If they don't catch the blight, they'll be a good crop."

We stood there, unable to think of anything to say. Then we both gave a nervous laugh at the same moment.

"Let's go over," said Astrid, glancing towards the railway. She seemed to have read my mind. At that moment the one thing I wanted was to get out of the bubble of The Hollies, into another atmosphere. I put down my hoe, and we went to the fence. The London Express had just passed, so no trains were due for the next twenty minutes, but I listened carefully anyway before we scrambled down and crossed the lines.

The wood was quiet and cool. Astrid took my arm and we walked silently. I felt the immensity surrounding us and Astrid warm beside me, and then, as if it came from outside, a great love seemed to flow into me—a love that was both personal and impersonal at the same time.

Astrid felt it too. She squeezed my arm and stopped, laying her head against my shoulder.

"Oh, Stevie," she sighed. "What would I do without you?"

I didn't know what she meant. I half turned and looked into her eyes.

"What would *I* do without you?"

She shook her head, smiling, and put a finger to my face.

"Oh no, you would be fine. You don't need anything. You are yourself."

Did she mean me? I couldn't quite believe it. Once upon a time we'd sat together looking at the Mediterranean, and she had put her head on my shoulder. It was the same now. Only now I was ready. Astrid looked up at me, and my eyes dilated, and my skin tingled with small electric shocks. She reached up and put her arms round my neck.

Michelle was no more than a memory. But Astrid

194

was there, present, with me. I had always loved her, I realized that now, and I always would, whatever happened. But this love was not possessive. It depended on nothing and no one. I was free.

My legs felt like jelly. I was nothing but desire for her, for her sweetness and purity. I fell onto my knees and she fell with me, until we were rolling in the bluebell leaves, clinging to each other as if nothing else mattered in the world.

We kissed, and our identities merged into a fullness in which the first intensity of desire eased, and the space opened up around us with a deep peace that included sadness, because beauty and suffering are one.

"What do you want?" I whispered.

She stroked my face.

"I want you."

There was still a doubt in me, though.

"You . . . and Spencer?"

She shook her head.

"Not for a long time. You know that."

"I am Brahmacharya," I said weakly. But even as I said it, I didn't believe it. It was just an idea.

"What does that mean?" she whispered, nuzzling my ear. "It means you dwell in Brahman. Anyway, it's only a word. You can do what you want. You are Stevie, that's all. My Stevie. Always."

Afterwards, we talked. It was almost the last time we talked properly, and I have tried to remember everything she said. It seems now so important. I want to bring back every word she spoke, to look at in a hundred different ways. But most of it has gone, along with the dapple of sunshine through the leaves and the robin that hopped onto a bush and watched us.

We talked about Spencer.

"Will he mind?" I asked. "About us."

"No, Spencer doesn't mind about things like that. He is not pretending. He is only present, with what is."

"He minded about Chinook."

She nodded.

"Yes. He did. He loved his dog more than anything. More than he ever loved me. He wouldn't grieve over me like that! But then the grief is over. He's finished with it. He moves on."

"Do you still love him?" I asked.

She didn't answer immediately.

"No," she said at last. "Not in that way. Because he doesn't love back. Not in the way I want. That's the price of it, I think. At first, he was my teacher, my lover, my friend, everything. It was so wonderful. We were going to make everyone free, like we were. But even then . . . That was when I saw you, in London. Do you remember? I was so happy to see you because I felt lonely. I didn't even know it at the time, but I was always lonely with Spencer. It's because—there's nobody there. It's not just talk. It's true somehow. He did show me something, though, showed me how to see things in a way I hadn't before, to feel—I don't know, it's hard to talk about, isn't it?—Brahman, perhaps."

I watched the movements of the leaves in the breeze.

She was right: Spencer wouldn't mind about us. It was as it was, that's all.

"He told me to be Brahmacharya, like you," Astrid continued. "Maybe it was best for me. Or maybe he had a reason—like to keep me quiet while he enjoys his Tantric teachings."

There was a note of bitterness in her voice.

"You're jealous," I said, smiling with my eyes.

"Of Anneke and Brigit? The Gopis? Okay, yes, I am. At least, I was. But if that's what he wants, that's fine now. I have you!"

She nuzzled against me.

"Why me?"

"Because you are real."

She raised herself and stroked my chest with her fingertips, looking down at me with her head to one side and her hair hanging around her shoulders. I looked up at her. Astrid. Beautiful, beyond my dreams.

We walked together through decaying bluebells and wild garlic till we came to the edge of the woods and looked out over a gate across sunlit fields. A herd of red cows eyed us curiously.

"One thing I don't get is how Spencer thinks we can buy a place. I know we'll have money coming in from the courses, but not that much."

Astrid laughed.

"That's easy. It's me."

"You?"

"I am rich, didn't you know? When I went with

Spencer, my father stopped all my money because he doesn't like Spencer, but I have also some of my own, from my mother. They made it so I couldn't have it till I was twenty-three. Now I am twenty-three."

"Will you give it to him?"

"I don't know. Maybe I will. What use is money? It never made my father happy. Or maybe I'll give it to you—would you like it?"

She smiled at me. It was such a big smile. And I smiled back, and our smiles got bigger and bigger until they took in the universe.

"I'd like you to meet my father," she said suddenly. "Maybe you would get on with him. I feel bad to be so separate from him, still fighting. He loves me, I know that. Shall we go and see him?"

"Why not?" I said. "We can do anything."

She squeezed my hand.

"Actually," Astrid continued as we wandered slowly back, "lots of people give money to Spencer. They always have done. Ray gives him money—a lot. I don't know where he gets it from. You wouldn't have thought Ray had anything, but he does. Ray's money has been keeping the house going."

"Is that why Spencer supported him against Carla?"

"No. He cares about Ray. And Ray loves him. He's probably the only person he's ever loved. He would kill for him."

I shivered at the thought.

"He gives me the creeps," I said.

And then, as we looked over the railway line to The

Hollies, the first thing we saw was the pink van. Ray was back.

We hugged each other tightly. We'd decided to carry on as normal in the house, at least for a while. Then Astrid pulled herself away from me, squeezed through the fence and started down the bank.

"Wait!" I shouted. I'd already heard that faint singing from the lines that meant a train was approaching.

Astrid froze on the bank, and the next moment a train thundered round the corner and sped past, the faces at the window almost close enough for her to touch.

I climbed through after her. I thought she'd be scared, but she was elated.

"The trains go so fast," she said, squeezing my arm.

"Didn't you hear it?" I asked, but she looked at me blankly.

The lines were quiet now. All the same, we crossed them quickly and ran up the other side, back to The Hollies.

Ray was sitting in the sunshine smoking a roll-up. He watched us approach across the lawn, his eyes narrowed.

"Hello, Ray," I said. "Where've you been?"

He took a drag on his cigarette. He didn't even look at me. His eyes were fixed on Astrid, summing her up.

"Baby's got new clothes," he said. "You've got a bit of stick on it, darling."

He reached out and pulled off a twig that had snagged on her dress.

"Been down in the woods today, have you?"

Astrid said nothing, but she blushed. Ray turned to me.

"So, it's Saint Stephen! You're looking in the pink, squire. Want to see what I've got in the back of the van?"

I didn't much, but it gave Astrid a chance to escape, so I went with him to his van. He opened the back and showed me a big, boxed color television set.

"What's that for?" I asked.

"That's for Spencer."

"Why?"

"Because he asked for it."

"But what does he want a television for?"

"For watchin'! Duh!"

I was puzzled. I never even thought of watching television. It was the sort of thing my parents did, people who were half dead to the world. I couldn't imagine Spencer settling down to *The Black and White Minstrel Show*.

We lifted it out and carried it up to Spencer's room. Spencer looked at me almost blankly, and I felt how he was still missing Chinook, that great loving presence. Perhaps the television was a sort of replacement.

I left Ray and Spencer to unpack the set and went out and did some more work in the garden. Later Ray went up onto the roof to fix the aerial. At least it kept him busy for the rest of the day.

*   *   *

I went to *satsang* that evening. It was the first since Chinook's death, and the room was crowded. I sat at the back, with Astrid a few places away from me. I ached to touch her, but we exchanged nothing more than a secret smile.

There was a buzz and then a silence as Spencer came in. He'd had his hair clipped to a short fuzz, which made him look strong and energetic, and he was wearing a new white denim jacket. He looked around the room at eager faces. Then he shut his eyes and went into silence.

It was a silence that pulsed with energy and expectation. If I shut my eyes, I saw colored lights; if I opened them, Spencer in his white jacket shone enigmatically.

At last, he opened his eyes and looked around.

"I won't speak for long. Silence is more powerful than speech. Or rather, speech comes out of the silence—words forming from nothing, and returning to nothing. Just dreams that we conjure. That's what our lives are too."

He was looking at me. I could feel his eyes, his half smile, probing. I thought of a line from *The Tempest* that I'd been studying not so long ago: *We are such stuff as dreams are made on.*

"And that nothing we come from and return to is also the Infinite," he continued. "Brahma, the Self, God, call it what you like. I think we can all see that. It's why we're here. So then, knowing that, why does one feel grief? Or for that matter, why does one feel love?"

He left the question hanging there, his eyes half closed, as if he was seeking deep inside himself for an answer.

"Can you imagine a love without attachment—the purest love, because it seeks no outcome, has no hopes or dreams of an idealized future? Do you know what that love is—its immensity? And a grief untouched by fear, that's a beautiful thing too, a pure contact with the suffering that gives meaning to our invented world. You think of suffering as your enemy, think you have to fight it and avoid it. You are wrong. To suffer knowing the source of it, knowing the immensity, is to be fully human. And human is what we are."

He paused again. The room was totally quiet.

"Chinook. You all knew Chinook. He'd welcome each of you when you arrived, make you feel comfortable, wanted. Dogs can do that. It's one of their gifts. And then he'd lie beside me here. As quiet as any of you, just present, taking it all in. He was love, pure love. He didn't expect anything, beyond the odd bone, but he got love back anyway, because that's how love is. And we miss him. There's a void where he used to be. Look in the void. Look now! You will see the ending of everything, of the trees, the house, the flowers— that train that just passed. You will see the ending of your body and of mine, and of everybody you ever cared about or will care about. But if you look hard enough, if you look without fear, you will also see the ending of your constructed self, your ego. And if you see that, you will see what does not end, because it

202

never began, because it is you, where the watcher and the watched become one. It's there now. It always was. It always will be. Immutable. Beyond grief. Beyond love. Beyond dreams. Gone entirely beyond . . . Look! Do it now!"

"Spencer wants to see you, in his room."

It sounded threatening, the way Anneke said it, as if I was being called in by the headmaster, and for a moment I thought he had heard or guessed about me and Astrid. But Spencer was at his most relaxed, all the intensity of the talk dropped away from him.

"Hi, Stephen. Have you heard the news?"

He gestured over to the television, which was on in one corner with the sound turned down.

"No. Why?"

"I just saw your mother. At least, I guess it was your mother. She won. She's an MP."

The election. Of course. I'd forgotten all about it, even though last time I rang home, my mother had gone on about how I had to vote, and arranged a postal ballot for me. I'd put a cross by her name and sent it off. But since then I hadn't thought about it at all. That was somebody else's world.

"Can I look?"

"Sure."

Spencer turned the sound up, and we sat together and watched Edward Heath, the new prime minister, with the glint of triumph in his eyes. Against all predictions the Conservatives had won. The camera cut to a dejected Harold Wilson, who'd lost, then the presenter speculated about the direction of the new government and introduced "one of the new members of the House, who will be taking her seat for the first time."

"This is it," said Spencer. "They showed this clip before."

And there was my mother, in full color, spouting into the camera about returning to "family values."

Spencer gave me an amused look.

"I think it's time you gave her a call and congratulated her, don't you?"

I rang from the phone in the hall. My father answered. He sounded flustered.

"Oh yes, Stephen, good. I'm glad it's you. We were hoping you'd phone. You've heard the news of course. Terrific. Your mother's over the moon. She's out at the moment, down at the Conservative Club. Well, she's been almost living there for the last couple of weeks. But it's not just that. It's your brother. Rob. He's getting married."

Married? Rob?

"Who to?" I asked, hoping it wasn't Gail.

"A girl called Melanie. Perhaps you know her. Nice girl. We met her. Anyway, it's all very sudden, I know, but we didn't have a number for you."

It was true. I'd never given them the number of the house. It was always me who rang them, and I preferred it that way.

"He wants you to come to the wedding of course. It's

in London. On Monday. I don't know why it has to be on Monday. It's very awkward. . . ."

He trailed off, and suddenly I felt a pang of love for him, his desire to do the right thing, his loneliness, his confusion.

I wanted to do the right thing too.

"I'll come up, Dad," I said. "I'll come tomorrow. Then I can go with you and Mum to the wedding."

"Oh, would you?" he said. I could hear the relief in his voice. "That would be splendid!"

That night, Astrid came to my room again. I was expecting her, and I lit a candle in readiness. She sat down at the other end of my mattress, neatly cross-legged and self-contained. Then she reached out and touched my fingertips.

"When I first met you, I was about the age you are now. I felt so old!"

I didn't say anything. I was too taken up with the electric pulses coming through my fingers.

"Am I too old for you?"

"Oh no. Never. Age doesn't matter, anyway."

She smiled at me, her face shining in the candlelight. I stretched out my other hand and stroked her cheek.

"Let's go back to Afghanistan one day," she whispered. "Just you and me together. I would like to see it again. Those mountains . . . It's like a landscape from my dreams that I cannot believe is real."

"Yeah," I said. "Me too."

"It's such a big world. There's so many places we

could go together, you and I. Let's leave. Let's leave soon. I want to get out of here—go somewhere different."

"You mean, go traveling? You and me? Just you and me?"

"Just you and me, and the great world."

In a moment we were wrapped in each other's arms. Just her and me and the great world around us, inside us, everywhere.

"Do you *have* to go tomorrow?"

Astrid sighed. We were lying side by side, still entwined. I could smell her hair, feel the softness of her skin.

"I do really. It's my brother's wedding."

"I wish you wouldn't."

She was running her fingers up and down my back. Remembering it now, I can still feel them.

"It'll only be a couple of days. You'll hardly miss me."

"Oh, but I will, I will. You don't know how much."

I was surprised, and for a moment I thought she was just saying it.

"Why?" I asked.

She raised her face and turned so that it caught the candlelight.

"You don't know, do you? It's not just because of what happened today. I am so alone here, especially since Tim left. Nobody even talks to me. I can't stand it here much longer, Stevie. I don't want to be near

Spencer anymore. That's all over for me. And sometimes, oh, Stevie, sometimes I'm afraid."

"Afraid? What of? Not of Spencer?" I asked incredulously.

"I don't know, it's just that . . . I think he wants to keep me here. He will say he doesn't want or not want, but he has plans, he has his "work." And I am important for that, like Ray, like Richard. So I can't go, but I can't stay. I feel like a moth in a trap, with a big light in the middle that pulls me in, but really I want to be out, out in the dark, with you. . . ."

She buried her head in my shoulder.

"Stevie, promise me something! Promise when you come back we will go somewhere. Somewhere far away."

I wanted to say "yes, of course," but I couldn't. I loved Astrid, but part of me still wanted to be near Spencer. I wasn't ready to leave, not yet.

"It's only a weekend," I said.

I felt her disappointment. And then I felt her forgive me.

"It's stupid, I know. I just have this sense that if you go now, I will never see you again."

I thought I knew what she meant. I thought it was how I'd felt with Michelle, the feeling that if I took my eyes off her, the world would sweep us apart. I thought I was wiser now, that I understood things better.

But I didn't. I didn't have a clue.

I put my arms around her. She was beautiful,

everything about her, inside and outside, and her beauty filled me with wonder.

Beauty is truth, truth beauty. That's what Keats said.

Beauty is truth, truth beauty, that is all ye know
Upon this earth, and all ye need to know.

Chapter 15

Beauty and truth. I thought about it on the train to my parents' the next day. Were they really the same? What Spencer said was often beautiful, but was it true? His talk last night had been powerful. It had moved people to tears.

And yet . . .

"I'm sorry, but there is such a thing as right and wrong." That was what Carla had said, and it still bugged me. Did Spencer really think that there was no such thing as morality?

"Of course there is," he'd said when I asked him. "But only within duality. When we hurt each other, it's bad for everybody; it makes for a nasty world to live in. That's obvious. But I'm trying to take you beyond that because there is a beyond. The place where right and wrong come from, where everything *is*— good, bad, ugly, beautiful, pleasant, unpleasant. It just is, that's all."

"So is it okay to lie, say?"

He watched me with his luminous eyes.

"Make up your own mind, Stephen. What's true for you may not be true for me. I'm not concerned with truth or lies in the way that you mean it. Lies are only lies if the past is solid. There are no lies in a dream."

It was good to be on a train. It was good to be by my-self again, away from The Hollies—and even from Astrid. What had happened between us had taken me by surprise. I needed time to let it settle, or so I thought. I didn't know that time had already run out.

"Whatever happens, it's fine. Everything is fine," she said as I left.

"Of course it is," I said, brushing away the emotion in her voice and kissing her.

I could still taste her kiss as I sat on the train. I loved her. Who wouldn't? But as she'd said herself, I didn't need her. I didn't need anyone because the immensity was always present and always would be.

I stepped out onto St. Albans Station. It was months since I'd been anywhere at all, and my perceptions were heightened. Everything was familiar and strange at the same time: the uniforms of the porters, the swing of the carriage doors, the peeling brown paint, the patterns the sun made through the ironwork, the whistle of the guard and the crunch of the carriages as the train pulled out. The sleepy hum of a hot June day.

The world was full and bright and easy. I slid my bag over my shoulder and sauntered out of the station.

The first person I saw was Jude.

She looked right through me at first, and then she blinked and a smile spread across her face. I thought she was going to throw her arms round me, but something stopped her, and she stood in the road a couple of paces away.

"You're back!"

"Only for the weekend. Thought I'd better congratulate my mum on her victory. Oh, and my brother's getting married."

"Uh-huh. So am I." She grinned. "Guess you'll get an invite."

"That'd be nice. Congratulations!"

"Where have you been, then? You look well."

"I'm living in a—a sort of commune."

"Sounds interesting. What do you do there?"

"I do the garden," I said, and a glow spread through me at the memory—the red soil turning under my fork, the early morning light, Astrid.

"Looks like it's done you good, anyway. Last time I saw you, you were a bit of a mess."

"Was I?"

"You came to our party and you ran away—don't you remember?"

I nodded.

"Yes. Christmas. That was a difficult time. Sorry."

"It's okay. You were right actually. It was a rubbish party. We're all pretty boring, and we get drunk to cover it up. I'm sure you know lots of people who are much more interesting."

She said it straight, with no hint of sarcasm, but it took me aback.

"I don't think you're boring," I said.

An engine whistled behind me as a train approached.

"No? Good . . . Gosh, there's my train. I have to run! See you sometime."

She ran past me and disappeared into the station.

Home. But it wasn't home anymore. It was just my parents' house now. I sat in the garden and listened to my mother telling me triumphantly how she had shaken hands with Edward Heath, the new prime minister.

"I wouldn't be at all surprised if Ted offered me a job."

"A job?"

"Only a PPS I dare say, to start with. But Ted said he wants more women in the government, so I should think I'm in with a chance. Have some more soup."

My father smoked his pipe quietly. He looked happy at my mother's success, but he seemed older, his hair whitening and his chin sagging.

"What about Rob?" I asked. "Bit of a surprise, isn't it?"

My mother's face changed.

"Your brother has always been difficult. I thought at least when it came to his wedding, he might see reason and do things properly. But I'm afraid it's one of these in-and-out affairs in a registry office."

"He couldn't really get married in a church, Mum. He doesn't believe in God."

Out of the corner of my eye I noticed my father smile, but my mother looked at me straight.

"What's God got to do with it? They could have married here if the girl's parents don't have a church."

"Melanie," said my father. "You should call her Melanie. She's a nice girl. They came to see us."

My mother turned her mouth down and said nothing. I knew what she was thinking: not good enough for Rob.

For myself, I was intrigued that Rob was marrying anyone. Marriage didn't seem to be part of his agenda. But I was pleased it was Melanie. Maybe he'd taken my advice after all.

The weekend passed pleasantly. I did whatever my parents wanted me to do, so there was no conflict. I even went to church with them on Sunday morning, amused by the quaint pointlessness of the service. After-wards I went for a walk on my own along the river. The poplars were in full leaf and sang in the breeze. I hardly thought of Astrid, or Spencer, or The Hollies. All that concerned me was what unfolded in front of me. Here. Now. It was the only way to live.

I found Vicky's *I Ching* in my room. For old time's sake I asked a vague question on the lines of "What happens next?" and threw the coins. I got Number 29: *K'an, the Abyss*:

Water flows uninterruptedly and reaches its goal:
The image of the Abyss repeated.

I looked up the one moving line:

Forward and backward, abyss on abyss
In danger like this, pause at first and wait,
Otherwise you will fall into a pit in the abyss.

It didn't sound too promising, but I didn't pay much attention. I didn't really believe in it.

The wedding service was oddly conventional. The registry office was packed with trendy people in ruffled shirts and embroidered dresses. There were a few faces I knew, but no sign of Rob's political friends, to my relief. This was a different crowd from the one that Rob used to hang out with: richer, better dressed. Rob arrived late, wearing a velvet suit, and sauntered down to the front with a guy whose face I knew but couldn't place. Then came Melanie, in white lace, on the arm of a bald, red-faced man I took to be her father, while a tape played "Here comes the bride." The registrar had smudged lipstick and read the service badly, but it all happened anyway: Rob and Melanie made their vows, kissed, and everybody clapped.

I looked at my mother beside me. She was wiping away a tear, and my father had his arm around her. As we went out, she hissed her disapproval in my ear: "So common!" Whether she meant the service, Melanie or just the whole occasion, I wasn't sure.

The reception was in a private house a short walk away belonging to Rob's best man. I'd worked out by now that he was a well-known rock musician. His face was on the front of one of my albums. He came up and talked to me as we strolled along the street. I felt awkward at first, but he was friendly and natural.

"You're Stevie? Hi, I'm Laurie. Heard a lot about you."

He had a pleasant Irish voice.

"From Rob?" I asked, surprised.

"He was worried you'd got involved with some sect or something. But you look all right to me."

"Rob should worry about himself," I said.

"Oh, Rob's all right." Laurie laughed. "He's been writing songs for me. Talented fellow, your brother. You must have heard him sing—he's a gas. I'm going to get him to sing on my next album."

So that was where Rob was at: moved on again, and suddenly making it. Just like my mother.

We had champagne and smoked-salmon sandwiches served by aproned waitresses in Laurie's sumptuous living room, with its white fluffy carpet and glass-topped tables; I could feel my mother tutting at what she'd call "bad taste." Spencer would have liked it, though. He had no hang-ups about luxury.

"Are you a friend of Rob's, then?"

A girl was talking to me. She had dark curly hair and was dressed to kill in satin and lace.

"I'm his brother."

She looked interested, then quickly hid it.

"So what do you do?"

What did I do? The same as everyone else. Breathed, ate, slept, sat in silence while the world turned.

"I'm a gardener," I said.

"Gardener? Far out!"

She was thinking the opposite, but she allowed herself to smile. She had small white teeth.

"What about you?" I asked.

"I work with Mel in the Roundhouse. We meet lots of bands. It's groovy." She touched my arm. "Your brother's really cool. He's really mates with Laurie now. He's gonna be big."

I wasn't listening much to what she was saying. I could see through her, past the pretty curls and careful makeup, to a hard, grasping little heart—and then the chaos behind that. But it didn't stop me being aroused by her, by the scent of availability. She offered me a cigarette: oval with a gold tip. No roll-ups for her. I took one for the novelty.

"Do you know the people here?" I asked. She glanced about languidly, blowing smoke through her nose.

"Pretty much. It's swinging London, isn't it? Swing, swing, swing. Everybody going somewhere. Everybody on the make. Except for you, darling, apparently, doing your 'gardening.'"

She came up close, looked in my eyes and brushed her fingertips provocatively across my cheek, then caught the eye of someone behind me, and in the same movement slid on past me with a "Hi, Joe, how are ya?"

"Who was that young lady?"

My mother was bearing down on me, a little tipsy.

"A friend of Melanie's, I think."

"She was taking quite an interest in you. Come along now. Rob's going to make a speech."

"What's all this about, then, Rob?" I asked him after the speeches.

216

He shrugged.

"It's what Mel wanted."

"I don't get it," I said. "You always said marriage was crap."

He grinned. "Well, we all have to have a crap occasionally, don't we?"

"So why are you doing it?"

"Why not? It's a party. Brings people together. Nice pad Laurie's got, eh? Anyway, what've you been up to? I'm relieved to see you looking so normal. I thought you'd got into some weird guru scene."

"Depends what you mean by weird," I countered. "Who's that guy in the shiny suit talking to Mum?"

"That's Alex, Laurie's manager. He probably thinks she's a good contact."

I watched my mother for a moment. It was strange: my father stood beside her awkwardly, half abstracted, but despite her straight clothes my mother didn't look out of place anymore. She was enjoying herself, and the big-nosed, long-haired manager was almost flirting with her.

"The Mouth of Darkness—doing business," Rob commented sardonically. "She'll probably make a speech in Parliament about how she's 'in touch with the young.' "

"You're quite proud of her, aren't you?"

"Yeah," said Rob. "In a way, yeah, I suppose I am. There's nothing wrong with getting on, Stevie. It's only the fools who don't make it."

* * *

I went outside into the garden and looked around at the backs of the grand Chelsea houses. It was a quiet, almost secret, place. I felt the vibration of a train passing under the ground.

The immensity was here too. I sat on a bench and closed my eyes and felt it.

Someone had sat down beside me. I opened my eyes to see Melanie smiling at me from behind her hair.

"So you did it," I said. "Man and wife! Great!"

"Yeah."

She sounded happy. She'd changed out of her wedding dress into satin trousers and a simple cotton shirt.

"What got you two to get married, then?" I asked. "I mean, I'm pleased, but I didn't think marriage was Rob's style."

"People change, Stevie. Rob's changed. He got friends with Laurie, and it's been real good since then. And . . ."

She paused and brushed the hair out of her eyes. There was a blush on her cheek, like a rose on snow.

"And I'm having a baby."

"You're not?"

She nodded.

"Don't tell anyone. Specially not your mother. She wouldn't like it, would she? I mean she's old-fashioned and that . . ."

"Don't worry," I said. "She'll forgive Rob anything. She already has."

She laughed.

"Yeah. I can see that. She's like him, isn't she?"

People changed. Melanie was right. Rob changed from day to day sometimes, changed scenes, changed clothes, changed opinions. In Vietnam bombs were still falling, kids were still dying, but Rob and I had simply moved on. Yet somehow also the essence of Rob didn't change. Perhaps none of us did. I hoped he and Melanie would be happy, with their baby. I hoped she'd give him stability. He needed it.

I heard a cough and turned round and saw my father.

"Ah," he said. "Here you are. Both of you." He laughed nervously. "Anyway, your mother and I have to get back."

We stood up. My mother was coming over with Rob, so we were a little family party. Rob put his arm round Melanie and she leant against him. I noticed they were both the same height.

"This is most irregular," said my mother. "You're the ones supposed to be going away, not us. Aren't you even having a honeymoon?"

"We're going to Ibiza tomorrow," said Rob. "Only we wanted to stay and party first."

"Are you coming with us, Stephen?" my father asked.

"Yeah, I guess."

"Oh no," said Melanie, taking my arm. "You've got to stay. We'll have music later."

"You should stay, Stephen," said my mother firmly. "There'll be plenty of trains in the morning."

So that was that.

* * *

Everything went quiet after my parents left. The aproned waitresses had already disappeared, and a lot of the guests had gone too. Rob and Melanie and Laurie went upstairs, and the rest of us relaxed, making tea in Laurie's kitchen. The smell of hash mingled with the evening scents of flowers from the garden.

I could have gone home with my parents. Or I could have taken a train to The Hollies. It was all the same, wherever I was. I had no plans, no expectations. I lay back in one of Laurie's plush armchairs and breathed.

People started arriving again with the dusk. A van brought a crate of wine and proper food—chicken legs in sauce, salads, quiches, boiled potatoes. Melanie's father reappeared and came over and chatted to me. He told me about Melanie's childhood—he kept calling her Liz, which was confusing till I realized she'd changed her name—and about her mother, who was ill, and how proud of her she'd be.

He patted me on the knee.

"Take life as it comes, my boy. I'm sure you won't mind the advice, now that you're one of the family, so to speak. Take it as it comes, and enjoy it while it's there, because you never know what's round the next corner."

When I look at it now, I suppose he was saying the same thing as Spencer.

The evening got going. The music was turned up on Laurie's expensive sound system, and the lights were turned down. Melanie and Rob came downstairs together, and people started dancing.

Someone was offering me a joint. I turned and saw the girl-with-the-curls.

"No thanks."

She raised an eyebrow, then inhaled deeply and blew the smoke into my face.

"Okay, what about a dance, then?"

It was a long time since I'd danced. Somehow it wasn't part of life at The Hollies. I felt the music pulse through me and let my body move while the girl-with-the-curls (I still didn't know her name) gyrated opposite me.

She had a weird way of dancing, twisting her body and making witchy movements with her arms. It was quite effective, so I let myself relax in the rhythm and watched her.

She was offering herself to me. She was offering sex, without ties, without future, pure pleasure, now.

I wanted her, and I didn't at the same time. She was pretty enough. I just didn't much like her.

Did that matter?

She could feel me looking at her. She snaked up to me and put her arms on my shoulders, opening her mouth and looking in my eyes.

We swayed together to the beat for a while. Then I kissed her.

It wasn't anything. Just two bodies and the music. I didn't think of Astrid. I was beyond guilt. I was nobody. I wasn't even there. My tongue touched hers, and electric sensations started from the bottom of my spine. She must have felt it, because she pulled her head back, surprised.

"You're hot!" she breathed.

Then our mouths joined again, and I felt her breasts hard against my chest.

I didn't like her, but I could sleep with her, and I would. I could do anything, be anything. Or not. It was all the same. I was free.

"Stephen?"

Laurie was in front of me, his face anxious.

"Your father's on the phone. I think you'd better talk to him."

The girl-with-the-curls rolled her eyes in annoyance. I stepped away from her, following Laurie upstairs to a bedroom, and took the phone.

"Hi, Dad, are you all right?"

"Ah, Stephen, yes. Yes, we're fine. It's just, we had a phone call from the place where you live, you know. They want you to get in touch. They say it's urgent."

"Okay, Dad, I'll ring them."

I put down the phone.

It was a warm night, but shivers were running up and down my spine. My mouth was dry and my hand was shaking.

"You okay, man?" asked Laurie, concerned.

"Yeah, it's . . . I've got to make another call. Do you mind?"

"Go ahead."

I misdialed the first time and had to start again. I was telling myself there was nothing to worry about, but my body knew otherwise. I felt Rob come into the room behind me, but I didn't look round.

The phone was ringing in The Hollies. And then Graham's voice:

"Stephen? Thank God it's you. We've been trying to get hold of you for hours."

"What's the matter? Is everything all right?"

"No. No, it isn't." Graham's voice was cracking. He was only just holding it together. "It's Astrid. She's—had an accident."

"Accident? Is she all right?"

But I knew from his voice, I knew already, that she wasn't.

"I . . . I don't know. She's at the hospital. She was hit by a train. Oh, Stephen, come quick. I'm afraid she's going to die."

Chapter 16

The night nurse allowed me to see her.

She was lying in bed, a sheet pulled up to her neck. Her head was bandaged, and a tube went through her nose, yet her face looked serene. The room seemed full of machines that ticked and hummed, but behind them was stillness. An incredible stillness. The peace of God that passes all men's understanding.

"Astrid!" I said softly.

No flicker passed across her face. She couldn't hear me.

One arm was full of tubes. I took the other hand, stroked it, then squeezed it. It was warm and limp, that was all. There was no response to my touch. I supposed I was meant to be emotional, but at that moment I was aware only of my own heartbeat, my own steady breathing. I kept hold of Astrid's hand and sat on a chair beside the bed.

I closed my eyes.

Immediately I felt her presence. I could even see her face, smiling at me from the depths of my consciousness.

"I'm fine. Everything's fine," she said. Her voice was speaking inside my head, clear and real.

"No . . . ," I started, but she put a finger to her lips.

"Shhh! It is. I'm going away for a while, that's all. You can join me later."

"I want to be with you," I mumbled.

"No, you don't. It's fine, Stevie. Everything's fine. You don't need me."

"I do, I do!"

Her eyes shone. She flicked back her hair.

"You don't need anyone. You are free. You can let go."

I opened my eyes. Astrid lay unmoving. The nurse came up beside me.

"Are you a relation?"

"No, just a friend."

"It's a terrible thing. Such a beautiful girl."

"Yes."

"They're looking for her husband. They weren't able to find him immediately. You know him, I expect."

Husband?

"You mean Spencer?"

"I expect so. Well, you'd better go back to the waiting room. Doctor said no one's to stay unless it's immediate family."

In the waiting room Rob was talking to Richard. They both looked at me, inquiring, but there was nothing for me to say. Richard looked terrible, white-faced with staring eyes. All his usual smoothness had dropped away.

Rob put an arm round me.

225

"Okay, bro?"

"You should get back to Mel, Rob," I said. "It's your wedding night."

Rob had driven me up there in Laurie's car, without question, and there was nobody I'd rather have had with me. We'd hardly spoken, but he was there for me, as he always had been when I really needed him.

"Yeah. We're supposed to be in Ibiza in eight hours' time. Funny, that's where I met Astrid."

"I know. She told me."

"Did she? What did she say about me?"

"You won't believe it, but she said you were a good singer."

He grinned.

"I guess she's tone deaf then. Tell you what, though, Stevie, I'll write a song for her. We'll put it on Laurie's next album. Yeah, that's what I'll do."

I walked out with him and watched him drive off in Laurie's sports car. Then I stood in the empty car park, alone in the predawn stillness. Already a faint pink light was showing in the east. It was midsummer, and the nights were short.

I was there, that was all, just there.

I went back in and found Richard sipping a coffee from the vending machine.

"What happened?" I asked.

He shook his head.

"I wish I knew. A train driver found her, down by the track. I suppose she was trying to cross. They say it's a miracle she wasn't killed instantly."

226

"Have you talked to the doctor?"

"Sort of. I came in with her—that is, I drove behind the ambulance. They've cleaned her up, thank God. It was terrible when we found her. She had a gash on her head and there was blood everywhere. I thought she was dead."

He grabbed my arm.

"Oh God, Stephen, it's been hell! And Spencer's not even here."

"Where is he?"

"He went to London with Ray. Earlier. Christ! Why did she have to go on the railway line? Why was she so stupid?"

"She went there with me," I said quietly. "A couple of times. We went over to the woods." I told him how close she'd been to the train the last time we crossed the line. I still felt quite calm, as if all this was normal.

He stared at me.

"What were you two doing over there?"

I didn't answer. I looked away. But he knew.

"Christ!"

"What did the doctor say?" I asked. "Is there any hope?"

Richard shook his head.

"He wouldn't really say. At first it was all go. They took her off and cleaned her up and did X-rays and stuff, put her on a ventilator and set her hip, which was broken apparently. Then the doctor came and said that she'd stabilized, but she was still in a coma, and there was nothing more that they could do for now, and he'd be back in the morning. I asked if she'd be all right. He shrugged and gave me a look. Then he asked who was the next of kin."

"She wants to go," I said.

"Yes. I guess she does."

We sat in silence. A big clock on the wall ticked ominously.

"Who *is* the next of kin?" I asked.

"Spencer. They got married last summer—I was a witness. It wasn't a big deal; it was just so Astrid could get a residence visa. Didn't you know?"

So the nurse was right. I didn't answer. Somehow it made me feel uncomfortable.

"You might as well go home," I said eventually. "There's no point in our both staying."

"Yeah . . . Yeah, okay."

He looked at me almost pleadingly. The old Richard who always took charge seemed to have disappeared.

"I'll be more use there. And God, I'm knackered. Will you be all right?"

"I'll be fine."

It was better being alone, with the slow movement of the clock in the fluorescent light. I sat on a plastic chair and thought. For the last few months I'd spent my time trying not to think, but I had to now. I had to.

The nurse brought me a cup of tea.

"Are you all right?" she asked kindly. "You don't have to stay, you know."

"I'm fine," I said. "Do you think I could see her again?"

She led me back into the room. I took Astrid's hand and sat down, hoping I'd hear her voice again in my head. But this time there was nothing, not even a sense of her presence, only her inert body and the hum of machines. I looked at her lovely face among the tubes and bandages. Her expression hadn't changed.

"Is there any hope?" I asked the nurse.

"Oh, there's always hope," she said brightly.

I went back to the waiting room and slumped down in a chair, watching the light grow slowly outside the window.

Why wasn't Spencer here? He hardly ever went away. He'd gone off to London with Ray, Richard said. What for?

My thoughts were dark, seeking answers that no one could give me. I had taken too much on trust, not asked the right questions. But I would now. I would now. . . .

I woke suddenly. My neck was stiff and my leg had gone to sleep. The morning bustle in the hospital had started, with the day shift arriving and a smell of bacon, but for a moment I was nowhere and nothing had happened.

Spencer was standing in front of me, holding two cups of tea.

"It's not true," I said, still half in my dreams, and

closed my eyes again, hoping to shut out the dreadful truth.

"She's dead," I mumbled.

Spencer sat down next to me.

"She's still alive," he said. "There's no change. They're waiting for the consultant now; he should be here soon."

I opened my eyes and took him in. He gave me one of the cups.

"Where have you been?" I asked.

"I was off on business. I came as soon as I heard."

I sat up and massaged my thigh to bring the circulation back. I drank some tea. Spencer sat calmly beside me. I had nothing to say to him.

"Look, Stephen," he said eventually. "We ought to be ready for something. Astrid got hurt pretty bad. . . ."

"I know. I've been here all night, remember."

My voice was bitter. I resented his coming in and taking over like this. What right did he have? He didn't care about her. She had told me so.

He watched me, taking in my distress.

"Yeah, I know," he said softly. "That's why I wanted to ask you something. I've been talking to the duty doctor. They don't know yet exactly what the damage is. I mean, to her brain. They're going to do more tests when the consultant gets here. We've got to face it, though, it's looking pretty bad. She might just, you know, stay like this. Look, Stephen, Astrid and I were married. You knew that, didn't you? So I'm the next of kin. If there's a decision to make, they'll ask me. . . ."

What would she have wanted, Stephen? If there's no chance of recovery, would she have wanted them to keep the ventilator going? I want to know what you think."

"Why me?"

"You know why."

I stood up and walked to the window. The day shift was arriving and the car park was filling up. I sucked my lower lip between my teeth, and then I bit. I bit with all the force in my jaw. I bit so that I tasted blood in my mouth, and felt the rush of pain.

I wanted the blood. I wanted the pain.

"You really are shit, aren't you!"

I turned to face him. I was spitting blood, my fists clenched, my body shaking.

"Why do you have to be so fucking right all the time? Astrid's going to die. Is that a fact, or is it just another dream for you? You're all bullshit, Spencer. You use people for your own weird fantasies. You married Astrid for her money, didn't you? To help you with your so-called work. And then you couldn't be bothered with her. I bet you'll be glad when she's dead. But don't ask me to do it. That's your decision. Don't try to put your fucking business onto me."

I turned away from him again, shocked by my own language. It didn't sound like me—it sounded like Rob. And I still couldn't help observing my breath, which came in irregular gasps and pants. I didn't want to do that anymore. I was through with all that stuff. I wanted to let go and rage. Because there were lies, and there *was* truth, and there *was* right and wrong—but there was no such thing as "liberation" or "enlightenment." That was just Spencer's trip.

"I understand how you feel, Stephen," Spencer answered smoothly. "And you've got a point. But maybe it won't come to that. Let's hope it doesn't."

I turned away from him again and dabbed at my lip with my sleeve. The anger was draining out of me. Behind it I could sense something else, something worse, but it hadn't arrived yet.

A different nurse came in. The day shift had taken over. "Would you two gentlemen like some breakfast?" she offered cheerily.

Bacon and eggs: I was hungry, in spite of everything. We ate in silence. My lip was still bleeding; it hurt to eat, and everything tasted of blood.

I had nothing more to do there, but I wanted to see Astrid again, one last time, so I left my plate half eaten and asked the nurse to take me in.

Spencer looked up at me as I went out.

"Stephen!" he called. I stopped and turned back to him.

"You got it, didn't you? You know that. You were the only one."

He smiled—his full, irresistible smile—as if I was the most important person in the world to him. I watched it and felt nothing. He was a person, that was all, with his own desires, his own conditioning, someone I'd met and spent time with, as unique and fallible as I was. Why would I ever have thought he was more than that?

"There isn't anything to get, is there?"

"That's right. And there's nobody to get it."

I turned away.

Astrid was the same, her life held suspended. I stood watching her for a long time.

"I love you!" I murmured, but she didn't hear or see. Gone, gone, gone beyond. Gone entirely beyond.

I didn't go back to the waiting room. I had nothing more to say to Spencer. I took the lift down to the entrance lobby. Two men were sitting there. One of them stood up and approached me.

"Stephen?" he asked. "Stephen Wiston?"

I stopped, surprised. How did he know my name?

"I'm Detective Sergeant Harrison. Look, I know this is a difficult time for you, but we understand you were a good friend of, er, the young lady. Astrid. We wondered if there is anything you'd like to tell us, anything that might help us with our inquiries."

"What inquiries?"

The man smiled unconvincingly. He had a mustache.

"Look, Stephen, you'll understand. We have to investigate accidents. Just a matter of collecting the facts, that's all. It's quite informal at this stage. You were a friend of hers, weren't you?"

"Yes."

"Then I'm sure you'll want to tell us anything that might be relevant, Stephen. Her relationship with her husband, for example. Her state of mind prior to her accident. There's also a character called Ray Mitchell who we're interested in. You'd help yourself by talking to us. We've been given to understand that the setup at your place of residence was, er, somewhat unconventional."

"I don't know anything, but . . . if you want me to answer questions . . ."

They looked at each other. They hadn't really been waiting for me, and they weren't quite ready. They were waiting for Spencer.

"No hurry at the moment, Stephen."

Detective Sergeant Harrison tried to smile again. He handed me a card with his name and telephone number.

"Look, I know how you must be feeling, Stephen, but if you think of anything, anything at all, give us a ring."

"Okay," I said.

"We'll be seeing you, Stephen," said Sergeant Harrison.

Rob had lent me some money, so I took a taxi to The Hollies.

Outwardly nothing had changed. Richard's car was parked on the gravel, and morning sunshine flooded through the woods beyond the railway line.

The railway line. A spasm went through me. I'd have to look at it. I'd have to see the place, the blood on the tracks.

It was my fault. If we'd never gone over together, she'd be in the kitchen now, welcoming me back. Perhaps she was there after all. Perhaps I had dreamed it all. I pushed open the back door. But in the kitchen there was only Graham sitting at the table with his head in his hands.

He got up and embraced me, his big frame heavy on my shoulders. He was the only person in the house who was taller than me.

"Stephen! Thank God! How's Astrid?"

"She's alive, just about. But she's on a ventilator, still in a coma."

"Jesus!" He slumped back onto his chair and ran his fingers through his hair. I put on the kettle automatically.

"Where are the others?" I asked.

"Richard's asleep upstairs. I heard him come back in the night, but I haven't seen him yet. Louise—I'm worried about Louise. She's taking it badly."

"What about Anneke and Brigit?"

"They left—didn't they come to the hospital?"

"No. Only Spencer."

He shook his head.

"I don't know, then. They all went off together in Ray's van."

"Have you had any sleep?" I asked.

"Not much. I lay down for a few hours, but I can't stop my head going. How can it have happened, Stephen? I still can't believe it."

I started to make tea, my movements slow and deliberate. I heated the pot, put the leaves in, poured the boiling water over them and put it on the table. I took a couple of mugs from their hooks and the milk out of the fridge. Then I sat down.

"Will you tell me about it, Graham?"

I poured the tea. It glugged pleasantly into the mugs. I passed Graham his mug and lifted mine to my face to feel the steam and aroma. My head was clear again, and every sensation was vivid.

Graham looked at me across the table.

"Will you tell me something first, Stephen? Tell me truthfully. Have you been having an affair with Astrid?"

I caught his eye and nodded.

"Christ!"

"It only just happened. The day before I left. But I suppose it's been in the air for a while."

"You bloody idiot!" said Graham quietly. "What are we all? Rabbits?"

"You don't think what happened to Astrid had something to do with that, do you?"

"No. Not that. No. It's just—oh, I don't know what to think about anything anymore! I wondered if Astrid was a bit unhinged, to be honest. I talked to her yesterday, just before she . . . We were in here. She was kind of nervy, so I asked her if she was okay, and she said she was missing you. I asked her what she meant by that, and she gave me a funny smile. I didn't want to understand. I said, 'Oh, come on, you've got Spencer.' Then she said it was time I got real; that Spencer had a scene going with Brigit and Anneke, both of them, and he'd had sex with Louise too. I didn't believe her. I thought it was some weird jealousy trip. I'm not sure now."

"Where had Spencer gone?"

"He went off with Ray early yesterday morning and asked Anneke to cancel *satsang*. They didn't say where they were going. It was all a bit mysterious. Oh God, I don't know! Astrid was in a funny state, sort of excited and a bit upset, but I didn't think she was suicidal or anything. Anyway, we drank some herb tea, and she told me she felt trapped in the house and wanted to get away. I said, 'Well, you can leave, can't you?' and she said, 'It's not that easy, Graham.' Then she went off to water your plants. Those were her last words—'I'm going to water Stevie's seedlings.' And that was it. Half an hour later I wanted to talk to her again because the things she'd told me were swimming about in my brain, so I went out the front, and I realized a train had stopped, and the engine driver was yelling at me from the fence, and I ran . . ."

Graham stopped. He passed his hands over his face. He didn't want to tell me, and I didn't want to hear it, but it had to be said all the same.

"She was lying by the track. She'd been hit by a train—only hit, not run over, thank God. It was bad enough anyway. She was all twisted up, with a gash down the side of her head and blood everywhere. I thought she was dead. The train driver said not to move her. He'd already done something to stop the bleeding and radioed the ambulance. I sat beside her till it came. Richard arrived about the same time. I wanted to go with her, but he told me to stay and handle things here. The cops came a bit later. They wanted to talk to Spencer. They seemed to know a lot about him, but none of us even knew where he was. God, Stephen, there've been so many things going on in this house, and I didn't know anything about anything."

He looked up at me, shaking his head as if he still couldn't believe what had happened.

"That's it, basically. As soon as the cops left, Anneke and Brigit started to freak out about their visas. As if that mattered. It was Louise I was worried about. She sat where you are now, not moving, not making eye contact. I managed to get her up to her room, and onto her bed in the end. Then about midnight Spencer and Ray got back. Spencer took it all in really quickly, like he does, and just told Ray to drive him straight to the hospital. Anneke and Brigit bundled all their stuff into the van and went with them. I thought I might as well get some sleep, so I went and lay on my mattress in the dark, seeing in my mind things I never wanted to see."

"How's Louise now?"

"She was asleep when I looked in, in the same position we put her in, like she hadn't moved. It's good. She needs sleep. We all do."

"And the others? You know, *satsang* regulars—anyone told them?"

"Yeah, I phoned Celia. She was great. She's got the list. She'll handle it."

I drank my tea. It was all too much. I was too tired to work anything out. Minkie the goat was bleating outside. Graham and I looked at each other, both red-eyed.

"Go and hit the sack for a bit," said Graham. "You look like you need it."

The stairs seemed to bounce back at me as I went up them, but I felt quite calm. I lay down on my mattress, and within seconds I was deep asleep.

I woke to a nightmare.

It was bright outside, hazy afternoon sunshine. But inside me everything was dark.

Pointlessness; deep, utter, total pointlessness. That was all there was.

It didn't matter what had happened or why. Astrid would die, that was all. Perhaps she was dead already. And with her died all my dreams, my delusions.

Outside, a train passed.

I washed and changed out of my soiled wedding clothes. Then I went downstairs. The phone in the hall was off the hook. I put it back and immediately it started ringing.

It was Celia, asking about Astrid.

"Yes, she's stable," I said. "Yes, we'll let you know. . . . Yes, Spencer's there with her. . . . Flowers? Yes, send them to the hospital. . . . Yes, tell everybody. Thanks, Celia. . . ."

I put the phone back, then took it off again. I didn't want any more calls.

The house was silent—as the grave, that's the expression people use.

I stepped outside.

A dog was barking in the distance. Nearer, in the holly bushes, a robin sang. Compared with the anxious rasping bark, it sounded pretty, but I knew it for what it was: a small, aggressive bird asserting its territory, the notes repeated again and again, exactly the same: repetitive and stupid.

I walked down to the vegetable patch. Even over the weekend everything had grown. Had Astrid really watered the seedlings, I wondered, yesterday afternoon? Was it the last thing she did? I knelt down and examined a lettuce, parting the outer leaves to reveal the soft green heart, where a small yellow slug lay curled.

Eat it, little slug! Enjoy it! It's all yours! Because I'll never touch these vegetables again.

There's another train—an express. Probably the 2:15. It speeds past, while everything else is slowing down for me.

The sound of the train fades. I step towards the railway line. Where did Astrid cross? Here. Yes, just here, the same place we went over before. Was she thinking of me? Remembering—as I am now? The touch of those long fingers, the beauty of those gray eyes . . .

She would have hesitated here, by the fence, listening perhaps to the birds in the wood.

At least the dog's stopped barking.

Did she want to die? Did it even cross her mind?

I don't know. . . . I don't know. . . . Can I bear not to know?

There was a shadow in her, a longing for escape. I know that. What was that light in her eyes after the train had passed so close last time? Could she have . . .

Could she have thrown herself forward as the train passed, embracing annihilation? Or did she wait on the tracks, heard the train coming, panicked and failed to scramble away in time?

Or did she just slip?

Or was . . . no, surely not. The hand that stretched out to help her, and let go. Or the hand that pushed her shoulder, knocking her off balance. No, it's not thinkable!

I am on the tracks. It's a double line, so I can lie down on one of them, and still have a fifty-fifty chance of survival. A kind of Russian roulette, but with worse odds. Beside me a small area is cordoned off by a police ribbon, though it's only symbolic; the police don't seem much interested. Inside the ribbon I can see a red stain on the chippings. Astrid's blood.

I lie with my head on the rail and watch the clouds. If a train came now, it would be quick. The express trains are round that corner in a few seconds.

The clouds are gathering, making shapes, obscuring the sun.

And suddenly I see Astrid. She is up there in the clouds, smiling, beckoning. We were going to go away together, weren't we? To Afghanistan, where clouds and mountains meet.

We could make dreams together, me and Astrid.

A tingle, that's all. Just the slightest vibration in the back of my skull where it touched the line, and my heart was racing with fear, my whole body pumped with adrenaline.

What on earth was I thinking of?

In a moment I was on my feet. I could hear the train now. I raced up the bank and through the fence as it passed, quite slowly, just below me.

I knew one thing now. I didn't want to die. And nor did Astrid.

I turned back to the house, breathing deeply. The shock had woken me up, given me energy. There were phone calls to make, Louise must be looked after, the chickens and the goat needed feeding. Life must go on.

What I'd thought earlier about the vegetables was nonsense. They needed watering. I'd do it now.

As I approached the house, I stopped because cars were driving through the gate, crunching the gravel, and men jumping out, an infusion of energy into the sleepy afternoon. Among them I recognized Detective Sergeant Harrison. They were rapping on the door although it wasn't locked and I was outside it.

I walked over to them.

Chapter 17

I knew what was happening. It just didn't feel like it was happening to me.

I was in the police station. I'd come there voluntarily. I'd walked up to Sergeant Harrison and said, "Do you want to talk to me now, then?" and he'd replied, "You'd better come to the station," and put me in the car.

Now he showed me into a room and offered me a seat, friendly enough. Another man, who I hadn't seen before, sat down opposite me and got out a notebook and pencil.

"Thank you for coming in with us, Stephen."

Sergeant Harrison tried to smile, then his face turned solemn. "Such a terrible business. A real tragedy. A beautiful young lady like that with all her life in front of her."

He broke off.

"Can I get you a cup of tea before we start?"

My throat was dry, but I didn't want tea. I already regretted coming. I wanted to get back out into the sunlight, be on my own.

"Just a glass of water, please."

Sergeant Harrison brought a glass of water while the

other man sat impassively, as if I wasn't there. I looked round the room. No windows, a table with a phone and a file on it, four hard chairs, a filing cabinet.

"I gather congratulations are in order, Stephen."

Sergeant Harrison put the water in front of me. I sipped it, then looked at him blankly.

"Your mother. An MP. You must be very proud of her."

"Oh—yes. Yes."

"I saw her on the television, as it happens. I'm sure she's got a great future. We need more women in Parliament, that's what my wife says, anyway."

He made an attempt at a laugh.

"And then there's your brother Robert, too. Just got married, I gather. Another politician, I'm told, though rather from the other end of the spectrum to your mother. Must be some arguments round your family dinner table, eh, Stephen?"

He smiled and raised an eyebrow. Why was he talking about my family? I'd come to tell him about Astrid. I wanted to explain why it had to have been an accident. But I supposed he was just being friendly.

"Do you take much interest in politics yourself, Stephen?"

"Not much. I voted for my mum."

"Did you now? Very loyal of you. I like loyalty. It's a fine quality, within reason. By the way, this is Detective Constable Walker, and he's from Special Branch. Do you know what Special Branch is, Stephen?"

"Sort of . . ."

He raised the eyebrow again. Suddenly there was an edge to his voice.

"Special Branch have the job of keeping an eye on people who are thought to be a threat to society. Terrorists. Subversives. They have a file on you, Stephen. Are you surprised?"

I wasn't completely surprised, yet it was still a shock. So they *had* been watching me, in London, maybe here too. And what had I ever done? Rob was right: the pigs always got everything wrong.

"A bit," I said.

"Good," said Sergeant Harrison evenly. He picked up the file—my file—and leafed slowly through it, pausing at certain pages, taking his time.

What was in it? My breath was speeding up. But I was there, that was all, in a room painted that green color I thought only existed in schools, with fluorescent light that made skin look like wax. And a fly. A single fly on the ceiling, upside down like the astronauts on the moon. The only wildlife in a sterile world.

Then am I a happy fly/If I live or if I die. William Blake wrote that.

Sergeant Harrison unclipped the file and took out a photo, looked at it for a moment, then placed it on the table in front of me.

"Do you know who that is, Stephen?"

My heart missed a beat. I reached out and touched the photo, picked it up.

"Michelle," I murmured.

It was a small photo taken in a booth, but her face

looked clearly out of it, straight at me. Those eyes that I used to plunge into . . .

"Michelle," agreed Sergeant Harrison. "Michelle who?"

I was still staring at the photo.

"I don't know. She never told me her surname."

"What do you know about her, then?" His voice was insistent, though I didn't know why. I'd come here to talk about Astrid, not Michelle.

"She's half French. I met her sister," I managed. Had they caught her shoplifting or something? I'd better not say anything that might get her into trouble.

"What did you do with her?"

"We went to the Isle of Wight Festival."

There was nothing wrong with that, surely. Sergeant Harrison was leafing through the file. The other cop looked bored. The fly woke up and buzzed round the light.

"I'm glad you told me that, Stephen. Because I've got a picture of the two of you here."

He took out another photo. This one was big but blurred, and showed a festival crowd listening to music. It looked peaceful and harmless. Michelle and I were just about recognizable. She was lying against me, looking up and smiling while I held a joint to her lips.

I remembered the exact moment, and how it had felt: the world stopped for a while and everything was perfect. Captured on film, apparently, by a cop in the crowd.

"She liked you, didn't she?" Sergeant Harrison

continued. "You can see that by the way she's looking at you. Did you shag her, Stephen?"

Shag?

"What?" I asked, unbelieving.

"You heard what I said. She's a very attractive young lady. You made it with her, didn't you, Stephen? Come on, admit it."

What could I say? I didn't want to talk about Michelle at all, certainly not to Sergeant Harrison. What had happened between us was private.

"I'd advise you to be truthful, Stephen." There was a threat in his voice now.

"All right. We made love. There's no law against it," I said defensively.

"Don't be too sure!"

He was leaning back, hands on the table. The backs of his hands were covered in dark hair, and he wore a signet ring.

"And then you hit her, Stephen. So I'm told. You hit her." His voice was contemptuous. "And after that you walked out and left her penniless in a squat full of junkies."

"No!"

"Do you deny hitting her?"

"No. But it wasn't like that . . ."

"Is that so? Then what was it like?"

I couldn't answer. I couldn't have told anybody what happened when I left Michelle because I still didn't understand it myself. The only person I could talk to about it was Astrid. . . .

247

Then I remembered. Astrid was in a coma. Compared with that, nothing else mattered, least of all this man asking me questions. I remembered her face on the hospital pillow, so serene, so absent. . . . I felt my eyes moistening. I bent forward and stared at my hands. I didn't want Sergeant Harrison to see my face. It was no business of his.

"How old was Michelle?"

"I don't know. It wasn't important." My throat was swollen, and I had difficulty speaking. Why did he keep talking about Michelle, anyway, when Astrid was in a coma?

"Did you supply her with drugs, Stephen?"

"No."

He jabbed his finger at the photo, suddenly insistent.

"What are you doing there, Stephen? You're giving her something, practically putting it in her mouth. Don't tell me it's a roll-up!"

I looked again at the picture: sweet days of innocence and wonder, gone forever.

"It's blurred," I said. "You can't see much."

"Come off it, Stephen!" Sergeant Harrison sounded annoyed. "Do you think I'm stupid? It's a reefer. We've got witnesses too. That's supplying drugs, Stephen."

"If you say so."

"So you admit it?"

I shrugged.

"We passed each other joints. Everyone did."

"You admit supplying drugs?"

"Yeah. If you want me to."

"Good!" Sergeant Harrison gave a satisfied nod. "You supplied her with drugs, and you had sexual relations with her. How old did you say she was?"

"I said it didn't matter."

"Oh yes, it did, Stephen. What if I told you Michelle was fifteen? That's underage, Stephen. Sex with a minor."

Fifteen? Michelle? No, it wasn't possible. He was bluffing. He must be. Michelle was seventeen at least. Her sister had her own car. But then Suzanne was older than her. And she had tried to warn me, hadn't she? I remembered her last words, shouted across the ferry: "It is not how you think it is!"

So how was it? I didn't know anything. I never had. Yet it didn't matter now.

Sergeant Harrison was watching me patiently. I looked up and met his eyes. He wasn't so bad. He was only doing his job.

"Assault. Supplying drugs. Sexual relations with a minor." He numbered out my offenses with his fingers. "You've committed a lot of crimes there, Stephen."

"Are you going to charge me?" I asked. I half hoped he would. But he never answered my questions. Instead he leant forward and patted my hand like a friendly uncle.

"You've come clean, Stephen. I like that. It wasn't the young lady who complained, as it happens. Her father reported her missing and asked us to find her for him. Which we did. She was in quite a state, and made a full statement. She liked you, you know. You could have done a bit better by her if you ask me, but there we go."

The fly settled on his nose. He brushed it off.

"How long have you been living at The Hollies, Stephen?"

The Hollies? Well, at least he was coming to the point now.

"Since January."

"And this man Spencer—he's your guru, right?"

"No. He's a friend."

"A friend," Sergeant Harrison repeated. "Funny sort of friend from what I can make out. You gave him all your money, didn't you, Stephen? You picked up your giro once a week and handed it straight over."

"Not to Spencer. To Richard."

"Richard. Yes, of course. But you knew where it was going, didn't you, Stephen?"

"It was for the house. I didn't need anything for myself."

"No. But you worked all day every day, from what I've heard. Building and gardening. And they didn't even allow you the money for a beer."

"I could ask for anything if I needed it."

"Yes, but you had to be careful what you asked for because if you got on the wrong side of certain people, you'd be in trouble. You might be asked to leave. Like other people had been. That's how it was, wasn't it? You all had to be with Spencer, didn't you? Because he'd promised you something. And he decided who stayed and who left. He decided everything in the end.

He even decided which of the girls got to sleep with him. Especially that, eh, Stephen? And no special favors, not even to his own wife."

"It wasn't like that." I was going to explain how it was, but he interrupted immediately.

"Oh, come on! What was his room like compared with the rest of the place? We've seen it. Thick carpet. Expensive furniture. A new color television. And the rest of you sleeping on mattresses and giving him all your money. What kind of friend is that, Stephen?"

I opened my mouth, but he didn't expect an answer.

"Are you such a fool, Stephen? Couldn't you see what was going on? Everybody else could—outside, I mean. Oh yes, when you moved in, it was all very nice and idealistic, young people trying to find somewhere to live, bringing the house back to life and so on. Your neighbors were quite enthusiastic, I gather. But they soon got wise to it. Nobody likes a cult, Stephen. There may not be a law against it, but people get frightened. They suspect drugs and sex, and they're not usually far wrong. They think their children are going to get sucked in and brainwashed and abused. Like you were, Stephen. Like you were."

"I thought we got on okay with the locals," I protested.

Sergeant Harrison snorted.

"Not what they tell me!"

He leant over me, staring down.

"Did you know Spencer was a heroin smuggler?"

I looked up at him, met his eyes.

251

"No," I said. "And I don't believe you."

"He's been doing it for years. Along with his associate, Leonard Carter, who also calls himself Ray Mitchell and is wanted by the police of several different countries, including the United States of America, who are seeking his extradition on charges of rape. Rape, Stephen, have you got that?"

Rape? It might be true. I could believe anything of Ray. But not Spencer. He might be a bullshitter, but he wasn't a heroin dealer. I shook my head.

"I don't think Spencer would smuggle heroin. It's not his style."

"Oh, isn't it? You'd be very surprised, Stephen, what people will do for money. Anyway, I believe you know a little bit about heroin yourself."

What was this about? I suddenly flashed back to Vicky and her little heroin joints. But they couldn't know about that. Sergeant Harrison exchanged a look with the other cop, then opened the file again.

"Your brother, Robert. You stayed with him last October, right?"

I was puzzled. What had Rob got to do with it? Suddenly I wanted to go, be outside in the sunlight. I hadn't been arrested. Perhaps I could just get up and leave. But I glanced at Sergeant Harrison and decided against it.

"And now he seems to have skipped the country."

"He's on his honeymoon."

"Conveniently, from his point of view. Special Branch have been watching your brother for some time. What were you doing for him, Stephen? You're not as smart as him, are you? But I expect you look up to him, admire him in a way. And I'm sure he found a use for you. Running errands perhaps. Dropping notes to his friends. Where were you on October 15 last year, Stephen?"

"I can't remember."

"Let me remind you then. You were at an anti-American demonstration in Grosvenor Square. What were you doing there?"

"Demonstrating, I suppose."

"Have you always been anti-American?"

"I'm not anti-American. I'm anti the war."

"And you hit a policeman while you were there."

"No."

"Don't get funny with me, Stephen. We've got photographs. Where did you go after the demonstration?"

"To someone's flat. We watched it on TV."

"And then you went home to bed?"

"Yes."

"Do the words 'Angry Brigade' mean anything to you?"

"No."

"That's strange because Special Branch believe you and your brother were implicated in their activities. They're bombers, Stephen. Terrorists. They attack Conservative associations and police stations. What would your mother think about that, eh? On the night of the 15th October, the Angry Brigade placed a fire bomb in the Imperial War Museum, causing extensive damage. You were there, Stephen, weren't you?"

"No."

"But you know who was there, don't you? Was it Robert, Stephen? Was it your brother?"

"I don't know what you're talking about."

"We'll see about that. Do you know this man?"

He held out a police photograph. I started, taken by surprise. It was Greg—the friendly dope dealer from the squat who'd moved down to Herefordshire for Sue to have her baby.

"That's Greg . . ."

"Friend of yours, is he? He's just starting his sentence for dealing narcotics. Nasty piece of work. I doubt we'd have caught him if Special Branch hadn't kept a tail on you and alerted us to some of the characters you were living with down in Brixton. What about this man?"

It was a blurry picture of the German guy who lived on the bottom floor. I hardly looked at it because I was still too shocked about Greg. What about Sue and the baby? How would they manage?

"He lived downstairs. I didn't really know him."

"No? Well, we do. He's a heroin smuggler, Stephen. You seem to know rather a lot of them, don't you? And this character . . ."

Another photo. This time Chet.

"Don't deny knowing him, because you were seen together frequently. A heroin addict and deserter from the U.S. Army. Disappeared rather suddenly."

"He went home," I said. "He went back to America."

"Are you certain of that, Stephen?"

"I saw him off."

"Did you see him onto the plane?"

"No, I . . . he didn't want me to."

Sergeant Harrison almost smiled.

"You know why that was, don't you? Because he didn't go to America. He went to Sweden. Where he has a wife and a child. You've been up to your neck in it, Stephen, haven't you? Associating with terrorists, drug dealers, deserters, con men. And you from such a good background. What would your parents think of you?"

He stood up and walked round the table so that he was behind me. Then he knelt over and whispered in my ear.

"I want the truth now, Stephen. The truth. Because a young lady is lying in hospital near to death, and I mean to clean up the whole sordid mess that got her there. You're not a bad person, Stephen. I can see that. You just made a few mistakes, that's all. Got taken in by the wrong people. So now I want the truth. It's the only way. As it says in the Holy Bible: The Truth will set you free."

He straightened up, went back to his own side of the table and picked up the file again.

"What were your relations with Astrid?"

I'd been waiting for this. I'd tell him everything I could about Astrid, except that we were lovers. That was none of his business.

"We were friends. I knew her before, years ago, and it was because of her I came to the house. Her father's wealthy, and she always seemed very glamorous. But at

The Hollies she was always just like everyone else, did a lot of washing and cooking. The other girls weren't very—"

"Yes, yes, yes," Sergeant Harrison interrupted. "What sort of 'friends' were you, Stephen?"

"Good friends. She helped me in the garden, and—"

Impatiently, Sergeant Harrison plonked down a photograph in front of me.

"Perhaps this will concentrate your mind."

I looked at the photo. I couldn't take it in at first. It wasn't like the others. It was quite artistic, with trees and bluebells, and in the middle distance two young people lying in each other's arms.

Then I understood. It was me and Astrid.

I felt a shiver down my back. Who did these people think they were? God? Wherever I'd been, it seemed a policeman had been snooping in the bushes to capture my most intimate moments. And who did they think I was? I'd never done anything to harm anybody, and nor had Astrid.

That was what they couldn't bear. They couldn't bear innocence, or kindness or love. They didn't know the meaning of love.

As I looked at the photo, I felt my spine straighten, then my hands and feet started to tingle, and my breath, which had been coming in harsh pants, settled to a slow, quiet rhythm. I knew what was coming: the electric energy that started at the base of my spine and then shot up in a rush of bliss through the top of my head and out into the universe.

I was nobody. I was nothing and everything. I was Astrid, and I was Michelle, and I was Spencer and Ray and Sergeant Harrison. I was the fly on the ceiling, and the other cop, who was suddenly staring at me in alarm.

Everything was fine. Astrid had said that too, her last words to me. Everything was as it should be and could not be otherwise.

"I want the truth," said Sergeant Harrison. "That's all."

"So do I."

I whispered it. He didn't hear me. His eyes were glazed with the stupidity that comes from thinking that you are real.

"Because this is not just about drugs, Stephen. This may yet be a murder inquiry. We need to know everything you know about the relations between Spencer and Astrid. Did you know they were married?"

"Only since last night. Richard told me."

I would tell the truth, like he said, in so far as he or I could understand it.

"So it wasn't generally known in your, er, community?"

"No."

"Did you know that Astrid had recently come into a large sum of money?"

"Yes, she told me."

"So who would stand to inherit from her?"

"Spencer, I suppose."

The fly took off from the ceiling again.

"Is it true that Spencer had sexual relations with the other girls in the house—singly and together?"

"It could be. I don't care that much."

Sergeant Harrison stood up and banged the table, raising his voice for the first time.

"Don't bullshit me, Stephen. Of course you care. And Astrid cared too. She'd had enough of him, hadn't she? She'd seen through him and all his so-called spirituality. She wanted out. She was going away with you, wasn't she? Already planning it. You and she were going to leave, and when you went, all her money would go too. That's the fact of it, isn't it?"

The energy was still flowing up through the top of my head, and his words couldn't touch me. Only the fly touched me, landing on my hand. I examined it closely, the translucent wings, the green tinge of its back.

"We hadn't made any plans," I said calmly. "And she wasn't bothered about the money, either way."

"Maybe *she* wasn't, but Spencer was, and that's why he got rid of her."

Did he really believe it? Then in a flash I saw what he wanted. He didn't want the truth. He wanted to get Spencer for something—anything—and he wanted me to denounce him.

"No. Spencer wouldn't hurt a fly."

As if to emphasize my point the fly got up from my hand and buzzed around the other policeman. Sergeant Harrison narrowed his eyes.

"How come then Ray Mitchell is wanted for rape?"

"That doesn't mean anything about Spencer."

"He's his oldest friend."

"Spencer doesn't judge."

"Oh, for Christ's sake! This guy's taken you for a ride. Can't you see that? He's a con man, Stephen, taking advantage of gullible people like you. What did he promise you, Stephen? Enlightenment?"

"I don't think he ever promised anything, but if he did, it was nonexistence."

Sergeant Harrison whistled with frustration. Then he pulled a piece of paper from the file.

"Listen to this: 'You can do as you like. This is not about morality. I'm not concerned with right and wrong. Stealing, lying, even murder, they are only actions like other actions, until the ego puts its twist on them and calls them "mine" and gives them a value.' That ring any bells, Stephen?"

"It sounds like Spencer."

"Indeed it is. One of his so-called talks. And what's he saying? He's saying stealing, lying, murder, they're all right. This is a deeply immoral person, Stephen. Worse than that, he's amoral. He can justify anything. Anything. Even murder, Stephen. Think about that."

I tried to think about it, but the flow through the top of my head had stopped as unexpectedly as it began, leaving a strange emptiness, and I couldn't focus so well. Sergeant Harrison put his face close to mine. I could see the small black hairs on his nose.

"Now listen, Stephen, I will give you the benefit of the doubt and say you didn't know what you were getting mixed up in, but we are talking about a dangerous man here. Spencer and Ray left the house some hours before Astrid's accident, but they could have come back, one or both of them. We have witnesses who claim to have seen Astrid by the track with a man. It wasn't you, because you've got an alibi. So who was it, Stephen? Who was it?"

Was he making this up? I wanted to go, that was all. I wanted it to be over.

"I don't know," I said. "I wasn't there."

Sergeant Harrison could feel me weakening. He put his hand on my arm and softened his voice.

"Don't you care, Stephen? A beautiful young woman with everything to look forward to is on a ventilator. And your so-called guru says he's beyond right and wrong. You don't buy that, do you? You don't seriously buy that rubbish?"

My breath was heavy and uneven again. I was going down now, fast.

"Actually I don't agree with Spencer about that. I think personal morality is important," I said feebly.

Sergeant Harrison looked encouraged. His voice was friendly, chummy almost.

"So why don't you help us nail the bastard?"

The fly was buzzing around him, trying to settle on his ear.

"But there's nothing I can tell you."

I looked up and met his eyes, and in that moment I think he finally realized I really didn't know anything. He looked away and coughed, then he continued.

"Remember this, Stephen, we can put you inside for

a year, maybe more, just on what you've admitted in this interview. Do you want to go to prison? Do you want to have a criminal record for the rest of your life? Do you want to put your mother to all that shame? It'll be all over the papers, with your background. Think about it, Stephen. Think hard. You might want to protect your guru for some reason I can't fathom, but is it worth it? Because if you will cooperate, you could be out of here just like that."

He sat back, and waited.

So that was it. If I denounced Spencer, he'd let me go. Even if he couldn't get anything else out of me, at least he wanted that satisfaction. I wasn't afraid. In a way I wished I had been. It would have given me an excuse. Instead I was thinking: it's a choice of dreams.

And the dream I wanted had birdsong and open roads, not court rooms and clanging doors. "Lies are only lies for those who believe in their own history." Spencer had said that himself. I could play Sergeant Harrison's game. A few words, and they'd let me go.

"Spencer . . . ," I started. My voice was strong but strange, not my normal voice at all. "He was conning us. I see that now. He fooled us all and I should have known better. Astrid told me. She told me Spencer was having sex with other girls in the house, and that he wanted her money. She said he thought he was beyond normal morality—that's what he always said—but she'd had enough of it. She wanted to leave. She wanted me to run away with her. But I couldn't accept it, till now. And I was scared of what he might do when he found out about me and Astrid. Perhaps he knew already. Ray knew. . . ."

I felt nothing, only a cold emptiness opening inside me, but I put my head into my hands in a pretense of emotion.

"I shouldn't have left her on her own. She wasn't safe. Oh my God!"

Was it enough? I peeked through my fingers. Sergeant Harrison was watching me with disdain. He didn't like me. I saw that now. That was all right. I didn't like myself either.

"Is that all?" he asked.

What more was I supposed to say? But at that moment the phone rang. Sergeant Harrison picked it up.

"Hello! . . . Yes." His face betrayed nothing. "Right!"

He put the phone down and turned to me.

"You're telling the truth now?"

"Yes."

"Well, you'd better, because she's dead. So let's get this clear. This Spencer character, he's a bastard, isn't he? A lying, cheating, con-man bastard, right?"

He was looking me in the eye. I was in shock. The roof of my mouth had gone dry. I didn't want to speak. The fly landed on Sergeant Harrison's nose, and he swatted it angrily away.

"Say it!" It was a command.

"Yes," I mumbled. "He's a bastard."

"A lying, cheating, con-man bastard."

"A lying, cheating, con-man bastard."

Sergeant Harrison nodded contemptuously.

"I've no further use for you. You can go."

He turned abruptly, as if I had ceased to exist, and headed for the door.

"Get rid of that fly, Jim!"

The other cop was already standing up. He took a spray can from the top of the filing cabinet and squirted at the fly, which fell twitching to the table. Then he looked at me.

"Go on! Get out!" They were the first words he'd said.

I picked up the corpse of the fly and followed Sergeant Harrison into the corridor. I hesitated, confused about which way to go, but the other cop was behind me and I felt his hand on my shoulder, turning me round.

"That way."

Suddenly his face was very close to mine. He was young, not much older than me. His eyes narrowed.

"Dirty fucking hippie!"

His lip curled, and he slammed his fist into my stomach. I doubled up, winded.

"Now get out!"

On the steps of the police station I stood taking in the early evening light and the soft breeze. My stomach ached, but that was nothing.

Astrid was dead. Sergeant Harrison had said so.

What did that mean?

I still held the corpse of the fly in my fist. I opened it and looked. The sheen had gone from its back, its wings. It would never move again. Killed casually for the crime of landing on Sergeant Harrison's nose.

> *Am not I*
> *A fly like thee*
> *And art not thou*
> *A man like me?*
> *For I dance*
> *And drink and sing*
> *Till some blind hand*
> *Shall brush my wing.*

The breeze flipped it off my hand into the gutter, another bit of dirt.

Chapter 18

The Hollies was deserted. The front door was locked, so I went round to the back door, which opened. I called but no one answered.

The kitchen had been left clean, washed-up plates in the rack, mugs on their hooks. There was a note on the kitchen table.

Hi Stephen,

I'm guessing you're the most likely person to get back here first. Richard went with the police too. God knows where Spencer is. Christ, what a mess!

I've had to go. Louise went hysterical when the cops came into her room. I've calmed her down, but she's got to get away from here. I rang Tim, and I'm taking her to his parents' place, near Manchester. We'll meet him there. I'm worried she'll have to go back to hospital.

I might be back sometime. I'm not sure. I'm pretty freaked-out by everything. I need a bit of time to think things through.

Best of luck.

Graham

I went upstairs to my room, my footsteps sounding loud in the empty house. At the top of the stairwell I stood for a minute, remembering the moment when I had first entered the house through the bathroom window, my shoe prints in the thick dust, feeling like an intruder on an alien world.

That's what the house would return to. It was all over. Astrid was dead, Spencer in prison, the rest of us dispersed like yellow leaves in the west wind.

The police had searched my room, and my books and papers were sprawled all over the place. I sat down on my mattress, resting my back against the wall. Here, where I had lain with Astrid through the warm nights, feeling her warmth, her aliveness.

Where had that gone?

And the immensity—where was it now?

It was not here, and it never had been. I saw that with sudden clarity. It was only chemicals in my brain, giving the impression of a wonderful experience, a high like no other, that somehow Spencer had managed to induce in me. But just a high. Another dream to disguise the only reality, which was dust and death.

A train passed, the 8:20 London Express, cutting through the quiet with an explosion of noise, reminding me of Astrid.

I couldn't stay here. God knows where I'd go. London probably. I could find a squat or sleep in a railway station. It was all the same. I stuffed a few things into my rucksack and left the house.

Outside, the sky was turning gold behind the trees and

a thrush was singing. Minkie the goat was bleating from the end of the garden. She'd been left there, forgotten. I'd have to at least milk her before I left. I walked down to her and she charged towards me, then butted me affectionately. I scratched her nose and undid her tether. Everything I did seemed to be in slow motion; my breath came in shallow pants and my chest felt like soup. I was tired, terribly tired, but it was more than that. It was an exhaustion of the soul.

Minkie bleated and wagged her tail. She was looking past me, so I turned, and saw Penelope.

I didn't know Penelope very well. She was one of the older women who Spencer seemed to attract, and she had given us Minkie. She came to talk to Spencer sometimes, and knew a lot about Buddhism and Hinduism, but she wasn't sociable. She lived on her own somewhere with goats and cats.

She nodded to me.

"I'm glad somebody's remembered the animals."

I wanted to answer. I opened my mouth to say something, but no words came out. I glanced at her, and then away. My whole body was quivering.

I felt her gaze, level, calm, honest, taking me in.

"Come along, then," she said. "You'd better both come home with me. And the chickens. No point leaving them for the fox."

I didn't look around to say goodbye to the garden or the house or the railway line or the rosebush or the holly trees by the gate, although I knew I'd never see them again. I took my rucksack and clambered with

Minkie into the back of Penelope's van, followed by a cardboard box full of chickens, the same box that Spencer's television had come in a few days before. I put a hand on Minkie to steady her and comfort myself as we clattered through the Suffolk lanes.

We stopped outside a cottage, deep in the countryside.

"You can have the spare room," Penelope told me. "Make yourself comfortable. I have to do the animals."

I still couldn't speak. She led me upstairs and showed me a small white room with a bed, a table and chair, and a framed print of the Buddha on the wall. I couldn't have asked for better.

Outside, darkness was gathering around woods and fields. A blackbird was chanting its last chorus outside my window. I lay down on the bed in my clothes.

I had no will to move or speak, but I was quite calm. I could cast a cold eye over my life and see it as Sergeant Harrison saw it. Michelle was a girl I'd shagged at a festival. Astrid was an adulterous affair. Spencer was a con man who had sucked me into his fantasy.

There were no demons and no immensity. No Hell and no Heaven. Nothing.

That was all.

Nothing.

Only my self, a monstrous ball of delusion consuming itself in a void.

Astrid was dead. Worms would eat her eyeballs.

Beauty, truth, love, what were they? Words, that's all.

I was nothing. A scream disappearing into the void.

Sergeant Harrison had unraveled the reality that I had constructed of my life—shredded it and thrown it back in my face. I was random actions, emotions, relationships, with no sense or meaning anymore to hang them together. A dream without a dreamer.

I lay there. The room grew dark. I heard Penelope come back in, but she left me alone. A little later she went to bed. A streak of green lingered in the sky outside the window, then that went too, and I lay in blackness and silence punctuated by an occasional call from hunting owls. My chest churned to the point of nausea, and my arms and legs ached. But I didn't move. There was no point. I slept in little fits, but there was no comfort in sleep; dreams of broken buildings in an arid landscape alternated with hooting steam trains charging towards me. Awake, I could find no steadiness in my thoughts, nothing to hold on to. Astrid was dead. There was no meaning in that. No meaning at all. Whether she had wanted to die or not, she was dead, and that was the end of it. No one would ever know what passed through her mind. . . .

I knew nothing about Astrid, nothing at all. I knew nothing about anyone; they were only shadows cast briefly over my consciousness—Astrid, Spencer, Michelle, Rob, even my parents—what could I see of their secret hearts?

Truth—what was it? Everyone thought they knew, but perhaps Spencer was right, and we all just made up our own stories. Could I make up a story in which Astrid wasn't dead? Where she was waiting for me somewhere, miraculously saved? No, that wasn't how it was, that's all. I was no conjuror of dreams. More like a prisoner of my own delusions.

Sergeant Harrison was certain about truth, and its power. That was what he had said: "The Truth will set you free."

Would it?

Without quite losing consciousness I started to dream again: Astrid's face, in the air in front of me, her gray eyes wide and pleading. She was trying to talk, mouthing something, but no words came out.

"Yes?" I said. "Astrid, where are you?"

I watched her mouth intently, trying to pick up the words, the words that must be so important, that she so wanted to tell me.

"Jellyfish," she whispered; then with a huge effort, "Jellyfish and eels."

Her face dissolved and became Michelle, smiling. And then another voice said, "It is all one."

I turned. Spencer was behind me in the shadows.

"Don't look behind," he said clearly. "Look in front. Always in front. The front is what matters. And don't forget to open your eyes."

So I looked in front again, but I couldn't see anything now because my eyes were closed, so with a huge effort I forced my eyelids open and saw the Buddha, cross-legged, serene in the early morning light.

The context returned: a print on the wall. A white room. Dawn.

I was alive. That was all.

I heard Penelope get up and go out to milk the goats. A rooster was making a lot of noise in the hen run, excited by the arrival of the new chickens from The Hollies.

I still hadn't moved. The churning in my chest had eased, but I had no reason to do anything. The world went on without Astrid, and it would go on without me.

The sun rose and the light changed.

Penelope came in with a tray. She glanced at me and put the tray down.

"Eat!" she said gruffly, and left.

I still made no move because I'd forgotten how; then, slowly, I raised my right arm. It was extraordinary how it worked. I had the thought to raise it, and then it just went up, apparently of its own accord. I formed another thought, visualizing my body sitting upright on the bed, with my feet on the floor, and at once my neck bent forwards and my arm pushed. It felt like a puppeteer pulling strings—except that I was both puppeteer and puppet. No division.

My body wanted the food too: a boiled egg and toast, and a mug of warm goat milk. I bit the toast, then put a spoonful of egg in my mouth and chewed. The food disappeared inside me, turning into something else. Turning into me. I sipped the goat milk, fresh from the morning's milking—straight out of the goat's body and into mine. I and the goat flowing into each other . . . strange.

After I'd finished, I stayed sitting at the table until I

could summon up the willpower to return to the bed. Then I lay listening to the changing sounds of the morning as if I was ill, though I wasn't. There was just no point in doing anything.

The afternoon passed. Penelope brought more food and told me to wash and change my clothes. I did as she told me and stood under a shower, but the sensation of the water pouring over me was overwhelming, and I was shaking by the time I lay down again.

There was nowhere to go and nothing to do. I wasn't afraid anymore, simply floating in a void. Thoughts arose—about Astrid, and Spencer, about my parents, even Penelope, but in a moment they had no meaning. They only repeated themselves like mantras: *"lying cheating con-man bastard lying cheating con-man bastard"* or *"did she commit suicide did she commit suicide did she commit suicide"* or *"she'll ask me to go soon she'll ask me to go soon she'll ask me to go soon."* Then they faded back into nothing.

The picture of the Buddha hung on the wall in front of me as I lay. It was a cheap print, but it had something—could you call it beauty? Another mantra immediately formed: *"beauty is truth truth beauty beauty is truth truth beauty,"* and then that gave way to *"the truth will set you free the truth will set you free."*

It was growing dark. Penelope had come in from milking the goats and putting the chickens to bed. I stood up uncertainly, picked up the tray with my empty dishes and went downstairs to the kitchen

Penelope was sitting reading in a crumbling armchair

in one corner, with two cats on her knee. She didn't look up. I took my tray to the sink, washed my plate carefully and put it on the draining board.

"Leave the rest. I'll put it away later," she said, still not looking up. I sat down on a hard chair by the table. She placed a bookmark in her book, took off her glasses and inspected me.

"Want a cup of tea?"

"No thanks."

They were the first words I had spoken since leaving the police station, and my voice didn't seem to belong to me.

"Do you want anything?" Her voice was gruff, but there was kindness in it too.

"Yes. I wondered if you could spare me some paper."

"Paper?"

"For writing on."

"Oh, I see."

She got up, gently removing the cats from her lap, and went through to her study. She came back with a sheaf of typing paper.

"That do you?"

"Thanks."

She sat back down, and the cats jumped eagerly back onto her lap. She picked up her book.

"I'll expect you down for meals tomorrow. And I've got a few jobs lined up for you."

I went upstairs and sat at the table. I turned on the light—it would be dark soon.

Truth. I should tell the truth, as Sergeant Harrison

had said. I would know who I was then. It would make it all clear.

I took a sheet of paper and tried to work things out. What was I doing a year ago? A year ago exactly?

I was doing my A-levels.

I thought: "All right, then, Sergeant Harrison, this is the truth, the way it all really happened."

Then I started to write.

I wrote all night in a kind of trance, till the mystery of the dawn brought me back to the reality of day with a blast of birdsong. Then I lay down and slept deeply till noon. In the afternoon Penelope gave me some jobs outside, cleaning the goats' shed and fixing fences. Then she cooked me supper. She didn't speak much— she had no small talk—and I was grateful. My senses had all become hyperactive. The smell of the goats, the birdsong, the taste of fresh vegetables all hit me with overwhelming intensity, and I returned to my room with relief.

I was in my own world entirely. I had no thought for the future. Often I didn't know where or who I was. At night I wrote, living among ghosts of my past, and by day the cottage and its two fields were all my reality.

One evening I was sitting in the kitchen in the dusk after supper—Penelope never put on the electric light till it was too dark to see—when she suddenly looked up from her book, took me in steadily, nodded, then started talking.

"I was born in India. My parents were Theosophists, do you know what that is? Well, you can read
up about it. There are plenty of books. In any case I
grew up familiar with the ideas of Hindu mystics,
though I always preferred the Buddha myself. I
remember Mrs. Besant, who was the leader of the
Theosophy movement. She was very old by then,
white-haired and deaf. She took me on her knee and
told me I was sweet. Sweet! I wasn't sweet. I've never
been sweet, and besides I was too big for that sort of
thing and it made me feel uncomfortable. I've always
been suspicious about leaders."

She stroked the head of the cat on her knee, and it
looked up at her lovingly.

"I know what you're wondering. At least you'd be a
damn fool if you weren't. What about Spencer? Is he
just another fraud? I can't answer that of course. He's a
good talker but that doesn't mean much. Rogues,
fools—the world's full of them, and they find each
other. The Theosophists were pretty cracked when you
look back at it, but they were also intelligent, well-
meaning people looking for a higher truth, and perhaps
some of them found it. I don't know. I'll tell you this,
though. Once, when I was about ten, my mother took
me to an ashram in India where there was a famous
guru. Spencer went there too, though that was later. I'd
been to plenty of ashrams with her, and I expected idols
and incense and a lot of self-important people, but this
one wasn't like that. The building was unpretentious,
and the guru was a shriveled old man on a mat, with

cropped white hair and a sort of glow around him. We sat down opposite him. My mother was going to ask him something, but he put his finger to his lips, and we just sat in silence. You could learn more from that silence than from millions of words. When it was over, he looked straight at me and smiled. . . ."

She paused. Her cat was purring loudly.

"Spencer has the same smile."

"And the same silence?"

She didn't answer. She looked down at the cat, playing with the fur behind its neck.

"All the same," she said eventually. "I'm not sure it matters. It's like the old proverb of the finger pointing at the moon. Only a fool looks too closely at the finger. Anyway, I have my own silence now."

Chapter 19

I was in a cemetery.

I walked along the neat paths between the grave-stones. So many, so many. People were always dying, there was nothing extraordinary about it: young, old and in-between, good people, bad people, rich people, poor people, they all died, and Astrid would lie among them. And so would I one day.

I was wearing someone else's suit, and I felt like someone else. The sky was overcast and it was muggy. There'd be thunder later.

I didn't know what time the funeral was, or how I would work out which was the right one. There were probably lots of funerals in the cemetery chapel, one af-ter the other. But as I approached, I saw a small crowd gathered on the gravel, ready to go in. A hearse drove up, and a tall, white-haired man stepped towards it. I knew immediately that he was Astrid's father.

I didn't speak to anyone. I just walked into the chapel with everyone else and sat at the back. I listened to the service without understanding; only the tunes of the hymns were familiar. I thought of Astrid, her beauty, her grace, her kindness. People in front of me were holding back tears—relations, I supposed, or friends of the family who had known her as a bright little girl, but I felt no emotion. I looked at the box that held her discarded body and knew she wasn't there. Whatever it was about Astrid that I had loved could not be broken, nor buried.

I followed the procession out to the family plot. The wind was blowing in our faces and ruffling the flowers on the coffin. I wished I'd brought flowers myself; I hadn't thought of it. Instead I clutched my rucksack awkwardly as the pastor said some words in German over the open grave.

I watched Astrid's father throw a handful of soil and turn away. It was over.

A hand was on my shoulder. I tried to turn away too, but I couldn't, and then the hand was shaking me.

"Wake up, Stephen!"

Penelope's voice. I opened my eyes, still half in the dream.

"Astrid," I murmured.

"You're wanted on the phone. I think it's your mother. Downstairs in my study."

She left and I got out of bed, rubbing my eyes. I didn't even know she had a phone. I'd never heard it ring.

My mother was shrill.

"Stephen? Thank God we've found you! Where have you been all this time? Your father and I have been worried to death about you."

"I've just been staying here. Sorry, Mum, I didn't think you'd be worried for a couple of days. . . ."

"A couple of days? It's been two weeks!"

Two weeks?

"Well, what are you doing now? Are you going to come home?"

"I don't know. I . . . I need to sort myself out. I'll ring you tomorrow. All right, Mum?"

In the kitchen, Penelope passed me a mug of tea without saying anything. I sipped it thoughtfully. Two weeks . . . Could I really have been there that long? If so, I had lost some time, somewhere.

"Penelope?"

"Yes?" The cats were rubbing her legs as she prepared their food. She didn't look round.

"What's been happening? At The Hollies, I mean."

"I expect the mice are having a good time, and the slugs are enjoying your lettuces."

"Nobody's there?"

"No."

"What happened to Spencer?"

"I don't know, but Richard's living in Colchester. I saw him in the market and told him you were here. He's been 'helping the police,' I gather."

"And Astrid . . . Was there a funeral?"

Without hurrying, Penelope put the cats' dishes down on the floor, and the cats scrambled to get their share. Then she turned and looked at me.

"What?"

"Astrid. Was there a funeral?"

"Yes, I heard what you said."

She sat down opposite me.

"Were you under the impression that Astrid had died?"

I looked back at her, confused.

"Sergeant Harrison told me. That's what he said: 'She's dead.'"

Penelope shook her head.

"Well!" A half smile crossed her lips. "You should know better by now, Stephen, than to believe a policeman. Astrid is certainly alive. Her father took her back to Germany."

I sat there, my mouth slightly open. I had nothing to say. In my head the clouds were parting, and the sun was shining through.

Once again, my world had been turned upside down. I had been so certain that Astrid was dead. I felt as if I had even been to her funeral. It was hard to get used to a world in which she still existed.

Penelope gave me Richard's phone number, and I rang him the next evening. He answered immediately.

"Oh, hello, Stephen. How's it going?"

He sounded normal. He'd got back all his self-possession.

"I'm okay." I didn't want to get into any small talk with him, though. "Listen, Richard. The police told me Astrid was dead."

There was a short pause while he took it in. I

wondered what they'd said to him—and what he'd said to them.

"Well, she isn't," he said matter-of-factly. "She's in Germany."

"How is she?"

"I don't know. Her father just came with an ambulance and took her back there. I've tried to contact him, but he puts the phone down. I'm afraid he doesn't like us very much."

"What if I went there?"

"You can try. I doubt he'll let you in the door. I have the address and phone number, though. I'll give it you if you like."

I wrote it down.

"Richard—where's Spencer?"

I had to ask.

"I don't know, and if I did, I wouldn't tell you right now. He'll contact me when he's ready."

"Was he arrested?"

"The police didn't press charges."

"What about everybody else?"

"Anneke and Brigit have gone back to Sweden. Their visas had expired. Graham and Louise are with Tim in Manchester. Ray, I'm afraid, is in police custody. I took care of the house. I've stored a few things, canceled the lease. It wasn't that good a place anyway. It'll be better to start again somewhere else."

I listened in disbelief. Start again?

"You can't be serious, Richard. Spencer was up to all kinds of stuff—"

"You haven't been listening to the cops, have you?" he interrupted. "You know where Spencer was that day? He'd gone to try and get Ray into a clinic in London because Ray was back on heroin. He was helping a friend, Stephen, that's all. The cops had nothing on him. They had nothing on any of us, except an old charge against Ray."

"Ray was smuggling heroin."

"If you say so. I certainly had no knowledge of it."

"Don't you see, Richard? Spencer lived for his own pleasure, and just abandoned us. Walked out as soon as trouble came. You can't 'start again' with Spencer. He's been an arsehole."

"I'm sorry you feel like that, Stephen, though I can understand it. But Spencer's not like other people. You can't judge him by the same standards."

"Bye, Richard."

I put the phone down.

The next day, I hitched to Germany.

Penelope drove me to the motorway. I tried to thank her, but she waved me away with her usual brusqueness.

"You worked your keep. Now go off and find Astrid. Help her get well."

I watched her drive away in her old van. She'd be happy to be alone again with her cats and her goats. I stuck out my thumb. The first car that passed gave me a lift all the way to Dover.

I took the night ferry to Oostende, sleeping an uncomfortable five hours on a bench. I still had no idea what would happen when I arrived, or whether I'd find out anything at all. Probably Astrid's father wouldn't let me near her. And even if he did, what could I expect? More than likely she was still in a coma.

But there was hope. A little flame of hope. Because I'd thought she was dead and she wasn't, so anything was possible.

At any rate, I had to know.

The lifts came easily, and I arrived in Cologne the next afternoon, dropped off opposite the cathedral by an old couple in a VW Beetle who spoke no English but smiled sweetly and fed me brown bread and sausage. I changed money at a bank, then went to a phone box.

My heart was in my throat, and my hand was shaking as the phone rang.

"Alfred Bauer." The voice was crisp and business-like.

I felt the sweat on my forehead. It was a clammy, overcast afternoon.

"Oh, hello," I managed. "I'm a friend of Astrid's. Do you speak English?"

There was a silence, but at least he didn't put the phone down.

"You telephone from England?"

"No. I'm here. In Köln. May I come and see you, please? I . . . I want to know how she is."

"You are from the house? The Hollies?"

"I was there, yes, but I knew Astrid before too. . . ."

"What is your name?"

"My name is Stephen."

Silence again. Then:

"You may come to my house. You have the address?"

"Yes."

"You come now."

Astrid's father was nothing like the tall, stooping man from my dream. He was stocky, strong, still youthful, the sort of businessman who plays squash twice a week.

He met me at the door and showed me into the living room. I sat in a leather armchair in a spotlessly clean room. All the furniture was new and expensive.

He looked at me coolly, unsmiling, appraising my dirty jeans and straggling hair, while he poured himself whiskey from a decanter.

"So . . . For what reason do you want to see my daughter?"

The way he said it made me feel encouraged. I might be able to see her. It was possible.

"Because she's a friend. I care about her."

"So where were you till now? Why were you not at the hospital with her?" he asked sharply.

"I was there—then I had to talk to the police. And then—I didn't know what had happened to her. I thought she'd died. Nobody told me."

He nodded and sat down opposite me, watching me steadily.

"This . . . Spencer," he said slowly. "He is your guru?"

I had always denied that, but not now.

"I suppose so. At least, he was."

He said nothing, just watched me again. He reminded me of a hawk, the sharpness in his eyes, the way he watched and waited.

"My daughter—she loved the man. She told me so. I will be honest with you, I didn't like him. I told her he was no good, he was after her money. I fought with her on this, but she would not listen. Perhaps I was wrong. So tell me please, what is now your opinion of Spencer?"

Was this a test? Would my answer decide for him whether I saw Astrid or not? Well, it didn't matter anyway. I could only tell him the truth, or the best truth I could manage. He was Astrid's father and deserved nothing less.

"To begin with, he was wonderful: kind, understanding, wise. Now I don't know. I really don't know. He did help me. He showed me how to deal with my own suffering, instead of wallowing in it. His words were often amazing, yet his actions seem—I don't know— selfish. Perhaps he was different from the rest of us, freer in a way. He doesn't seem to have shame or guilt or fear, or follow any moral code. That makes him strong, but then he seemed to use his freedom to follow his own desires."

I wriggled uncomfortably. Astrid's father watched me with halfhooded eyes.

"Astrid said something to me about him," I continued. "She said he couldn't love her, or anyone else, not in the way we understand it, because he wasn't really there."

I stopped. I was blushing. I had already said too much. Astrid's father kept watching me, but his face gave nothing away, and I had no idea what he was thinking. He sipped his whiskey.

"The police said he tried to kill her. Is it possible?" he asked quietly.

"No." I was certain now. Not Spencer, not Ray. Nobody.

"No! Of course not!" Suddenly Astrid's father came to life, banging his fist on his chair fiercely. "He is a little rat who runs for his hole in trouble, but he is not like that." He altered his tone again. "Did she want—to kill herself?"

Did she? Could she have? After all that had passed between us? Suddenly I knew.

I shook my head

"No. It was an accident. I'm certain. I'd been across the railway line with her, two days before, and she nearly fell then. It was easy to slip, more dangerous than we realized."

He winced.

"Was she happy, the last days?"

"Yes." As he asked me, I knew. "She'd been unhappy, but she was better. She was planning to get away, to go traveling. With me."

"With *you*?" The hoods came up on his eyes, and he looked at me intently.

I could only nod, aware of my long, greasy hair and the odor coming up from my socks.

"Well!"

He emptied his glass and stood up.

"My daughter has spoken of you," he continued. "She has said your name. That is why I asked you here. She is in the hospital. We will go there now."

Hope. The flame was growing, and I could hardly contain it as we drove in Astrid's father's Mercedes. Astrid was conscious. She had said my name. She was going to recover.

"She is still very weak," her father warned me. "Her memory, it comes and goes. Sometimes she speaks, makes sense, sometimes not. It is possible she will not know you, but if she does, that will be good for her, I think. That will help her. The visit will be only short. It is important you do not upset her or disturb her."

"Will she make a full recovery?"

He didn't answer immediately. We'd stopped at traffic lights. They turned green, and the powerful car raced forwards.

"Let us just be thankful that she is alive, that she can speak, be with the people who love her. I have learned something too. When you think your child is going to die, you forget everything else, because nothing is important, nothing, except the life of your child. If she lives, that is enough. If she lives, everything is forgiven."

We were at the hospital—a private hospital with flower beds and shining plate glass. We must have looked an odd pair, Astrid's father so immaculate in his gray suit, me scruffy and unwashed from a night on the ferry, but the nurses smiled at both of us equally.

Astrid's father led me down a corridor. My heart was beating. I wished I'd brought flowers; I hadn't thought of it. Instead I clutched my rucksack awkwardly.

He opened a door. I hung back, suddenly uncontrollably nervous, but he strode forward to the pool of golden light round the bed, bent over and kissed his daughter. Astrid was propped on pillows, her head bandaged but her face clear, looking up at him. They talked in German, and then her eyes moved from her father's face, out towards the door where I stood, looking at me, taking me in.

She stretched her hand out towards me. Astrid's hand—her long fingers soft and white.

"Stevie!"

Her father stepped aside and I moved towards her. She smiled at me. Astrid's smile.

"Stevie! You have come back."

Chapter 20

I've almost finished now.

It's autumn. In the public gardens by the cathedral, where I work, the leaves are falling—yellow and black and pale and hectic red. I spend a lot of time raking them up. The days have passed easily. I've had a job with the parks department and been living with my parents, back in my room with the view of the beech tree. It's been fine. The demons have gone. My mother's mostly out, and my father seems to like my company, though we don't talk much. But I've been saving up, and soon I'll be ready to be on my way again.

When I'm at home, in the quiet of my room, I think about all that has happened and try to write it down. This sheaf of paper that I started at Penelope's has turned into quite a bundle.

It's strange how quickly everything fades into the past. The immensity that once I felt everywhere, that I thought was permanent, has dissolved as suddenly as the community at The Hollies. One tragedy was all it took to blow away our dreams of enlightenment. Yet there's still something—a kind of silence between the sounds.

I never heard any more from the police, and I never

went back to The Hollies, but I did have a letter from Graham. He and Louise joined up with Tim again. Louise had a spell in hospital and got a lot better, and now they're all helping to set up a Tibetan Buddhist monastery in Scotland. I also had a card from Chet saying he was clean, and going to "clown school." I'm not exactly sure what a clown school is, but the card had an American stamp and a New York postmark, so I know that Sergeant Harrison was lying about that too. As far as I can see, he lied about everything.

I'll never forget Chet, his strength and his honesty. In Vietnam the killing goes on, and even when it stops, it will start again somewhere else. I wonder sometimes how it's possible to have any kind of fulfillment in life with so much pointless suffering in the world. Maybe I should give my life to trying to make the world a better place, after all. But you can't do it alone, and as Chet said, maybe we ought to start by setting ourselves straight.

In the top drawer of my desk, which I can lock, I have my letters from Astrid. I read through them every night before I go to sleep. The early ones are short and hesitant, but as they go on, you can feel her getting stronger. She tells me she's had to teach herself to walk again, that she has gaps in her memory and strange moods. She tells me not to expect too much. But she's getting better. Of everything at The Hollies, Astrid is what remains to me. In her last letter she said she was fed up with being stuck at home and she wants to see me, so I've decided the time has come, and once again I'm packing up my rucksack.

I often wonder about Spencer. I can't help it—he had such a big effect on my life. But still I don't know. Usually I agree with Astrid's father that he was a "little rat," a good talker who could get people under his influence while he pursued his own pleasure. Nonduality—what does it mean? It was only another idea to feed our delusions, to make us feel more important, to disguise the nothing that we are.

I'm not certain, though, because whatever he said about morality, Spencer never tried to deceive me. At worst, he let me deceive myself. I was lost in a meaningless world, desperate for love, and he helped me open to a mystery that can't be named or defined. It was Sergeant Harrison, urging that the Truth would set me free, who lied—lied, it seems, for the sake of it.

I enjoy my job. I'm outdoors with living things, which is what I like. I meet people too. Yesterday Jude came past on her lunch break—sweet, pretty Jude, always so happy and uncomplicated. So I took mine as well and sat with her on a bench.

"I'm still waiting for my invite," I said by way of conversation. "To your wedding," I added, because she was looking at me funnily.

"Didn't you know? It's off."

"Oh, I'm sorry," I said.

"It's okay. It's a good thing really. We weren't that

well suited. We were both just taking what was available."

She said it so calmly. I was impressed.

"You seem to have handled it well."

She threw me a look.

"Do I? Good. Well, it's been awful actually. But there we go."

There was nothing I could say, so I chewed my sandwich.

"You've changed, Stephen," she said suddenly. "You seem more—I don't know—ordinary. You used to be sort of stuck-up and not quite there, like you thought you were better than everybody."

"Thanks!"

She blushed.

"Oh, I'm sorry—that sounded—I didn't mean . . ."

"It's fine," I said. "I'm pleased." I smiled at her. I really like her.

"Are you still working in the Steiner Community?" I asked.

"Yeah, it's good. They're going to send me on a training course. But then sometimes I think it's not quite enough. There must be more in the world than this. Do you know what I mean?" She sighed, then brightened. "How about you? Going to work your way up the St. Albans Parks Department?"

The autumn sun was shining on my back, and her question made me feel dreamy. None of us ever knew what the future would bring, not even in the next moment. And then my mouth started talking for me.

"I'm going away soon. I'd like to be on a slow train to nowhere, keep moving and watch the world from a carriage window, and feel my thoughts slow down until I know who I am. Which is nobody. As I already know."

I blinked. Jude looked surprised.

"Cool!" she said. "Can I come with you?"

I turned to face her. She wasn't serious, was she? She was looking at me earnestly, so fresh, so generous. In another life I might have married Jude, had kids, worked my way up St. Albans Parks Department. It wouldn't have been a bad life. But it wasn't this one.

I grinned.

"Maybe one day."

She put her hand on mine.

"You've got a girlfriend, haven't you?"

"Yes," I said.

She smiled.

"Tell me about it all one day, will you, Stephen?"

She stood up. Her lunch break was over. I watched her walk away through the falling leaves.

My heartbeat slowed. I was just there on the bench, watching Jude go.

And it was there. Not the immensity, but something else, something that lies behind even that, and for which there are no words. Whatever Spencer is, he did give me something. There is a beyond. We were not entirely deceiving ourselves.

I'm going to pack up this pile of paper now, put a rubber band round it and leave it in a drawer and forget about it. The past is over. Maybe my children or grand-children will find it one day and laugh at what an idiot I was. In a few days I'll be on my way to Germany to see Astrid. I might stay there for a while, get a job, learn German, see if we still get along. And then—who knows?—maybe we'll set off together to Afghanistan, or Morocco, or Tibet. To any of the waste and solitary places where we taste the pleasure of believing what we see is boundless.

As we wish our souls to be.

ACKNOWLEDGMENTS

Among the many books and articles I read while researching this, Jonathan Green's *Days in the Life* (Heinemann) and Richard Neville's *Hippie Hippie Shake* (Bloomsbury) gave valuable and entertaining background to the late-sixties scene in London. From the point of view of the hippie-on-the-street, though, easily the most vivid account I found was Chris Faiers' *Eel Pie Dharma: a memoir/halibun,* published on the Web.

To these and all the others who helped me write this book, many thanks.

ABOUT THE AUTHOR

Patrick Cooper, the author of *I Is Someone Else*, *O'Driscoll's Treasure*, and *Wings to Fly*, lives in England.